"A compelling mix of passion, revenge, and a gallant people's quest for freedom. With the historical accuracy of a L'Amour novel, the characters are well-drawn, leaving the reader to feel the openness and harsh challenges of the Texas frontier . . . Don't expect to get any sleep when you start this one."
—*John J. Gobbell,*
Bestselling author of THE LAST LIEUTENANT

Praise for MAD MORGAN:

"Colorful, old-fashioned adventure . . . Awash with treachery and romance, this well-spun yarn fairly crackles with danger and suspense. Vigorous historical fiction." —*Booklist*

"Swashbuckling adventure!"   —*Indianapolis Star*

THE LEGEND OF MICKEY FREE

KERRY NEWCOMB

St. Martin's Paperbacks

THE LEGEND OF MICKEY FREE

Copyright © 2002 by Kerry Newcomb.

ISBN: 0-312-97931-2

Printed in the United States of America

St. Martin's Paperbacks edition / April 2002

St. Martin's Paperbacks are published by St. Martin's Press, 175 Fifth Avenue, New York, NY 10010.

10 9 8 7 6 5 4 3 2 1

This book is for the shining lights of my life—
Patty, Amy Rose, Paul Joseph, and Emily Anabel.

I give glory to God.

I give thanks for love.

*I am deeply grateful for the patience and support of
my friend and agent, Aaron Priest.*

*Thanks to Marc Resnick, my wonderful editor,
and the other good folks at St. Martin's Press.*

*And blessings and peace be upon you, dear reader,
and on us all.*

I was born on the prairie where the wind blew free
and there was nothing to break the light of the sun.

—GERONIMO, *from his autobiography*

This is a Godforsaken country and a
Godforsaken people living in it!

— CAPT. HENRY LAWTON,
Indian fighter, on entering Apache Territory,
from The Journal of Leonard Wood

Part I

Prologue

Well now, you want me to say all this is gospel? Choose what to believe and where to hang your hat; I don't give no never mind. Mickey Free lived, he walked the white man's path and the good red road and was at home in neither. This is his story. Mine, too. Maybe it's the story of us all. There's the truth of history and the truth of legend, but what really happened often lies somewhere in between.

And that's the undiscovered country you hold in your hands.

—Apacheria: Being the Personal Memoirs of an Indian
Fighter and Arizona Lawman
—R. D. JORDAN, 1901

Chapter 1

It was the summer of 1876, in a time of his life when the spirits called him by name, Dabin-ik-eh . . . One Who Is Free, in a time of his life before he stepped outside the Great Circle to follow his own path.

It was summer and he was Mickey Free and the Great Desert baked beneath the sun; a heated breeze rattled the branches of the ocotillo and cholla on the hillsides and sounded for all the world like the bones of dead men dancing to the whispering wind. These lower elevations, the kingdom of the rattlesnake and cougar, scorpion and javelina, offered a series of flat, harsh basins streaked with rust-red ridges that looked like the spines of gargantuan beasts protruding from the rocky soil. In the hazy distance the escarpment swept upward to isolated, thickly forested plateaus, like emerald islands in the sky where snow settled upon stunted forests of piñon pine and spruce and carpeted the trails worn into the earth by white-tailed deer, black bears, and the elusive pronghorn antelope, whose meat was always a welcome addition to any Chiricahua feast.

Despite the harshness of reservation life, these had been good days, a time when it seemed possible to Mickey that he could live in two worlds, that of the Apache and that of the white man. But that was before the Run of the Arrow, before the killing began . . .

* * *

The elders of the tribe had warned that the desert took no prisoners; it would call the thirteen-year-old boy to his death. But if not death, then manhood. Mickey Free knew the beliefs of his adopted people. But why should one so young risk making the Run? There were other ways, less harsh, said the elders, other ways for the thirteen-year-old to prove himself.

(*Ah . . . true. But if the All Father comes to you, if He sends Ba-ts-otse, the Coyote Spirit, to whisper in your ear, then what can you do but obey and proclaim your vision and endure the Run?*)

So Mickey Free had heard Coyote speak, as did his adopted brother, Chato, older by a year. Now some said Mickey Free was lying. Some said the foundling only pretended to hear Ba-ts-otse, so that he would undergo the same rite as his brother and not be left behind. Some said Gray Willow's adopted son was too young, too proud, and would meet a fool's fate and die alone in the mountains.

But who can defy the will of the All Father?

Try to reason with a Coyote.

* * *

The Run of the Arrow began in the cold of pre-dawn, on the outskirts of San Carlos, the Apache settlement, beyond the last of the wickiups, in a dry wash where flat rocks lined the banks like overturned tombstones. Geronimo was there, one of the chiefs who refused to become a tame Apache. Already a legend, hunted and feared by the Blue-coats, Geronimo knew he risked capture or death by bringing his warriors down from the mountains. But the Run of the Arrow was sacred, and he had heard there were two boys who sought to prove themselves worthy of becoming Apache warriors.

With his war party standing watch, Geronimo confronted the two brothers. He held two small pouches hung from leather strings and handed one to Mickey Free and one to Chato. Both of the youths immediately hung the spirit pouches around their necks. Even then Mickey Free was

tall for his age and could look Geronimo square in the eyes.
It was like staring into the face of a cougar; in that fierce
gaze burned the fires of defiance and grim determination.
But there was recognition, too.

"Dabin-ik-eh . . ." said Geronimo. He looked deep into
the thirteen-year-old's cold blue eyes. "I see the infant I
brought from the Great Desert. Your cries carried to me on
the wind." The wily war chief remembered the desolate-
looking wagons and what little the vultures had left of the
party of homesteaders who had been claimed by the wilderness they had attempted to civilize. But the baby had
been secured within one of the wagons, shielded from the
sun by a weathered canvas cover, a child still too stubborn
to die. "Do you still have a warrior's heart? We will see
today."

Gray Willow came forward with a water gourd. It pained
her to sense the bitterness in Chato. But she made no mention of it. The Run was neither the time nor the place for
family disputes. Gray Willow embraced them, her elder son
first. Chato endured, growing stiff in her arms. Three years
ago he had buried his father, Cuchillo, and still Chato could
not reconcile the fact that it was his mother's counsel that
had brought her husband back to San Carlos, to live as a
tame Apache. Chato had watched this cunning and
invincible-seeming warrior die in bed, not battle, his once-
strong body wracked by one of the white man's diseases.
Three years ago was only yesterday to Chato's grieving
heart.

Gray Willow ladled out a dipper of water. Each of the
boys would be allowed a mouthful of water. Their mother
cautioned them to resist the temptation to swallow.

"Hold the water in your cheeks until you most need it,"
the slender woman said, her silver-streaked hair caressed
by a gentle breeze that tugged at the hem of her red cotton
skirt and the sleeves of her patterned blouse. A leather

conch belt circled her waist. Firelight gleamed off the tiny mirrors that added glitter to her necklace of shells and trade beads. She adjusted her serape blanket about her shoulders and fixed her warm gaze upon Mickey Free and Chato, so different from each other, yet so much alike in their fierce pride. But Chato carried his anger like a festering sore that would not heal. Mickey Free seemed to accept things as they were. He, too, had grieved for Cuchillo, but the boy was no stranger to death. All he had to remind him of those he had lost long ago was a name scrawled on a locket that someone, perhaps his own mother, had tucked in her infant's blanket.

Mickey. Not even a last name, but no matter, the Chiricahua had supplied the rest; the name . . . and the life.

He reached out and took the gourd from Gray Willow's hands. "Thank you, Little Mother," he said. And drank. She could not hide her pleasure. From the day Geronimo had placed the squalling infant in her arms and she took him to her breast, Gray Willow had loved him. Her bond was no less than if he had sprung from her own womb.

"There will come a time when your throat will feel as if you are choking on hot coals, when the earth beneath your feet becomes soft and difficult to stand upon, when your suffering becomes too much to bear; then a mouthful of water will mean the difference between life and death." Her breath clouded the cold night air, fanned their faces so that it seemed as if she were blowing part of her soul into each of her sons. As she was a woman in her late thirties, her once-youthful features were tempered by a scattering of lines that fanned out from the corners of her eyes.

Chato glanced at his foster brother. Their eyes locked. They were always competing. Now would be no different. The two had been close once, inseparable companions. But lately, Chato was finding it harder and harder to see past the color of Mickey's skin. Dressing like an Apache didn't make him one. Chato was determined to prove which one of Gray Willow's sons was the real Chiricahua warrior.

But the thirteen-year-old would not be intimidated, though he had never understood Chato's growing animosity. In the early years, as children, they had played as brothers, shared both good and bad times. Mickey Free would not allow the anger gnawing at Chato's heart to drive him away.

Mickey Free grinned and winked at his brother, despite the solemnity of the occasion. Chato scowled and looked away. Then Geronimo addressed them both. The thirteen-year-old grew serious. For more than six years Geronimo had carried on a war with the Bluecoats. His warriors were the scourge of the territory. Even in the pre-dawn darkness, danger and menace seemed to radiate from the war chief. When he stepped close, Mickey could see the walnut grip of a Colt dragoon tucked in the gun belt circling the warrior's narrow waist. It was said Geronimo could become invisible, that soldiers would ride by within arm's length and never know the warrior was near until he struck. Mickey could believe it, for the very air seemed to crackle around Geronimo and an aura of almost supernatural power dogged his every step. The warrior had never known surrender, and it was said he never would.

"I have left a spirit arrow for each of you on the summit of Blue Mountain. Place the arrowhead in the medicine pouch and return it to me, place it upon the ground at my feet, that I may see you are no longer a boy, but Apache!"

And that was the Run, nothing complicated, only to cover a long, hard distance, endure the desert's brutal heat, drag weary limbs up one hill, down the next across a barren landscape where there were no water holes, across a plain of volcanic rock that would leave a horse lame—in brief, to run to hell and back, with only a mouthful of water to sustain them.

Geronimo fixed his gaze upon the two boys who would be men, then turned on his heels and returned to his campfire around which fourteen battle-hardened warriors sat, leaning on their Winchester carbines, while another half-dozen of their companions patrolled the perimeter of the dry wash.

Mickey Free glanced back at his mother, standing in the starlight, so beautiful, her long black hair adorned with a single beadwork braid holder. The same whisper of wind that played upon her hair tugged at the fringes of her dress. She waved to the thirteen-year-old and chanted softly, a prayer meant only for him, to guide him and guard him and keep him safe.

Chato turned away. Then he vanished in the twilight. And Mickey Free could not help but follow.

Chapter 2

The heated air rose from the dry earth in brutal waves; the rock-strewn summit underfoot felt like bricks in an oven, warming the soles of his feet through his moccasins. Memories faded, driven from his mind by thirst and the heat that made it difficult to catch his breath, that hammered him upon the anvil of this arid, unforgiving landscape. Mickey Free stood unsteadily, his naked torso caked with dust, the sweat long since leached from his pores by the wind's heated breath. He wavered, here on the crest of Bear Butte, and the land below tilted crazily. Chato glanced aside; his features betrayed the effects of the ordeal he shared with his foster brother.

Thirteen-year-old Mickey Free had already eclipsed his older brother in height; his shoulders were broad and his reach longer. Chato was short but powerfully built, with eyes like chipped flints that peered at the world from below a wide, flat forehead, his iron-clay features framed by a mane of coal-black hair bound, like Mickey's, by a wine-colored bandanna.

Behind them lay hours of running and climbing, scrambling up treacherous slopes where the ground gave way and threatened to send them hurtling down into ravines, traversing the spiny backbones of volcanic ridges, following the winding creek beds devoid of even a trace of water, with only the debris left by flash floods to taunt them with memories of rushing, foam-flecked streams of rainwater. Dry springs and dust devils lay behind them and before them, and always the sun, a single baleful orb, beating and breaking them down, scorching the air and blinding them with its white-hot glare.

The freezing temperatures of pre-dawn that left Mickey's teeth chattering were a distant memory. How long? How much farther? He tried to read the shadows. But his vision blurred. Grains of sand stung his eyes.

"Downhill from here, then across Fire Creek Basin," Chato rasped, his gravelly voice shattering the silence. "And back trail through the arroyo to San Carlos." He had taken his drink, here when he needed it most, with the end in sight, though not at hand. The mouthful of moisture eased his tortured throat.

Fire Creek Basin was a broad, flat plain that looked harmless enough from the skyline but at close hand was bedrock seamed with black tendrils of volcanic rock. The two had already crossed it once today, in the early hours of their ordeal. It would be worse now, with the bloated sun beating down on them, more difficult because they were tired and might miss a step and stumble.

Hours earlier, Mickey had lost his purchase and slid a few yards down a slope of loose shale and nearly plummeted to his death in one of the ravines ringing Blue Mountain. He had bruised his ankle and knee and opened a gash along his hip.

"Stay here and I will send someone back for you . . . as soon as I have handed my arrowhead to Geronimo." Chato was anxious to stand before the war chief of the Chiricahua Apache and demonstrate his superiority over his younger brother. "Nan-sh-dah! I will come back."

Chato started down the slope, his muscles bunched and glistening as he picked his way along an antelope trail to the flatlands. Mickey wavered and then sank back against an outcropping and sat on the ledge, shoulders slumped forward, pain shooting the length of his right leg. He watched Chato disappear through the shimmering heat and continued to stare long after the image of his brother was lost to the haze. Mickey felt like curling up here and dying. The elders were right. He was too young. He had been too proud.

Shadows of circling buzzards glided soundlessly across the broken ridge. He shielded his eyes and gazed upward at them, spied them, black against the lurid white sky, patient, waiting, if not now, then later.

Dabin-ik-eh . . .

He heard the name reverberate in his skull, creep into his consciousness on velvet paws, a voice rising out of the earth, borne on the radiated breeze, drawing his gaze to a coyote who watched him from the darkness beneath an outcropping of stone. The animal stood and walked in a tight circle, never leaving the haunted shade, then reclined on its paws.

Dabin-ik-eh . . . is this all, then? The end of your journey? No. Only the beginning. You cannot imagine where the path leads.

Trickster . . . ha. I see you. Play your game elsewhere. I am dying.

I do not think so. My blood is your blood. I came to you long ago, I found you alone, alive among the dead, and gave you my spirit and afterward brought the People of the Desert to save you for me. My spirit in you, and both of us Free. Stand up.

He should have never trusted the Coyote, for he was a trickster, always working mischief.

Leave me, Trickster. I will not be fooled. You are a beast. What do you know of men?

I know their cruelty. I know their empty wisdom and their pride. I know their courage. Come, Free One. Show me your courage.

What must I do? Curse you, what more must I do?

Hear beyond hearing. See beyond seeing.

What did that mean? The thirteen-year-old boy would have wept, but he lacked the strength and the tears. He wiped a bruised forearm across his eyes. The scrapes and nicks were caked with dirt and dried blood.

He stared at the Coyote, saw the animal stir, shudder, reshape itself, become a man draped with pelts, a man with eyes like live coals, a man whose feral grin made the boy's blood run cold. The shadow of a beast seeped out from the shado and flowed across the sun-baked slope and engulfed the battered, broken youth.

Mickey Free shuddered as the patch of darkness flirted with his limbs, then washed over him. And in that second he heard not only the whispering wind but also the voices on the wind, heard Gray Willow calling his name in her heart, heard the groaning earth, the song of distant clouds, the cadence of the breeze in the junipers. He saw that what had been to him an open empty expanse was bursting with life. He became aware, in an instant, that the green fuse that burned in man and beast and winged creature also connected him to the tiniest twig of columbine, to hyacinth and ironweed, to scuttling insect, to painted stone, to the past, to the present, all of it pulsing with life, pulsing in him, until the enormity of his discovery forced him to stand, to outstretch his arms because he could not even hope to take it all in.

Dabin-ik-eh . . . now you know. Ha-ha-ha.

The Coyote, a beast once more, settled its narrow jaw upon the rocks, licked a paw, snorted, then suddenly rose and bolted from its concealment and scampered out along the slope and disappeared among the boulders and cacti and creosote bush.

Mickey Free stood, unsteadily trembled, then placed one foot forward, followed with the other, and so forth and so forth, one step at a time, still shaken by the vision, troubled, yes, confused by all he had experienced, and yet certain of one thing.

He would not die today.

And now you know.

Chapter 3

"Woman, you are in my shadow. It is not your place, for this will be a warrior's night," Geronimo said without glancing up at Gray Willow. She did not back away from the campfire but held her ground. Let the shadows fall where they may.

"*My* sons . . . *my* place."

"*Tsaaa* . . . so you say. But do not think to run me. Watch your words, lest they weave the same trap for your sons that they did for your husband."

"Cuchillo walked a different path than you because he thought it was a good thing."

"And became a tame Apache who died of the white man's sickness." Geronimo scowled and shook his head. "Heii-ya. A warrior should die with his eyes open, so he can see his death, so he can show death that he is not afraid."

"I choose that my sons live with their eyes wide open, so they can see their lives and choose the right road."

"The tame road?" Geronimo spat into the flames. "We will see. I have need of warriors."

"No. They shall not take your words into their hearts. Let them be men. But let them live."

Geronimo glanced at her, his expression gun-barrel cold. The war he carried to the Bluecoats was a one-sided contest. His force was always outnumbered, always outgunned. And the fallen were difficult to replace. "We will see."

Gray Willow felt her heart sink. She knew the power of Geronimo's words, knew they could turn a young man away from the path of peace. How could anyone compete against such power? The war chief's magic was stronger than hers. His words had already lit a fire in Chato. Perhaps even Mickey would succumb to the war trail's call and be lured into living by his wits and his courage, into becoming a warrior like so many others of the tribe who had followed Geronimo into the distant mountains.

A pair of sullen-looking young men cautiously approached the war chief, uncertain whether or not they should intrude on his thoughts. But he waved them forward. Gray Willow recognized them both. They had been Chato's friends but had abandoned their families and become renegade Chiricahua.

Although they were older than Chato by a few years, Gray Willow knew them all the same: Tzoe, the taller of the two, was a braggart who imagined himself the subject of songs and tales of bravery. His companion, Mansaana, was lean and dangerous-looking. War suited him. It was said he preferred the smoldering homesteads of his enemies to the confinement of San Carlos, and the smell of powder smoke to the aroma of a cook fire.

"The trails are clear; the Bluecoats are asleep behind the walls of their fort." Tzoe puffed out his chest. Both men carried Winchester carbines, and bandoliers crisscrossed their faded checked shirts. They wore breechclouts and leggings of brushed buckskin. Both men had streaked their features with ochre war paint to frighten their enemies. "We were close enough to count their horses," Tzoe finished.

"The patrols they sent to the mountains to look for us have not returned," Mansaana added. "Not so many remain."

Still several times the number of men in his war party, Geronimo reminded himself. "It will not be a good thing if you were seen," he added by way of a warning.

With Fort Apache to the east, only a half hour's ride from the village at San Carlos, and the bustling settlement of Rio Seco with its armed and suspicious populace only a few miles to the north, Geronimo was keenly aware that he had brought his force into the very heartland of his enemies. He considered an attack on the house of the new Indian agent, McDunn. The man lived with his family on the outskirts of the village, protected by the tribal police. But such an action might turn some of Geronimo's own people against him. And besides, any trouble would result in a fast and furious retreat to the mountains. He preferred to avoid a running gunfight, especially when he might run into one of the search patrols returning to the fort.

"We must choose our battles wisely," said the war chief.

"We were not seen," Tzoe assuredly replied. "We were like the wind."

Mansaana nodded, proudly concurring. He was confident of his own abilities and contemptuous of the soldiers asleep behind the walls of their garrison.

"The wind leaves its mark. Next time be like a shadow," Geronimo quietly admonished them.

The two men nodded respectfully and withdrew, pausing for a moment to confront Gray Willow, who appeared unaffected by their fierce demeanor.

Mansaana lifted his blousy shirt and patted the hilt of an army-issue Remington revolver jutting from his waistband: the weapon's chipped walnut grip was as brown as his hard belly. The blued metal cylinder had been wiped clean; the hammer rested on an empty chamber. "This is for Chato. I am keeping it for him." Mansaana grinned. "I think he will kill many Bluecoats with it."

"But he will have to bring his own rifle," Tzoe chuckled. "Maybe his father's, eh? Cuchillo has no need of it now."

"Tsaaa. He had no need of it when he was alive, either."
Mansaana chuckled, glancing aside at his companion. "No
tame Apache does." His nostrils flared as he caught the
scent of *cabrito*. He licked his lips and glanced hungrily in
the direction of a butchered goat roasting on a spit over an
open fire. The two men were of one accord; their growling
bellies overruled any need to find humor at the widow's
expense. They followed the scent of their supper, leaving
Gray Willow to think and to plan.

She must save her sons. But first they must save themselves. *How distant and lonely the hills. Wisdom sits in
such places, yes, but also death, swift and sure.* She kept
a worried, silent vigil while the night crept across the landscape like a stalking wolf. The western horizon was its
bloodlust; the gilded wisps of clouds against that crimson
sky, its fading dreams.

"Do not worry for your sons," Geronimo said, reading
her heart as easily as he could track his victims. "They are
warriors."

"I would prefer they be men."

"Am I not a man?"

"You are the fear," she said. "The white eyes punish
their children by warning them that Geronimo will come
for them if they do not obey. The Apache are their nightmares. Geronimo is the unstoppable storm that claims
mothers, fathers; you strike with the whim of the whirl-
wind, taking what you will and leaving grief and terror in
your passing."

Geronimo straightened. He rose from the campfire, the
flames glinting in his brown eyes. "It is good to be feared."

"Not good for your people."

"Ask these men . . . Ask Tzoe and Mansaana and all the
others, woman . . . They will tell you. They are my people."

"Yes," Gray Willow said, concern for her sons embold-
ening her. The ground was losing its heat; a chill, more

pronounced with nightfall, settled on the land. The air was fragrant with the aroma of the cook fires and the distant scent of wildflowers and creosote bushes. "But we are also your people, here at San Carlos. We have chosen to live in peace. But the Bluecoats keep a heavy hand upon us and the people of Rio Seco will not accept us, because they look at us . . . and see *Geronimo.*"

"And that is as it should be. Let them know this is Apache land and they do not belong."

Gray Willow shook her head. She knew her words had little chance of reaching his heart. How could it be otherwise? She looked into the fire and saw warmth, thought of her hogan and the comfort of knowing her children would not die in battle but might someday walk a different road. The war chief only saw the faces of his victims, the dead he had left behind them, and the battles yet to come. Gray Willow had her eye upon a future that wasn't written in blood. A new Indian agent had been assigned to the reservation, to act on their behalf. Maybe things would be different now.

"I will never come in," Geronimo said. His voice had an edge to it. "And one day the white eyes will hold council and say to themselves there are other lands for them; the price of our mountains is too high. They will seek a place where they can know peace. And when the Bluecoats are gone, we will break the arrow and I will fight no more." A breeze stirred the dust at his feet. Something whispered in his heart. He sensed . . . an approach . . . and held up his hand to silence the woman, then turned his attention to the opposite end of the arroyo. Gray Willow held her breath, then exhaled in a rush of short-lived happiness as Chato appeared out of the dusk.

The young man was unsteady on his feet, his steps leaden; he wavered from side to side, and the warriors along the rim of the arroyo lifted their carbines in salute and exhorted him onward and slapped their brass-plated rifle stocks against the rocks underfoot. An arrow was lit from the flames of a campfire and sent arcing across the deepening sky to plunge downward and be lost to the night.

Chato willed himself forward. His dust-caked features failed to conceal his triumphant expression as he staggered up to Geronimo and placed the pouch containing the arrowhead in the war chief's outstretched hand.

The war chief casually tossed the pouch into the fire. Chato looked startled by the man's cavalier treatment of what he had assumed was an object of power and worth. Confused, he glanced past Geronimo and spied Gray Willow, whose relieved expression bespoke her mother's love. But Chato noticed how she continued to study the night-shrouded entrance to the arroyo; her features still held worry as well as joy.

No matter what my triumph, there will always be Mickey Free, Chato thought, scowling. He shifted his gaze and saw Tzoe and Mansaana, grinning and motioning for him to join them by the cook fire. Mansaana held up a sizzling morsel of *cabrito* skewered on the tip of his knife blade, juices running down the steel to the hilt. Then Geronimo blocked Chato's line of sight and that indomitable visage of his that seemed chiseled of wind-eroded stone captured the young man's attention.

"How have you suffered?" Geronimo asked, peering into Chato's eyes. "Tsaaa. What have you learned?"

Chato wavered—he wanted a drink of water from the clay jug his mother held; he wanted that bite of cooked meat. But he resisted the temptation, steadied himself with his back to the blood-red sunset. He wiped a forearm across his dust-caked features.

"I have run the Arrow," he rasped. "And I have bested my foster brother who ran with me but who could not finish. He was not Apache. That I am here and not Mickey

Free proves I will be a great warrior. I held the water in my cheek until I could no longer endure the thirst. I took my drink upon the mountain. I have learned this: An Apache can live where no one else can, but he must be hard as the land."

"Chato, son of Cuchillo, it is an answer." Geronimo nodded, then cautioned, "But your words about your brother trouble me." He shook his head and placed his hand upon Chato's shoulder. "The Run of the Arrow is not a contest. It is a way of knowing the Grandmother Earth, a way of finding the All Father. Here." He placed his hand upon his chest. Then he motioned for Gray Willow to approach. She hurried forward and Chato made a hurried grab for the water jug and drank enough to ease the burning in his throat.

"Where is your brother?" she whispered.

A coyote howled in the distance, a lonely cry taken up by other voices out among the broken hills.

"Ha . . . woman, ask them."

She sensed the change in his tone; indeed he was a man. He had made the Run. There was no returning down that trail to childhood. But she worried where it would lead him. He stepped around her and hurried over to the cook fire, where Mansaana handed him a chunk of seared tender goat. Tzoe threw a blanket upon the ground and Chato slumped upon it.

Gray Willow watched him with sinking heart, then confronted Geronimo yet again. The short, bow-legged man with the sloping shoulders and the burning gaze suffered her to harangue him.

"My son . . . you must send your men to look for him." The canopy of sky had become flecked with stars, like miniature campfires lit one by one, then by hundreds and thousands.

"It is for Mickey Free to find his way here, not for me to bring him. At least not alive."

"But you saved him long ago."

"That was then; this is now—it is a difference. I will not shame him." Geronimo tucked his thumbs in his cartridge belt. The temperature began to drop as the land released the day's captured heat. "Mickey Free has chosen his own path, the way of the Run. It is for him to make his way. Or for us to give him time to die. Then we will find him. The vultures will be our guides."

They waited together, watched, a man and woman with more than one secret between them, for Gray Willow and her husband and the war chief had all been young once, and had their moments of foolishness. An hour crept past.

"I will not have it," Gray Willow suddenly snapped.

"Woman, you have no choice."

"I can—"

Again Geronimo silenced her. He listened to the chorus of coyotes in the distance and frowned, stepped out of the circle of firelight. Could it be? The soulful baying of the coyotes seemed to be drawing closer. The first might have sounded from the foothills of Blue Mountain. But the others, heard every fifteen or twenty minutes, seemed to be drawing closer to the arroyo. Geronimo nodded and returned to the campfire. Gray Willow and Chato, who had come to join her with the water jug still in his hands, retreated a few steps as the war chief motioned them back.

At a wave of Geronimo's hand, the men lining the arroyo retreated into the shadows, silently repositioning themselves in case a troop of cavalry came charging out of the night. Only one man was left alone in the center of the light, one man waiting. Gray Willow, on the fringe of the firelight, wanted more than anything to ask what was happening, what words the ghosts and the darkness had spoken to Geronimo. But she knew better.

Not now.

Wait.

Worry and . . . wait.

Be silent and . . . wait.

Listen to your beating heart . . . and wait.

The minutes creep past, unmarked until time loses all meaning and there is only the Now. And still you wait.

Geronimo blinked, squinted, glimpsed the slouching beast beyond the reach of the light.

Tsaaa . . . *Trickster, I see you. Who have you brought?*

Geronimo watched the Coyote trot a few yards down the arroyo, its tongue hanging out. The animal sniffed the air. And in his mind Geronimo heard the animal tell him, *Wait and see.* The Coyote as quickly turned and scampered into the darkness. Geronimo continued to listen, his ears searching the night where his vision could not reach. Then he heard the step, the scrape of loose rock, a stumbling step, and then another.

Now Gray Willow heard it and her grasp tightened on her son's arm. Chato's jaw dropped as Mickey Free emerged from the darkness. The thirteen-year-old appeared to lose one step backward for every three forward; he staggered from side to side, blood crusted on his scrapes and cuts and his gashed thigh. His leggings were torn. His big-boned frame trembled from the effort. And every time he started to collapse he caught himself and, through sheer force of will, stood aright. No one made a move to help him. No one lifted a hand, except the warriors along the rim of the arroyo who once more tapped their rifle stocks against the stones underfoot and began to chant.

And then it was over and Mickey Free stood before Geronimo and held out the pouch containing the arrowhead from Blue Mountain. Geronimo accepted it and once more tossed the buckskin pouch into the campfire. Mickey Free looked as surprised as his brother.

"Mickey Free . . . how have you suffered? What have you learned?" Geronimo asked. The Coyote had brought young Mickey Free out of the howling wilderness for a reason. There was strong medicine here, and the war chief was determined to divine its wisdom.

Nothing, only silence. Why did he not speak? Geronimo resolved to give the youth time to collect his thoughts. After all, there was no denying the ordeal. To cross all that distance in the burning heat and endure the thirst and deprivation with only a mouthful of water to sustain him, a single swallow to momentarily ease the torture. What greater control could a warrior show?

Mickey Free's vision blurred. He willed himself to focus. He saw Gray Willow. Judging by her expression, he must look pretty rough. Well, he felt pretty rough, damn rough. The world tilted, he shuffled forward a step and almost lost his balance, braced himself. *Not yet, not yet.* He had lost blood and was clearly dehydrated and sick with exhaustion. He could not even remember the journey back, only the effort of placing one foot after the other. The cry of the Coyote who called him by name had been his guide and brought him home. What was the question? Geronimo's words reverberated in his skull.

How have you suffered . . . suffered . . . suffered? . . .

The pouch and the arrowhead he had carried, he had endured this torture for, tossed aide as if it meant nothing. Nothing. *Tsaaa,* it meant everything, every damn step, every tortured aching muscle, every cut and bruise. He knelt and, ignoring the flames, plucked the smoldering pouch from the fire's embrace and patted out the flames.

How have I suffered? See for yourself.

Mickey spat his mouthful of water onto the singed buckskin, the very same water Gray Willow had given him, the same mouthful of water he had refused to swallow out in the desert because he had chosen the course of greater sacrifice; he had chosen to test his will, to suffer and endure, while knowing relief was on the tip of his tongue.

Chato looked startled. He lunged forward. "What is this? He found a spring to drink from! He has not made the Run!"

"There is no spring," Geronimo said, never taking his gaze from the youth before him. "Your skin is white, Mickey Free. But your heart is Apache."

Geronimo grunted, nodded, and took the water jug from Chato and handed it to Mickey Free, who lacked the strength to bring it to his lips. Chato watched, fuming, as Gray Willow hurried forward to press a water-soaked bandanna to Mickey's cracked and bleeding lips.

"There are two warriors here!" Geronimo shouted out.

And the men along the arroyo answered with a chorus of war cries that would have chilled the heart of any raw cavalry man or townsman within hearing distance. The coyotes among the hills took up the challenge and joined in.

Mickey stared down at the seared palm of his hand, at the blackened buckskin pouch he had extinguished. Its contents might be worth nothing to the war chief, but it was everything to Mickey Free and had been hallowed by his blood and sweat, by the Run of the Arrow. He removed the flint arrowhead from the tattered remnants of the pouch, held it up before Geronimo, and closed his fist around it as if daring any man to try to take the relic from his grasp.

A whirling vortex started as a single fleck of obsidian, then expanded to engulf every sight and sound. Mickey thought he heard himself speak. Then his knees had buckled and he collapsed. He hit the ground hard enough to jar his head back and nearly crack a rib. But Mickey Free never lost his hold on the arrowhead, even as the world around him faded away; his fist remained iron hard, defiant to the end.

And that was how he suffered.

And that was what he had learned.

Chapter 4

Mickey opened his eyes and looked up into the face of an angel and fell in love.

She speaks . . .

He heard a sound in his head like a great rushing river. He tried to focus on her lips (her lips the color of wild strawberries), to concentrate on her voice. He blinked, wondered if the image would fade. The angel's hair was fine as spun gold, her cheeks smooth as spilled cream. Her round emerald eyes were filled with a tender mercy. She was beautiful like the morning and not any morning, but the first morning, the first blush of sky and cloud and parting rain and blowing breeze, the first morning at the beginning time when the All Father breathed over the empty earth and said, "Let it be as it will be."

She speaks again . . .

"I am Colleen McDunn. The daughter of Angus Mc-Dunn. Your mother brought you here a couple of days ago. You were quite sick." The young woman, a few years his senior, tucked a strand of hair behind one exquisitely shaped ear. She dabbed a cool cloth across his fevered brow and then spooned some broth between his lips. "My father was a doctor before he accepted the post of Indian agent here at San Carlos. We've barely settled in, but then you know that."

Well then, he wasn't dead and she was mortal. That didn't make her any less an angel, though. Mickey swallowed. The broth was salty but good, and tasted of chicken.

Colleen was seated upon a ladder-backed chair alongside his bed. She wore a pale yellow cotton dress and had draped an embroidered shawl about her shoulders to ward off the evening chill.

Mickey quietly appraised his surroundings. He was in a room that smelled of mesquite and lilac water and home-made soap. He shifted his weight, heard the bed slats creak beneath the cotton mattress. A pair of coal oil lanterns cast their sallow glare upon bedroom walls draped with hand-woven Indian blankets. An end table with a pitcher and basin of water had been left near his bed. A small wooden dresser dominated the far corner of the room.

He heard other voices, propped himself up on his el-bows, grimaced, and then realized for the first time he was bandaged, on both his side and thigh. Salve had been ap-plied to the several cuts and abrasions on his feet where the rocks had worn through his moccasins. He recognized the sound of his mother's voice and caught a glimpse of Gray Willow through the open doorway. She was seated in the front parlor, hunched forward as if bowed by guilt. Her fists were clenched; she was oblivious to her son, lost as she was in earnest conversation with a squat, imperturbable man wearing a nightshirt tucked into his gray woolen pants. The man adjusted the wick on an ornate-looking lamp and replaced the flue while listening intently to what the woman had to tell him.

Angus McDunn looked to be about forty. His brown hair was close-cropped and had been slicked back with water. His features, dominated by a bulbous nose, were scarred from a childhood bout with the pox. When he turned to pour himself a glass of sherry, Mickey could see that a bushy salt-and-pepper mustache concealed all of his upper lip and most of the lower. The Indian agent sensed he was being watched and glanced toward the room.

Mickey tried to call out, but the words wouldn't come. He was just so weak, and his throat felt raw and parched. He closed his eyes, and settled back on the pillow. Colleen's hands continued to apply a cooling cloth to his features. She had a soothing voice. He relaxed, closed his eyes and slid into a dream state where Coyote came to him and walked a circle around him while he stood alone upon the desert floor. Then the animal started down a well-worn path. Mickey tried to follow, but his feet would not keep to the tracks the animal left in the dirt. Coyote softly laughed as if in derision. *So you think you can follow where I go? I live in the places where dreams die. Make your own way, boy.*

There were other visions throughout the night. . . . Once Mickey thought he heard the sound of distant gunshots. He imagined blood on the walls of the room and heard a cry of rage. Then the Coyote returned and spoke to him, but his words and counsel were lost upon the wings of the wind.

* * *

Sunlight streamed through the open window. A wasp buzzed lazily overhead, then heeded the call of the Warm and drifted out to the world beyond. Mickey sat upright and swung his legs to the floor. He blinked and stretched; his muscles warned him with a sharp twinge of pain. He held out his hand. It was steady. He heard a girl's voice; it was Colleen, humming to herself from somewhere at the rear of the house. Mickey stood, steadied himself, was relieved to see he could stand and was wearing his buckskin trousers. The room was as he remembered, only it seemed meager without the "yellow-haired angel" who had tended him. He noticed his calf-high moccasins on the floor and pulled them on, catching his breath as his bruised and battered torso protested each and every motion. He found a fresh coarse cotton shirt and leather belt his mother must have left for him on a nearby chair. Mickey gingerly donned them. Where was Gray Willow? How long had he been a guest of the Indian agent here on the edge of San Carlos? Maybe McDunn's daughter had the answers; at least it was an excuse to see her again. He followed the sound of her voice down a narrow hallway and into the kitchen at the back of the house. The kitchen was uncomfortably warm, the result of the fire in the wood-burning cookstove. But despite the heat the whole rear of the house was fragrant with the aroma of freshly baked bread.

Colleen had just delivered another crusty round loaf from the cast-iron oven that commanded its proper place against the opposite wall. She placed the steaming hot bread alongside an earlier loaf that had been allowed to cool on a broad-beamed table in the center of the room. Colleen glanced up and gave a start at seeing her youthful patient leaning against the edge of the doorsill.

"I didn't hear you," she said.

"You weren't supposed to," Mickey replied. "You never hear an Apache warrior unless he wants you to."

"Apache indeed," she chided. Although in truth, she had to admit her guest looked a bit wild and as unpredictable as any savage. Maybe it was the way he stood there, watching her, like a young wolf in repose. "Do many Apaches have red hair and blue eyes?"

"No. I am the only one."

"You really shouldn't push yourself. You looked in a bad way last night."

Mickey walked to the doorway, realized it faced west. The sun was already dipping toward the distant hills, which meant it was late afternoon.

Colleen frowned and poured a cup of coffee for her guest and gave him a thick slice of bread. Mickey Free gratefully accepted both, wolfed down the bread, and then continued out the back door and into the afternoon light.

He took a sip of coffee, his gaze sweeping across the dry wash and the bridge that separated the agency from the village. A troop of soldiers rode past, the shod hooves of their horses beating a cadence upon the hard-packed earth. He watched them ride off through the slanting sunlight. Then the silence returned.

Suddenly he frowned and set the enamel cup on the steps, straightened, and then his youthful expression seemed to age and became more intense with each passing minute that he listened. Something was different. Across the wash, the collection of hogans that made up the Apache settlement would have looked abandoned except for the smoke that rose from several of the dwellings. But there was a disturbing absence of activity in the village. In fact, an unnatural stillness clung to the world around him. He could not see or hear a single cactus wren, and the little birds were normally plentiful unless frightened off. And as for the San Carlos Apache, only a few people stirred among the hogans, old men who lingered outside only as long as they had to, to gather wood for a fire or carve a strip of dried meat to carry to a cook pot. Where was the usual activity, the playing children, the packs of yipping dogs, the young women gossiping beneath the arbors?

Now that he thought of it, why were soldiers from the fort patrolling the perimeter of the village? He recognized Reverend Doctor Jordan lounging with a half-dozen of the tribal police near the well in the center of the village. Their horses dipped their muzzles into the cool, still waters held by the stone cistern.

A horse whinnied and pawed the earth off to Mickey's left. He watched another trio of soldiers in their faded blue uniforms approach Jordan, who waved them forward and made room for them to water their mounts at the well. The soldiers exchanged pleasantries with the scout and passed around Mexican cigarillos among themselves and continued to engage in muted conversations with Jordan and the tribal police. Despite the casual appearance, the mere presence of police and soldiers put the youth on his guard. One of the soldiers noticed the thirteen-year-old and said something to his companions. Mickey felt the hairs rise on the back of his neck. Was he suspected of wrongdoing? Jordan immediately came to his defense. The soldiers looked away from him.

No matter. Something was gravely amiss. Mickey Free could read it in the wind, in the dancing heat, and the shadows on the earth, the silence itself, spoke of trouble.

"What has happened?" Mickey asked.

"I'm not really certain," Colleen told him. She retrieved the cup from the steps, tossed out the coffee, and wiped the cup clean on her apron. "I thought you might know. It seems it started shortly after your mother brought you here."

"Gray Willow?"

"Your mother left with my father and that man over there, the big ugly one who claims to be a preacher or physician, but I don't think he is either."

"Reverend Doctor Jordan?" Mickey Free smiled.

"Yes. He went with them, late last night. No telling what my father is up to. But that Mr. Jordan is a most unusual character."

"They will be safe with him." Mickey frowned. What was he saying, safe? Why did his mother need to be safe? San Carlos was her home. These were her people. He glanced past Jordan and the soldiers to Gray Willow's stacked-log hogan, a large, round structure with a roof of mud and bear grass and log beams that rose to a center smoke hole. An arbor had been added on to one side, and it was here during the warm days of summer that Gray Willow could often be found, weaving on her loom, cook-

ing, and tending to the needs of her two sons. But today
she was nowhere to be seen.

Colleen started toward the back door, speaking as she
went. She held the door open for her thirteen-year-old
charge. "Well, like I was saying, everything changed
around here the moment your mother began talking about
someone named Geronimo." Colleen reached for the back
latch. "Well, I suppose there's nothing left for us to do
but—"

Mickey Free was gone in the afternoon heat, trotting
across the bridge over the dry wash that separated the
agency from the village, past the soldiers at the well,
through the lazy sunlight on a direct course toward home.

Too bad, thought Colleen, puzzled by his behavior. She
liked having a visitor near her own age. These Apaches
were certainly an unpredictable lot, even the white ones.
Was it something she said? The young woman re-entered
the house. Standing in the kitchen, she began to feel so
alone. Where exactly was her father? The sunlight grew
more oppressive than cheery. And who the devil was this
Geronimo anyway?

Chapter 5

Mickey Free ducked through the opening of the hogan and froze as cold steel kissed his throat. Tzoe pressed the knife against the youth's jugular and pulled him through the entrance, then shoved him toward the center of the hogan where Gray Willow and Angus McDunn were seated by the cook fire.

"Come in and be quiet, Brother," Chato said, stepping out from the shadows.

Mansaana walked up behind Mickey and gave him a shove. The thirteen-year-old whirled about, his fists clenched. But the odds were against him. Mansaana held a revolver; its business end jabbed Mickey in the belly and forced him to back down.

"Put the gun away. He won't go anywhere," Tzoe said. He gestured with his knife. The double-edged weapon was assurance enough. Mickey swallowed his pride and retreated toward the fire. He stood by Gray Willow. His mother, in her full blouse, long skirt, and serape, reached out and took his hand.

Mickey noted that Chato brandished his father's rifle, a Yellowboy Winchester .44. Firelight glinted off its brass casing. Chato also sported a pistol tucked in the cartridge belt circling his waist. There was a fire in Chato's eyes, a look of anticipation, a sense of excitement and danger that made him seem older than his fifteen years.

"*Bilah*, Brother, what are you doing?" Mickey asked, puzzled. He glanced around the hogan, his gaze sweeping

over his brother's deadly companions, holding them in disdain. Even before they had left to join Geronimo, Mickey
had never thought much of the two warriors. They had
never fully accepted him into the tribe and were not to be
trusted. He didn't like the way Tzoe and Mansaana were
dressed for battle. Each man carried a rifle and pistol, and
their features were streaked with war paint, adding to their
fierce appearance. Not to be outdone, Chato had mixed
ashes with a paste made of moistened clay and was busily
streaking his brow and lower jaw.

"Be still; we haven't much longer to wait," Tzoe said,
and returned his knife to the sheath he kept tucked in his
calf-length moccasin. "It will be night soon enough."

"Once it's dark we will be on our way," said Mansaana.

"What has happened? Why are their soldiers patrolling
the village?" Mickey asked, looking to his foster brother.
"Chato?"

"Ask her," Chato grumbled, finishing his task.

Shadows cast by the dancing flames flitted across the
faces of the Indian agent, the Apache woman, and their
captors. The air was heavy with the scent of burning mesquite wood, gunpowder, and fear. Angus McDunn shifted
nervously. Perspiration glistened in his mustache and trick-
led down his cheek. His hair was sweat-slick and plastered
to his skull like a cap.

"Your . . . uh . . . mother told me that Geronimo had
come down from the mountains and was hiding near San
Carlos," McDunn said. "I of course alerted the troops and
the tribal police. They already have a number of the renegades in custody; however, Geronimo has apparently
slipped past the patrols."

"You will never catch him," Tzoe blurted out.

"We will join him," Chato said. "As soon as it is dark,
we will take what horses we need." He stepped around the

fire, fixed his angry gaze upon Gray Willow. "My mother . . . our betrayer."

"Leave her alone," Mickey warned. Chato glanced angrily at him.

"Geronimo wanted you both to join him," Gray Willow said. "I told him I would stop him, that he could not have my sons. Too many of our young men follow him. But he can only lead our people to ruin."

"Then your treachery has failed you, for I will ride with Geronimo and bring death to the white eyes," Chato boasted.

"You will follow him to your death."

"Better to die fighting than like my father, sick and feeble and broken by your peace." Chato crossed to his friends, who nodded in approval.

"Enough talk," Mansaana said, cradling his rifle in his arm.

"There are soldiers everywhere," Mickey Free spoke up, ignoring the Apache's warning. "You will have to fight your way to the horses."

"Not with the agent leading us. No soldier will fire on us as long as we have McDunn to shield us," Tzoe chuckled.

"I will not help you," McDunn told them.

"Then I will gut you like a calf," Tzoe said.

"Chato . . . my son," Gray Willow entreated. "Try to understand. The Old Ways are finished. Our people must live in a new way if they are to live at all. Listen to my words."

"No. You are my mother no longer." Chato held his hand up to silence her. "Comfort the foundling. He has turned your heart as white as his skin."

Mickey reached out and took Gray Willow's hand in his. He gave a tug and encouraged her to sit beside him near the fire. Her eyes brimmed with tears. He hated to see her so distressed, but there was nothing he could do. Chato,

Tzoe, and Mansaana continued to pace about the hogan, pausing from time to time to peer from the opening at the horses by the well.

Time crawled. Minutes measured by the silence, by the prospect of slaughter, seemed an eternity, so slowly did they pass. But at last the sun dipped below the line of hills to the west, blanketing the earth in forgetful sleep. A mantle of shadows drifted over the village. They could hear the passage of soldiers from without the walls, the occasional barking dog, but for the most part there was only an unsettling stillness. And still they waited, for the night to stretch on, for the Apache police stationed by the well to begin to doze at their post.

"Get up," Tzoe said, nudging Angus with the rifle he held. "There's four of them police by the well. That's a horse for you, too, Agent."

"Me?" His eyes widened in alarm.

"We'll take you with us. Trade you for our brothers the Bluecoats captured today," Chato explained. "It was my idea." He beamed, then jabbed Angus in the ribs with his Winchester.

"You mustn't take him," Gray Willow said. "It will go hard for all of us. Think of your people."

"My people are hiding in the mountains," Chato replied, and started Angus toward the entrance. He cocked the rifle and kept it against the Indian agent's side.

Mansaana stood in front of Gray Willow and Mickey Free. "Remain here until we leave or it will go bad for you." He turned his back on them and followed the others out of the hogan.

Mickey stood, his expression grim. He glanced at Gray Willow as she rose and headed for the entrance. Mickey caught her by the arm. "No, Little Mother, stay here."

"I must stop him. Chato must not leave with Mr. McDunn."

"There is nothing we can do."

"There is always something." She placed a hand on his cheek. "Whatever happens, try and love your brother. He is lost; he walks a bad trail, I do not know if he will find his way home again." She pulled free of Mickey's grasp and darted out into the night. He stood there in the silence, staring at the entrance, for a moment, frozen in time, a youth becoming a man, for there was only one recourse, and that was to follow Gray Willow into the night.

What happened next would be repeated in his dreams, would take root in a place impossible to purge, and start him down his own dark path.

Chapter 6

Mickey emerged into the cool night air. His vision took a moment to adjust to the shadowy scenario unfolding at the well. Mansaana and Tzoe walked abreast of each other. They cradled their rifles beneath their blankets as they advanced on the Apache police lounging by the well. Reverend Doctor Jordan and the soldiers were nowhere to be found, but Mickey presumed they might be patrolling the perimeter of the village. Off to his left, Angus McDunn led the way with Chato just behind, his rifle thrust between the agent's shoulder blades.

The tribal police, seeing the Indian agent, assumed they were being relieved. Men nudged one another awake and struggled to look alert as the agent approached. The blue-coated Apaches had yet to realize the three men accompanying Angus were not in uniform. Darkness hid the war paint masking their features. For several seconds, everything was peaceful, orderly. Mickey was loath to interfere in such a volatile situation.

Suddenly from the shadows Gray Willow lunged forward. She moved quick as a cat, pouncing on her son and placing herself between Chato and the Indian agent. She made a grab for the rifle barrel, caught it by the sights, and forced the weapon toward the ground.

Angus saw his chance and darted toward the dry wash and the bridge. "To arms, to arms, renegades among us!" he shouted.

The Apache police grabbed for their weapons. Tzoe and Mansaana tossed aside their blankets and opened fire. Muzzle blasts blossomed in the dark. One of the tribal police, a young man no older than his attackers, howled, twisted as a slug tore through his shoulder; a second struck above his cartridge belt. He dropped his Springfield rifle and fell forward clutching at his belly

The horses tethered by the well shied and tugged at their reins while their owners attempted to make a stand. Another of the blue-coated Apache broke ranks and ran for his life. Bullets fanned the air around him and sped him on his way. Mansaana and Tzoe kept up a steady stream of gunfire as they advanced, forcing the remaining tribal police to retreat.

Chato struggled to bring the Yellowboy Winchester to bear on the fleeing agent. Gray Willow clung to the rifle barrel in a futile attempt to stop the violence. Chato twisted, shoved, then gave a violent tug. The Winchester bucked in his grasp. A lurid orange tongue of flame spat from the rifle, illuminating the woman for one brief horrid moment.

Gray Willow was blasted backward by the impact and slammed into the hard-packed earth. Chato stared at the Winchester in his hands as if the weapon had a mind of its own. The weapon slid from his grasp.

"No!" Mickey shouted, and rushed forward. He brushed past Chato and dropped to his knees alongside Gray Willow. The front of her blouse was singed and blackened, and blood oozed from the terrible rent in the fabric. He glanced up at Chato, whose eyes were wide with shock. The Winchester slid from his grasp and clattered to the ground. Mansaana and Tzoe appeared behind him, both on horseback and leading the other mounts they had stolen after driving off the last of the tribal police.

"Chato, hurry. The gunfire will bring the soldiers down on us!" Tzoe shouted.

His words had the desired effect. Chato spun on his heels, staggered toward his companions. He swung up astride the first mount offered him. But his movements seemed stilted, benumbed by what had just transpired. She shouldn't have pulled on the gun; his finger had been curled around the trigger. It was an accident, an accident. He never meant . . . no. It was her fault, her own fault.

"I warned her," he said, choking back a sob. "I warned her!"

Mickey Free rose up and charged his brother, his long legs covering the distance with catlike speed. He was like a lunging cougar, his lips curled back in a snarl. Barehanded he intended to avenge his mother's death. Chato swung the horse about, let it rear and paw the air in Mickey's face. Mickey ducked under the flashing hooves and came up on the left. Chato had his revolver out by then, thumbed the hammer back, and aimed the weapon at Mickey's forehead, right between his eyes. Mickey halted, arms half-reaching out to drag Chato from horseback.

"Kill him and come on!" Mansaana shouted, and galloped off through the village. Tzoe was only half a length behind him. Both renegades loosed their war cries and fired their guns to announce to these *tame* Apache that there were warriors among them.

Kill him . . .

Kill him . . .

Kill him . . .

On the edge of the village something stirred, distracting the man with the gun. Chato caught a glimpse of a coyote slinking off between the hogans. Suddenly it vanished. Had it been there at all?

Gray Willow . . . what have I done? What have I done?

Chato eased the hammer down on the cylinder. He hauled on the reins, causing the animal to turn sharply on its hind legs. The animal slammed into Mickey and knocked him off balance. By the time the thirteen-year-old had recovered, Chato was out of reach and riding at a fast clip in pursuit of Tzoe and Mansaana.

Mickey could only stand there and watch his brother gallop off through a cloud of dust. He remained still as a statue, powerless, until the horsemen were out of sight and the sound of their hooves had faded.

"Gray Willow saved my life."

Mickey glanced over his shoulder and found Angus McDunn had returned, this time armed with a shotgun. Colleen McDunn had also left the Agency House, and disobeying her father's instructions she, too, had ventured into the village. The girl knelt on the ground alongside Gray Willow's broken, lifeless body. Colleen removed her apron and tenderly draped it over the dead woman's features.

Mickey had to look away. He spied his father's rifle in the dirt and, leaning down, took up the gun. He felt a terrible weight crushing his chest and stumbled forward, struggled to breathe while the grief welled up in him, a grief that had nowhere to go. He stared at the darkness, blind to the men and women cautiously venturing from their hogans. Mickey Free could only see his mother being blown backward into the dirt and after that his brother's spectral form, staring down at him from horseback, Chato's face peering at him from over the gun sight.

Somewhere in the night a coyote mournfully howled.

Mickey wiped the moisture from his eyes with the back of his hand. He managed to swallow; he forced the pain deep inside, an effort that aged him where he stood, until he could speak without sobbing. Alone again, this time he did not waver. Mickey Free levered a .44-caliber round into the Yellowboy's chamber and, confronting Chato's apparition, coldly whispered, "You should have pulled the trigger."

Where is she going? Who will guide her?

"I am going to where the moon is a silver song."

Why is she going? Who goes with her?

"I go to gather the starlight. I go alone."

My heart is bitter. It grieves for her.

"The owl is flying downward, tired of all your tears."

Now she is gone. Now she is written on the wind.

"One day I shall call you by name."

My heart shall know her among the bones of the rain.

Chapter 7

1886

Colleen McDunn knelt on her hands and knees in the dirt, arranging rocks around the blooming cacti she had transplanted and nurtured out of the dry earth. She was a woman in her mid-twenties now, lithe and tawny beneath the noonday sun, and oblivious to her own beauty, which seemed as much a part of nature as the rarest cactus flower. A pale blue bonnet shielded her features from the sun's harsh glare, but a few errant ringlets gleamed like twists of straw gold, and beads of sweat glistened against her tanned and sandy cheek. She heard the sound of approaching horses and glanced up from the cactus garden. The bonnet shaded her eyes and allowed her to identify the visitors to the Indian agency.

Major James Buell and Reverend Doctor Jordan walked their army mounts across the front of the agency, for the two men had spied the young woman tending her desert garden. Both riders continued on around to the prized plot of earth she had created outside the storage room she had converted into a makeshift schoolhouse for the children of San Carlos. Buell dismounted and, sweeping his hat before him, bowed.

"It takes a fair flower to coax a blushing bloom from this godforsaken land," he said.

Colleen was surrounded by a variety of cacti, many of which were proudly arrayed in the colors of spring. The orange flower of the prickly pear mingled with the butter-yellow blooms of the barrel cactus. Delicate pink petals crowned the silken-looking spiny stems of the hedgehog cacti that formed a formidable perimeter around the garden.

"Why, Major Buell, you talk like you've come a'courting. But I suspect your true intentions are to speak with my father about which of our tribal police would make the most trustworthy scouts to help you track Geronimo."

"Morning, Miss McDunn," Reverend Doctor Jordan said, climbing down from horseback. The big man flashed her a knowing grin. "By God, you are a winsome sight for these tired old eyes." Jordan sighed. "Now if I was only a few years younger . . ."

She was a rare treasure indeed. Most women would have been married long before their twenty-fifth birthday, but not Colleen McDunn. Her sympathies for the plight of the Chiricahua Apache of San Carlos were widely known and had cost her the attention of many a suitor. It was hard to blame the local settlers, though. A man only had to find one massacred family and burned-out homestead to learn to hate the Apache with a vengeance. The woman's comeliness was no match for the inherent mistrust and outright bigotry of the local population of settlers and soldiers.

Colleen noticed Buell's brown eyes flash an angry look in Jordan's direction. Buell resented the chief of scouts' familiarity with the woman, not to mention the fact that Jordan probably had revealed the army's marching orders against the renegade Apache. The agent's daughter felt compelled to rush to Jordan's defense. The big, bull-necked Indian fighter was hardly an attractive man. He had a brawler's face. His nose had been broken and reset more times than he could count. Ridges of scar tissue formed a lurid half-circle around his right eye where someone had tried to blind him with the jagged remnants of a whiskey bottle. And yet for all his colorful nature, Reverend Doctor Jordan had never shown Colleen anything less than courtesy.

"Really, James, now don't get your dander up. Reverend Doctor is like a great big ol' huggable uncle to me. And as for the army's intentions," Colleen said, "why, they were the talk of the town on my last visit to Rio Seco. I may even have read something about them in the *Clarion*."

Buell frowned and pursed his lips and stroked his close-cropped goatee while he considered just which of his aides might be leaking the contents of his private dispatches. There was some information in the last communiqué that was best kept private until Geronimo was dead or safely in irons.

"So you say, the *Clarion*! Why, I never . . . Gossip is one thing, but actual orders are . . . are . . ."

"News!" Colleen chuckled. "Why don't you come around to the porch and I'll bring out some lemonade and you and Father can have a nice visit? You might even get an invitation to supper." Colleen smiled and dabbed the perspiration from her features with the hem of her apron. Her gingham dress felt wet and clammy from working outside for so long. "I must look a sight."

"I've never seen the blossom that can hold a candle to you, Miss McDunn."

"Hmm . . . compliments from a lonesome man don't count for much. I hear that you have already purchased a tract of 'godforsaken' ranch land down on Saledo Creek. Who can guess what an ambitious young man like yourself might aspire to?"

"Certainly more of your company," Buell replied. Whatever fates had robbed Reverend Doctor Jordan of physical beauty had heaped an abundance of blessings upon the dashing major. Buell was of average height, with keenly wrought features, a brown-eyed wonder for whom soldiering and politics was a family tradition. Jordan had seen the kind before. They usually wound up worm food. Although untested in battle, Buell felt confident in his ability to prevail both in battle and in love. " 'Shall I compare thee to a summer's day? Thou art more lovely and more temperate.' "

Jordan, standing off to the side, could endure no more of such talk and dissolved into a series of coughing spasms that doubled him over and was so obviously staged that Colleen almost broke out laughing. When the fit subsided, Jordan cleared his throat, scratched the back of his head, and beneath the major's baleful stare muttered a semblance of an apology.

Lordie, as chief of scouts it's gonna be my job to keep this moonstruck greenhorn from getting himself and his men killed, Jordan thought. *And just listen to all this dad-blamed hinting and hemming and hawing between two adults.*

Life was much easier back in Rio Seco, at Calico Annie's; there it was three dollars a poke for one of Annie's regular gals like Sí Sí Quezada, who never said no. Or for an extra two dollars a gent could try something special with Mademoiselle Brigitte, who hailed from Paris, France, or Mai Ling, "the Chinese Princess," who not only rumpled the sheets but also played the piano and lute.

"Major, reckon I ought to rustle up the Kid?"

"You are going to take him out again?" Colleen asked, perturbed. "He was going to help repair the windmill out back."

"My chief of scouts says we need him." Buell searched her expression. "Hmm, I assume repairing that windmill is the only reason you want him to stay." It was common knowledge Free lived at the agency now. Buell had always managed to conceal his disapproval until now. He didn't like the arrangement.

"He's like a brother to me."

"Free is an Apache."

"Nonsense! He was just raised by them," Colleen insisted. "And he stayed with us after his mother's death. I like to think I helped to civilize him some."

"Your father fears he helped *wild* you," Buell chided, offering his arm.

Colleen's eyes flashed emerald fire and the officer backstepped, knowing he had crossed the line. She would not be mocked, not by anyone.

"Er . . . uh . . . what I mean is . . ." Buell stammered. And when she did not slip her hand through the crook of his arm the soldier knew he was in trouble. "Oh, see here, Colleen. All I am saying is that there will come a time when Mickey Free will have to choose one road or the other, the Apache way or ours."

"Seems like he's done that, ain't he, sir?" Jordan interjected. "By scouting for us. No man at the fort has brought in more renegades than the Kid."

"Yes . . . precisely," Buell coldly replied. "The *Apache Kid*. And seeing as it takes a savage to capture a savage, let's bring him aboard, what say you? Why don't you go and find him, Mr. Jordan?"

"He's out by his mother's grave," Colleen told him. She did not bother to gesture toward the hilltop off to the east where, on the fateful morning following Gray Willow's killing and Chato's escape, Mickey had dug his foster mother's grave, alone, refusing help, and alone laid her to rest.

"I know the place," Jordan said, hauling his big-boned frame up into the saddle. He nodded to the officer and Angus McDunn's daughter, then touched a boot heel to the flank of his stallion and cantered off toward the hilltop where a solitary figure lingered amid the scrub oaks and yellow-gold cactus flowers.

Hilltops are fitting places to while away eternity. Too bad, though, this one sheltered one who had died so young, and too damn needlessly.

*   *   *

It was only in passing that Jordan first hung the moniker Apache Kid on the orphaned boy. But by the time Mickey Free was old enough to scout for the army, three years after Gray Willow's death, the handle had stuck. He was Mickey Free, the Apache Kid.

Free stood a head taller than the Apache tribesman with whom he had lived, who had raised him after finding him, half-dead, among the windswept ruins of a fatal camp. And yet if it weren't for the cold blue of his eyes and his shoulder-length red hair trailing in the wind, Mickey Free could have easily passed for a renegade. His lithe, wiry frame was bowed beneath a burden of grief, though his blood still boiled at the mention of Chato's name. Mickey Free still carried a thirst for a vengeance that had gone unslaked.

He knelt and sprinkled a handful of dirt on the marker he had erected over Gray Willow's burial mound. The earth had settled, leaving little but a wooden cross draped with a beaded belt to mark his foster mother's resting place.

"Little Mother . . . if only you were here now to advise me. Angus McDunn has been good enough to me. I am grateful. He gave me a place to live and set a place for me at his dinner table. And his daughter taught me to read the white man's words. She has been like a sister to me, until, uh, lately. I mean, it seems like more and more when I see her I start hurting inside, like my heart's fixing to bust out of my chest." He placed a hand on the beaded belt, opening himself to his mother's spirit. "Colleen McDunn . . . I like the sound of her laughter. I cannot tell her how I feel, how even now her face hangs in the air before me, like a sunrise."

"You got it bad, Kid!" Jordan gruffly called out, breaking through a thicket of ironwood and buckhorn cholla. The chief of scouts followed a narrow, winding deer trail that brought him out onto the summit. Reverend Doctor reined in his mount at a respectful distance and removed his hat out of deference to the gravesite and the woman awaiting Judgment Day beneath the land of the Chiricahua. "But you better saddle up and come with me, 'cause Major Buell's down there with your lady and I'd say he sets quite a store by her."

If Mickey Free minded the intrusion he did not show it. The young man stood and retrieved his Yellowboy Winchester from where he'd leaned it against a tree. "Major Buell talks to many people." Free took the carbine in one hand and leaped astride his own Appaloosa mustang; his calf-high moccasins slid effortlessly into the stirrups. "So the major has learned that Geronimo's escaped the trap General Miles set for him down on the border."

"You know?"

"This is Apache land. News travels faster than orders and dispatches from generals."

But there was never any question that Mickey Free wouldn't take up the hunt. If he found Geronimo, then chances were good he might find Chato and avenge Gray Willow's murder. Free had no animosity toward Geronimo. But the war chief's capture would undoubtedly ease the tension between the white settlers and the Chiricahua of San Carlos. And that might finally bring about the peace Gray Willow had envisioned.

"Then have your coyote friends told you where to find Geronimo and his renegades?" Jordan pressed.

"Tsaaa," the Kid scoffed. "Who has heard of such a thing? Coyotes. . . . talk!"

Chapter 8

I am your killer.

A coyote howled. It might have been that four-legged Trickster, Ba-ts-otse, or one of the Chiricahua Apache who were born to this arid landscape with its dry wind and harsh hills, its barrancas like scars in the earth, this land of jagged skylines and apricot sunsets and brisk nights.

Isaa! I, too, am of the desert born.

He heard the call once more. Was it a man or beast who tolled his presence with a mournful cry on the crisp night air, signaling others of his pack?

Come forth, you wary trickster with your hide burnt by the sun, curl back your dark muzzle, and bare your fangs.

The call of the wild echoed down the wind, drifted from Skeleton Canyon, sounded lost and lonesome in the velvet night. The clouds coiled and twisted, and moonlight washed the barren cliffs, shifting shadows, made menace of the cholla and flowering ocotillo cacti that sprouted from the dry earth; the undulating dark gave marching orders to the spiky undergrowth, presented an illusion that whole columns of desert plants were shifting position and advancing down the slope toward the soldiers' encampment.

Yes, I hear you. Oh, my inscrutable brothers, we share an understanding of this howling wilderness the likes of which no Bluecoat ever shall. Brothers, we must both be hunters this night. But you will not hear me; a shadow will make more noise ... when I come for you.

"Mickey Free?" said Reverend Doctor Jordan, ever the rough-hewn, thick-necked bruiser in army-issue trousers and faded red flannel shirt.

"Hey, Kid!" Jordan called out while knowing full well that the noise he had made walking up the path had already announced his approach to the twenty-three-year-old. Jordan hadn't kept his hide this long by being foolish. Caution and a healthy respect for men like Free enabled him to function as chief of scouts.

A man couldn't be too careful. The good citizens of Rio Seco, not to mention the local settlers, figured there was no such thing as a tame Apache. To most folk and the army Jordan scouted for, that's what Mickey was ... Apache ... despite the circumstances of his birth, a boy raised by the Chiricahua, raised wild as any *coyotero*. But that didn't make Jordan like the younger man any less. Reverend Doctor Jordan reckoned they were as close to being friends as a loner like Free would allow. Coyotes were the same way: you might coax one to drawing near your campfire, but you'd never get one to eat out of your hand.

It was toward the end of Taa-nachill, the time of rebirth white men called April.

Rebirth ... a time of change ... and change it was, for these were the last days of a warpath that began more than a decade ago. The moon slipped from behind a cloud and draped its silvery mantle upon the earth, illuminating the entrance to the canyon up ahead and the outcropping of sandstone behind which Mickey Free kept his vigil, waiting for the right moment when he must go.

Gray Willow's face drifted across the harsh landscape of his memory, her oval face, long black hair, kind eyes, his Apache mother, who had taken him into her hogan, suckled him, given him life, and reared him along with her own child.

Gray Willow, if not for you . . . ah, but those days are past. The Apache Kid walks alone.

Tender thoughts were dangerous to him now. He pressed a hand to the medicine bag he wore about his neck. The small beaded pouch contained a lock of Gray Willow's hair, a locket from the site where he had been found, a sliver of eagle feather, a lead slug covered with dried blood—mementos of a life and a death. He willed his mind to shed the trappings of what had gone before. To be here, now, in the present, was all he needed, if he wanted to survive the next twenty-four hours.

Mickey doffed his cotton shirt, retied the faded yellow headband that held his neck-length rust-red hair in place. His flesh was burned dark by the sun till it resembled the dusty brown stone outcropping behind which he kept his silent vigil, leaning forward, lost in thought. At a glance, there was hardly the look of an Irishman about him. One would have to look past his Apache upbringing and, in the light, catch his gaze. His eyes were the color of an approaching blue norther. Even now they swept the lay of the land with an understanding and an accuracy that defied the powers of the soldiers of the Third Cavalry, huddled round the comfort of their campfires.

Reverend Doctor Jordan had never encountered a man with a keener sense of observation. Mickey Free could read the irregular configurations of shadows and darkness like a book, finding whole chapters in the rustling breeze where Jordan would sense a page.

The chief of scouts leaned upon the same rock, loomed over it, a hulking brick house of a man whose fondness for whiskey and women meant his fall from grace among civilized society. But General Miles and the army always had a place for a white man whose knowledge of this Arizona Territory was nearly the equal of that of the Apache and the Spanish who initially called it home. And yet when hunting a wily Chiricahua Apache like Geronimo "nearly" wouldn't do. So the army had needed a man like Mickey Free.

The dust settled on the winding path Reverend Doctor Jordan had followed out of the circle of campfires that blocked the entrance to Skeleton Canyon. Reaching the outcropping, Jordan suddenly winced, gave a yelp, and removed his battered cap and slapped the brim against his leg.

"Damn, something bit me," he growled. "Crawled up my blasted trouser and attacked my leg. A little higher and I'd be whistling Dixie in falsetto. What is it with this damned country? Something's always on the attack."

"It's the only thing the desert knows how to do," Mickey dryly observed, a trace of amusement in his voice. He glanced aside at the Indian fighter, twenty-five years his senior. "An old jehu like yourself ought to know that after all these years."

Jordan ignored the admonishment and slapped again at his leg, then, satisfied he had killed whatever had dug its pincers into him, returned his cap to its rightful place, covering the evidence of his thinning hair.

"Did Major Buell send you to check up on me?" asked Free, his voice barely above a whisper.

"Well, it's true General Miles is counting on him to carry the day tomorrow. A dispatch from Miles arrived today ordering Buell to launch an assault on the canyon. The major's giving it some thought. You know he's got the cannons in place on the high ground and can bring those canyon walls crashing down. He'd have buried 'em all by now, Geronimo's whole bunch, but I put a bee in his bonnet how it would look bad on his record, blasting women and children to doll rags and all." Jordan carved a wedge of tobacco from his plug and stuffed the black leaves into his cheek. "And I told him if he gives you a chance to talk the red devil out, why, the general would be plumb tickled to bring those bucks back in leg irons. Nelson Miles is partial to parades. Buell, too, for that matter. Give him something to preen and gloat about in front of Angus McDunn's daughter . . . but you wouldn't care about that, I reckon."

"I know very little about General Miles," Mickey said with a shrug. He wasn't about to be drawn into a conversation about Colleen McDunn. "I never had words with the man." The general was always protected and had refrained from associating with the likes of enlisted men, much less a half-wild scout. But Mickey Free had glimpsed him from afar, seen the man in his buffalo robe coat in the winter, watched him astride a coal-black charger, riding proud and self-assured.

But a handful of armed renegade Chiricahua Apache had added desperation to that image. With more than a thousand troops scattered across the mountains, Brigadier General Miles was confronting the specter of a public failure. Nor could the general's subordinates like Major James Buell abide such a disgrace. There was more than one career at stake here.

"It is said the Apache Kid is the white man's dog, that men like Major Buell run me." Mickey stared at the boulder-strewn entrance to the canyon. "But I am my own man," he muttered.

"Yessir," said Jordan, spitting a stream of black juice on the ground. "Hell's hinges, I'm here to tell you Buell be damned. Geronimo, too. I didn't figure this to come down on your head. I ain't left nothing up that canyon and neither have you. The artillery will do the job. There's no way in or out. Geronimo knows he's boxed up. Let him choose for himself to come out with a white flag or be blasted into perdition." Jordan spat again for emphasis. "I've got thirty years on you, Kid. And if Gray Willow were—" Jordan caught himself, realized he had set foot down the wrong path. He sensed how Mickey Free stiffened. "Well . . . now . . . if she were standing right alongside us she'd be telling you the same thing."

Mickey studied the varying degrees of shadows and shapes, rehearsed his approach, walked the trail in his mind's eye, until he could picture every footfall. Geronimo would have left at least one man to watch the entrance. Maybe two. He'd have held council with the rest. But it was the *ndeen* left to guard the mouth of the canyon that bothered Mickey. He would have to fight them. And kill them without warning the others.

"Any bucks catch you in there and sound the alarm, you'll have Geronimo's entire band of renegades to deal with," Jordan emphasized, stating the obvious.

"Once I am among them, the sentries will not cry out for fear of giving away their positions. No, they must hunt me in silence."

Jordan noticed Mickey's Yellowboy propped against the rock. The Winchester's characteristic brass casing and butt plate gleamed in the moonlight's baleful glare. It suddenly dawned on Reverend Doctor that Mickey intended to walk into the canyon armed only with a knife. "Kid, you can't be serious. A knife won't save your hide when you come up against Geronimo."

"Nor will a rifle, or a thousand rifles. Or those cannons on the rim above us." Mickey Free chuckled mirthlessly. "For me it can only be this way."

"Then I guess I got to come along."

"We have ridden many trails together, Jordan, but where I must go this night, you cannot follow."

The chief of scouts considered the warning, then sighed in resignation. "Reckon not." Reverend Doctor shrugged, seeing the wisdom in the words. "So be it." He studied the same expanse of night and saw nothing. "When do you figure on heading"—he glanced around—"out . . . ?"

Mickey Free had already slipped away.

* * *

Three companies of weary soldiers out of Fort Apache clustered about their campfires. The artillerymen supporting Companies A, C, and D likewise huddled in protective groups about their deadly guns and waited for morning and an end to a long campaign that had eaten up most of 1886. Troops B and K, the garrison's complement of infantry, and a handful of scouts completed the encampment, blocking the pass and fanning out across the valley.

The chase had begun last fall, when Geronimo and a dozen Chiricahua warriors had taken their families off the San Carlos reservation and headed south for the mountains of Old Mexico. General Miles had immediately ordered his men into the field. It had been like chasing a ghost, following a trail of burned-out farms, looted settlements, the grisly remains of some poor prospector's encounter with the Apache. A ghost, yes, and you needed one to catch one. Now it was Major Buell's turn. Only he had luck and a redheaded hellion called Mickey Free.

"I seen the Kid just standing there, he ain't so much as budged for the longest time, and then he was gone," a trooper muttered to his companions, bone-weary and butt-tired. He took a chaw of tobacco and passed his plug around. "I heard the renegades got their own name for Free. Seeing he was raised by 'em, then turned agin' 'em. I can't get my tongue around the Injun word, but I heard it means 'Killer.' "

"Well, I'll be gawddamned," another trooper muttered, helping himself to the plug. "Still, he ain't no better than the red devils we're after if you ask me. But I reckon we gotta trust him for now."

The two men nodded in accord, imagining the lone figure stalking through the dark expanse of Skeleton Canyon, its black open maw waiting to crush the unwary intruder. The troopers were grateful for their campfire and the safety of their numbers.

"Geronimo's in there, I tell you, the wily ol' devil himself," a third soldier sighed, his voice carrying to a detachment of artillerymen lounging uncomfortably by pyramids of nine-pounder explosive lead shot and wadding and sacks of black powder.

"I wouldn't walk in that damn canyon if I had General Miles hisself at my back with a battalion of angels. No, sir. A man could catch his death in a place like that," observed a grizzled sergeant down from the artillery camp. He drank from his canteen and leaned on the iron-rimmed wheel of the caisson he had driven down to collect some hardtack from the commissary wagon.

"Or his death catch *him*, you mean," one of his subordinates chuckled. He was seated on a keg of black powder, legs draped over the caisson's bench seat, a pocketknife in one hand, a length of whittled wood in the other.

"You mean to say that blue-eyed killer has got more sand than all of us yellow legs put together," a sallow-faced trooper sourly observed, approaching the first campfire, his eyes on the coffeepot. "Now don't that beat all. Haw-haw."

"I didn't hear you volunteer to go talk Geronimo into surrendering!" someone called out from beyond the light. "You better hope that there Apache Kid succeeds. 'Cause tomorrow noon, if the red devils don't show, we got to go to hell and run them to ground."

The soldiers glumly studied the broken walls of the cliff surrounding the entrance to the canyon. Artillery be damned. Every man jack of them knew the Apache were cornered all right. But Geronimo, with no way out and his back to the wall, would die hard. Real hard. And he wouldn't die alone. . . .

*   *   *

"What do you mean he's gone?" Major James Buell growled, nursing a cup of cold coffee, catching the grit in his teeth. For a young man he looked haggard this night. The lantern's sallow glare added age and discoloration to his finely etched features. A few weeks' growth of added beard aged his youthful appearance, although these days it was the campaign that had seasoned him.

Jordan considered his commanding officer's poor state. Nothing robbed a man of his youthful good looks like a couple of long weeks spent afield, far from the comforts of home and hearth, chasing an elusive enemy that at any given moment might turn and strike without warning.

The chief of scouts sensed James Buell was tired and trying to suppress his misgivings. A gruff demeanor might be the major's way of coping with the fact that he didn't feel up to the task at hand. All Buell knew about chasing Geronimo's renegades he had learned from Jordan and the Apache Kid.

"Just what I said, Major," Jordan replied, staring past the enameled coffeepot on the officer's desk to the silver-embossed whiskey flask lying flat upon a hand-drawn map of the terrain. Buell was an artist; his maps were things of beauty. And he had the temperament of an artist, quick to anger, to judge, a man unaccustomed to the desert and the patience it took to survive in this harsh land. But he was smart. And he could learn.

"I told him to check with me first," Buell said.

"Free has a way of doing things his own way."

"See here, I gave the man an order."

"And I'm letting you know. He's gone in."

Buell could see there was no point in belaboring the matter now. He would take it up with the white Apache at a later date, if the man survived.

Buell brushed back an unruly strand of curly brown hair from his forehead. He rose from his travel desk and motioned for the scout to follow him outside. *Reverend Doctor,* he mused. Now there was a peculiar handle. The major had heard Jordan was so named because his mother had hoped her son might either aspire to the higher calling of her Calvinistic upbringing or pursue a career in the healing arts. Mother Jordan obviously had not taken into account her son's proclivity for sinning and his disdain for any kind of formal education.

Jordan followed the officer into the night air, momentarily glancing over his shoulder to cast a lingering look at the silver flask as he exited the tent. The scout stood alongside Buell, their collective breath clouding the night air.

"What a land," Buell muttered. "You bake in the saddle by day, freeze at night."

"A man can't let it bother him, Major. I promise you ol' Geronimo don't pay it no never mind."

Buell shrugged. He took the man at his word. The officer found some comfort in the sight of the campfires holding back the night, sensing rather than seeing the artillery on the high ground. Skeleton Canyon was just one of several box canyons in a maze of ridges and ravines that made up the Chiricahua Mountains. Its entrance was so heavily choked with underbrush, the troopers might have ridden past and never paid it any notice, save that Mickey Free had brought them here, elaborating on the times the Chiricahua hunting parties had rested up in the *rancheria,* secure from discovery.

Buell tried to judge the distance from the encampment to the canyon's darkened maw. The silence was deafening. He could spy no movement. Indeed, he could see little beyond the firelight, only the black expanse his troops had successfully blocked off. He half-expected the rattle of gunfire and muzzle blasts to blossom in the dark. Of course, Mickey Free might not have even reached the entrance to Skeleton Canyon.

"How long will it take him to cross the open ground? How long before Free reaches the canyon?"

"Be patient, Major. After all, it's taken the Kid ten years to come this far," Jordan muttered.

"What is that supposed to mean?"

Jordan glanced aside, met Buell's quizzical expression, pursed his lips for a moment as he paused to gather his memories (a drink would sure help, but damn if that was coming), and continued, "It was back in '76 . . ."

Chapter 9

Mickey Free heard the lookout breathing nearby, a sound so faint most men would have failed to take notice. But the Apache Kid was not "most men" and the walls of Skeleton Canyon acted as a sound chamber, amplifying the simplest disturbance for the experienced hunter.

Crouched among a blunted forest of piñon pine and ocotillo cacti, Mickey placed his hand upon the hillside, imagined he could sense the warrior's pulse through the red rocks and catch the scent of the sentry's fear sweat. Somewhere close by, in the night, the Apache was waiting for Mickey to make the first move.

Mickey knew the sentry would not raise an alarm to warn Geronimo and the band of renegades back in the canyon. No, the warrior would handle it here, quietly as possible so as not to alert other . . . intruders . . . who might be lurking in the dark.

I can feel your hatred, my brother, but it will not find me. You will not hear me come for you. A shadow will make more noise. We have come to the end of the hunt, you and I. Heii-ya. Here is your death.

Mickey Free leaned back, pressed his spine against the flat outcropping of stone. Throughout the long hours, Skeleton Canyon had spoken to him, revealed its secrets as he stole from brush to ledge to shadowy recess, pausing now and then to read the sounds and the silences of the place. He judged each step. It wouldn't do to slip and lose his purchase. The canyon floor a hundred feet below promised a rough and painful descent to the careless.

It took another fifteen minutes to cross a couple of yards as he picked his way toward the Apache. Mickey silently cursed the loose rocks and crushed sandstone underfoot. This was hard going. The subtlest sound might give him away.

Life was harsh in these mountains. And they were old and broken by the elements. It was said the Old One, the Grandfather of All, first walked these barrancas in a time more distant then memory, when the world was young. It was here the Old One first dreamed his dream of men and beasts. If a man was quiet and still and patient, he could almost hear the footsteps of the elder gods echo down the whispering wind.

Mickey Free had not come to commune with dreams but to end them. The scout slowly inhaled, his nostrils flared. He smelled water. Perhaps there was a *tinaja* close at hand. Such shallow basins of rainwater worn into solid limestone were lifesavers to thirsty men. Mickey reconsidered. No. He had caught a scent of the spring at the upper end of the canyon.

Although he had only been here once before, a long time ago, before the Run of the Arrow and the San Carlos incident, he recalled that a pool of spring water, masked by a grove of shrub live oak, bubbled out of the cliff face. The box canyon was an oasis ringed with steep overhanging battlements. The cliffs were embedded with great boulders that threatened to topple down and bury anyone desperate enough to make his camp upon the floor of the canyon. But after ten long years and countless skirmishes, Mickey Free had no doubt Geronimo was desperate.

An owl glided past the scout and headed toward a cluster of piñon pines, then at the last second veered aside and flitted off among another stunted growth of trees that eked their dry existence from this arid soil. The scout licked his lips and felt his muscles tense. It was time. The one who made the first mistake, who revealed his presence to the other, was a dead man.

Mickey studied the grove the owl had so pointedly avoided. He knelt, picked up a couple of pebbles, and tossed them ahead. The stones went skittering down the slope, creating a miniature avalanche of rocks and shale. Suddenly a figure hurtled from a patch of darkness. The Apache's lithe form sprang from shadow into moonlight with a ferocity that almost caught Mickey off guard. But he only hesitated a second and then launched himself, a knife blade glittering in his fist.

The two men met in midair, their bodies colliding with a loud crack, followed by a muffled thud and a groan as they hit the hard earth, rolled over and over, pummeling each other, knives slashing, glancing off rocks and limestone rubble. Patches of cacti whipped them with thorns. Neither man uttered a sound. But the sound of their struggle echoed on the night air.

Mickey caught his opponent's wrist. He dug his heels into the hillside, braced himself, and thrust upward; his knife slid beneath his quarry's guard and sank into his chest. Mickey pressed his forearm across the wounded man's throat to keep him from crying out. He continued to apply pressure as the Apache struggled in an attempt to bring his own blade into play, but Mickey pinned the man's weapon with a well-placed elbow and held the sentry in check long enough for the warrior to weaken. The man gradually ceased struggling, shuddered, his arms dropped to his side, and his body grew limp.

Mickey rolled free, withdrew the knife, and wiped the blade clean in the dirt. He gathered his legs beneath him and managed to stand, his sides heaving as he caught his breath. He winced and touched his side. There was a gash on his left side, and blood was dripping down onto his pants' leg. He gingerly probed the torn flesh. It was a superficial wound, painful as sin but not life-threatening. He glanced down at the lifeless form stretched upon the hillside. The moon drifted out from behind a cloud and bathed the slope in its lurid light.

Mickey knelt by the fallen Apache and took a moment to study his features. No. It wasn't Chato. Even after ten years, Mickey was certain he would know his foster brother. And this dead man wasn't him. Just another nameless renegade to join the others Mickey had hunted down the labyrinth of time. Maybe tomorrow. Maybe the next day. Mickey Free had learned the value of patience. It was the Apache in him.

It was this same upbringing that saved his life in the very next instant.

One moment the Apache Kid was lost in reverie. The next he dropped and ducked. And a split second later a war hammer whirred past his skull. The rawhide-encased stone at the end of the club was the size of a big man's fist and hard enough to kill with a single blow.

Two sentries! Geronimo had been cautious with an overwhelming force of U.S. cavalry and artillery blocking his escape. Mickey had no time to admonish himself, not if he wanted to stay alive. His attacker reversed himself and dived forward. Mickey back-stepped and lost his footing. The war club caught him on the right hip as he fell back. The warrior tried to leap atop Mickey's chest with both feet. He used his own momentum to roll out of harm's way, then caught a handful of dirt and pebbles and threw them in the warrior's face. The Apache swung wide. The war club missed the scout's head by mere inches.

Mickey made a pass with his knife that opened his attacker up along the belly, leaving a bloody but superficial wound. The Apache yelped in pain, then abandoned the contest and scrambled down the slope until he reached the floor of the canyon, where he broke into a run toward the main camp with Mickey Free in hot pursuit. Mickey could not allow the warrior to alarm the camp in the canyon. Once they were aroused by his warning there would be no time for a council, no time to explain his errand of mercy. This was a contest the army scout could not afford to lose.

But the Apache sentry had a head start. And two good legs. Mickey made a game effort, but his right leg was numb from the blow he had received. Moonlight illuminated the narrow passage, the sharply steepening walls, and, ahead, a dogleg turn that would open onto the interior of the box canyon with its cluster of trees and the makeshift shelters of Geronimo's renegades.

It was now or never. With split-second timing Mickey came to a dead stop. He shifted his hold on the weapon, gripped the knife blade between thumb and finger, judged the distance, snapped his arm forward, and hurled the weapon. It cut a deadly glittering arc through the night air and sank to the hilt between the running man's shoulder blades. The Apache arched his back, staggered ahead another few yards, then sank to his knees. He sank forward and braced himself with his hands.

Mickey limped up to the man and squatted in front of him.

"You have rubbed me out," the Apache gasped, crimson spittle flecking his lips in the moonlight. His lean features looked vaguely familiar. The man turned his face full to the light. Mickey's blood ran cold. It was Tzoe. The dying man furrowed his brow, dim recognition reflected in his gaze.

"Are you the one called Nizhee, the Killer?"

Images came flooding back, like a storm held in check by wind currents and atmosphere, unleashed at last, exploding in a torrent of electricity and thunder. At last, one of the three who had been responsible for Gray Willow's death. "Where is Chato?" Mickey snarled. "Is he with you? Is he here?!"

"Are you the Apache Kid? Are you the one called Nizhee, the Killer?" the dying man repeated.

"I am Mickey Free."

"Heii-ya," Tzoe whispered, with his last breath on earth. "One and the same."

Chapter 10

Private Marcus Dolan died quickly. He never saw his attacker spring from the shadows, failed to heed the faint rush of air or the whisper of the steel blade that came unwelcome out of the still night and carved a crescent wound across his throat. By the time Dolan had the wherewithal to cry out, his mouth and throat had filled with blood and all he could do was choke out a garbled prayer, an outpouring of his own wished-for salvation. Every sinner's dream, to be forgiven again and again. He died listing his transgressions. And the blood spurting from his severed jugular mingled with his tears.

Chato knelt by the fallen man, lifted him by the hair, craned the man's head back, opening the wound even farther as he stared into the soldier's blank expression, dead man's eyes like pennies, round and vacant, once for a brief moment preoccupied with sorrow and regret. Now Dolan's eyes were no longer of this earth.

The Apache lowered the man to the ground and crept past his body. A few horses shied as he drew near, unused to the Apache's smell. Chato retreated from the rope corral and tore off the dead man's blue coat, donned it, and ducked beneath the tether line. This time the animals allowed him to approach. Chato was a keen judge of horses. He took the time to check hooves, run his hands over their flanks, listen to each animal breathe. At last the Apache made his choice. He'd found three steeds to his liking. Using their own bridles, he led the mounts from the corral and out onto the valley floor. He retrieved his Winchester carbine from where he'd concealed it among a cluster of ocotillo cactus. He paused every few yards to check the way ahead and behind him. On a night like this the quick and the dead were one and the same. Chato intended to be neither.

He had not been sent for horses but to scout the Blue-coats and judge their chances if Geronimo's band attempted to fight their way out of the canyon. Or tried to defend it. Either course was self-slaughter. Chato wanted no part of it.

Waiting in the night, listening to the muffled chatter of the soldiers, the mournful melody from a harmonica drifting on the cool desert air, the creak of leather, and the gruff voices of the soldiers with whom Chato, Geronimo, and the other Apache had dueled for so many years. The Chiricahua Mountains were a dark and bloody ground.

Chato wiped a forearm across his features. The light of distant campfires flickered in his obsidian eyes. *You are out there, Mickey Free . . . Nizhee, Killer, my brother of many names.*

"Chato, my son . . ."

The Apache gasped in horror and spun around. Who spoke? Was that her voice? How many times had he heard her calling in the night? Was there no end to Gray Willow's wandering? He had not meant to shoot her. No matter how his heart had turned against his mother for seeking to make him a tame Apache like his father.

She pulled on the rifle. His finger caught on the trigger. *Not my fault. Hear me.* And now Mickey Free hunted him, driven by a need for vengeance. One day they must meet. But not this day. Chato would choose his own time and place to turn at bay. And that would be a time for reckoning.

He stared off toward the entrance to Skeleton Canyon. He could return undiscovered and tell Geronimo what he had seen, but it wouldn't do the war chief any good. The long knives finally had him. Chato had considered his options. He saw no purpose in returning to make a suicidal stand. Not when he was free. And while he lived the war went on. The Apache were trapped. Not even the great shaman warrior was going to get them out. Chato had seen the artillery; he had counted the campfires and estimated the number of soldiers. Major Buell and his Bluecoats had finally succeeded, and there was nothing to be done for it.

So Chato turned his back on the campfires, on the remnants of the Apache war party, on the enemy encampment and Skeleton Canyon, and on his own honor. And rode away.

* * *

"One man dead," Buell muttered. "Damn these red butchers!" He glared at Reverend Doctor Jordan's weathered war map of a face. "Three horses stolen. I ought to give the order to open fire right this minute and the hell with their surrender. It appears we have been played for fools." The major rubbed the sleep from his eyes, scratched at his stubbled cheek, cleared his throat with a swallow of brandy from a flask he kept hidden in his shirt pocket. He used his campaign hat to slap the dust from his gray woolen trousers. Then returning the hat to its proper place, he finished fastening his shirt's brass buttons. Buell adjusted his gun belt and looked to the east at the swath of stars twinkling above the skyline. The moon peered out from behind the ghostly galleon of a cloud. Shadows retreated from the valley floor like a tide ebbing back toward the line of hills and broken-backed ridges.

"Beggin' your pardon, Major sir," Jordan said, "but those horses were stolen about the same time as Mickey Free was heading off for Skeleton Canyon." The chief of scouts had joined the major on the edge of the encampment beyond the smoky haze of the campfires. Behind them, the camp was awash with activity. Men scurried about from cook fires to tents, gathering their weapons and equipment and trading opinions about poor dead Marcus Dolan, a private whom everyone seemed to remember and fondly regard. Or at least they pretended to.

His death gave a man pause. After all, it could have been any one of them murdered in his sleep by one of these red devils. Buell began to fume and pace, uncomfortable with the knowledge that he had placed his career in the hands of a man like Mickey Free.

"You'll forgive me if I do not share your confidence in this white Apache," Buell pointedly observed. He shook his head and folded his hands behind his back and sighed. He wished he were back at San Carlos, sitting on the porch of the Indian agent's house enjoying a lemonade in the company of the fair Colleen. Now there was a pleasant thought. A man could happily lose himself in the twin pools of her emerald eyes. For a brief moment the notion of that happy fate took him away from the harsh reality of the present.

"Seems that rushing the canyon in the dark would only get more men killed; they'd probably wind up shooting one another while Geronimo slips clean away." Reverend Doctor Jordan spat a stream of tobacco juice into a nearby patch of cacti, then wiped the spittle on the sleeve of his right arm. He cradled his Winchester in his left. "No, sir. Better you wait for the dawn. I'll warrant you Mickey has the old bastard's ear. If anyone can talk Geronimo into the net it's the Kid. I'd stake my life on it."

"You have, Mr. Jordan," Buell steadily replied, his expression hard enough to strike sparks off of. "Believe me. You have."

Chapter 11

Geronimo, wrapped in his blanket beneath the spreading branches of a shrub oak, opened his mind to the secret of the flames. Glowing embers from the campfire drifted upward on the sacred smoke that twisted and twined about him, then drifted toward the entrance to Skeleton Canyon.

Ghostly talons of smoke summoned what lay beyond the darkness, enticed the stillness, beckoned the unknown. Geronimo's hands trembled, not from fear. He had made war against the white settlers and their armies of Bluecoats for more than ten years. And more than ten years was a long time for a man to be hunted, to watch his back trail for pursuit, to fight his way out of traps, to win battles but never victories against a foe who would not be denied, a foe whose numbers were like the stars in the skies.

More than ten years was a long time to see his friends and cousins die one by one, until all that remained of his renegade band was eleven warriors, half that number of women, and a few scraggly children, all of them hungry, all of them weary, all of them finished. So his hands trembled.

Earlier this night he had seen a flaming star shoot across the heavens and vanish in the blackness of the great beyond. It was the sign Geronimo had been waiting for. And so he had walked out away from camp while the rest of his people slept. He had made his fire as the voices in the wind told him to do. He knelt on his faded red blanket, sat back on his heels, placed his army-issue Remington .44 revolver before him within easy reach. And waited.

He could hear the owls back in the trees, the muffled gurgle of the spring where it bubbled out of the cliff and spilled over the rocks, the horses cropping the dry grasses, an insect buzzing past, his own breath, his beating heart, the crackling embers. But in the end he knew without hearing; he sensed the man approaching, drawn by the undulating embrace of medicine smoke to the shaman's fire.

Mickey Free materialized out of the gloom and, favoring his right leg, stepped into the circle of firelight. The wound high on his left side had begun to cake over thanks to the poultice he had quickly fashioned from the flesh of a prickly pear cactus back in the canyon. He looked like a man who had been in a fight, and since he had emerged from the passage Geronimo could only surmise his force had been diminished by two.

"So, foundling . . . look at you. We have seen many seasons. And now you are a man and along the way you have found two new names, the Apache Kid . . . Nizhee, the Killer. Have you come to kill me?"

"If I had," said Mickey Free, "we would not be talking right now." He knelt across from the war chief, on the opposite side of the fire, and slipping the knife from its sheath tossed the weapon on the blanket alongside Geronimo's revolver. "I come to save lives, not take them."

"*Heii-ya* . . . there is blood on your knife."

"It could not be otherwise and you know it."

"Too bad you did not choose to ride the red road and join me."

"Then we would both be hunted men and I would not be able to save your life and those of the rest of your people."

Geronimo's eyes narrowed to slits. His muscles tensed. For a moment Mickey Free thought the man might spring upon him like a wild beast. War chief, shaman, man of power, he was still someone to be reckoned with. And Mickey Free didn't like his chances in another fight. But Geronimo did not move toward him except to stir the embers in the sacred fire.

"You carry the words from the soldiers?"

"They come from General Miles himself, carried by Major Buell and now by me."

"Speak for the long knives. I will listen."

Mickey sighed in relief and then spoke the words he had been instructed to say, the words he had memorized several days ago when Buell had offered to allow the Apache to surrender.

"It will be dawn soon. Shortly after first light the soldiers will open fire with their artillery. They will knock down the canyon walls and bury you. Then they will march through the canyon and shoot the rest."

"Many of them will be rubbed out, eh?"

"But not all. You cannot shoot them all. You do not have enough bullets in your guns, and when they are finished the Apache will be dead. But if you bring out your people, if we walk out together, no more blood will be shed."

"And what will happen to my people?"

"The women and children will be fed and returned to San Carlos."

"My warriors?"

"Surrender their guns. And they may also return to the reservation, where they can farm and tend cattle and never more take up the gun."

"And what of Geronimo?"

Mickey Free never considered lying. Geronimo was a warrior, a man of courage. And men of courage deserved no less than the truth. "You will be sent to prison. Probably to Fort Pickens in Florida."

"I do not know this place. But it sounds like death . . . the living death."

"I will not lie and say otherwise," Mickey told him, his voice softening in tone. He felt like a target in the firelight. "I ask this. . . . will Geronimo 'die' so his people might live?"

"*Heii-ya,* your words are hard. They cut like a sharp knife, like truth." Geronimo shook his head. "This night I saw the flaming death write my name in the sky." The warrior shaman seemed to age in the glare of the crackling flames. He was like an ember, pulsing with life but destined for the dark at the end of days. "A man cannot escape his fate, especially when it is written in fire."

He stared down at his fist; reddish brown like the desert mountains he loved, his hand looked to be carved of stone yet made of flesh and blood, one and the same, scarred, yes, like the land was scarred. But suddenly he realized his hand no longer trembled and he knew then what his answer must be. "It will be as you have said. So my people will live."

Mickey Free nodded. He looked relieved but still on his guard. He glanced past the war chief toward the shadowed grove at the rear of the canyon. "Does Chato still ride with you?"

"Old hates die hard," Geronimo ruefully laughed. "You may have passed him in the dark. I sent him to scout the soldier camp."

Mickey scowled. Chato had eluded him again. Of course there was the chance his foster brother might surrender with the others. Yeah, a snowflake's chance in hell. If Chato found a way to escape he would take it and his comrades in the canyon be damned. And with Chato running loose there could be no real peace.

Using a broken branch for a crutch, Geronimo struggled to his feet. He winced as an old war wound reminded him of his bloody past. Then the war chief stood, transfixed for a few moments, watching the sky, listening to the wind in the branches of the piñon pines, dancing in the sage.

Geronimo took it all in, breathed deeply, savored every lungful, as if this might be his last taste of freedom.

It was.

Chapter 12

Geronimo and his men had offered no resistance as they emerged from Skeleton Canyon, even when the soldiers clamped them in irons. The renegades remained impassive, accepting their fate with stoic resolve. Geronimo clung to his dignity and seemed to ignore the jibes and insults hurled his way by the relieved soldiers who bought their bravery with iron bracelets. Buell claimed the shackles were for the old warrior's own good, so that the soldiers would not be tempted to exact their own brand of personal revenge for the war chief's depredations.

Throughout the trek from Skeleton Canyon, Free had tried to see to the needs of the women and children of Geronimo's band. At his behest, they had been fed and cared for as much as an army in the field could allow. But no matter what his kindness, in the eyes of the surrendered warriors he was still some kind of Judas who had betrayed the great war chief of the Chiricahua.

* * *

Mickey breathed a sigh of relief when, six days later, the wind-scarred collection of adobe buildings that comprised Fort Apache materialized out of the shimmering heat waves. In another hour the Apache scouts would be heading back to San Carlos, back to the reservation and their "civilized" lives. And he would return to the Indian agency and resume his duties working for Angus McDunn. He might even get around to fixing the windmill for Miss Colleen.

Perhaps one day he would find the courage to speak his true feelings, for she had enchanted him since the day he first woke in her room, bone-weary and suffering from exhaustion after the Run of the Arrow. And Colleen's friendship had been the one bright spot in the dark days that had followed the death of Gray Willow. Colleen had been like a sister . . . to him and then one day, without warning, he began to see her in a new light. She became more than a sister . . . to a young man in love. But sweet memories died aborning and reality set in like a leg cramp as the prisoners nervously began to mill about, their iron shackles disturbing the sudden ominous silence. Mickey had brought in the last of the Apache. But he felt no elation, only a numbness of the heart.

As Buell's column arrived within sight of the sturdy-looking adobe walls of Fort Apache, Reverend Doctor Jordan left his position at the head of his Apache scouts and brought his lop-eared old warhorse back to where Geronimo and the other Apache who had surrendered formed a ragged line of prisoners flanked on either side by U.S. Infantry troops that Buell had brought with him into the field. The cavalry companies up ahead reined in their mounts at a command from the major. In kind, the rest of the column came to a halt.

A ginger-colored cloud of dust billowed over the troops and their prisoners, settling on sweat-stained blue uniforms and ragged cotton shirts alike. The soldiers used their hats to slap the dust from their shirts and trousers; the prisoners and Apache scouts waited in silence, unmoving, oblivious to discomfort.

As Jordan approached him, Mickey Free could hear the officers up ahead suddenly begin to bark their orders to the cavalry. Free was glad to be out of earshot. Officers were always issuing orders. He hadn't found all that many worth following. Perhaps it was this land. The harshly beautiful craggy ridges and serrated canyons had a way of tempering orders. A man had to bend with the wildness or it would break him.

Mickey found it curious they should have come to a halt with Fort Apache in plain sight. But there was nothing for him to do about it but wait astride his Appaloosa. He glanced over his shoulder at the solemn-looking faces of the Apache scouts, full-blood reservation warriors in army-issue uniforms. Though he knew each of them by name and had hunted with them in the past, in the years following Gray Willow's death he had become more of a loner, a man unsure where he belonged, for both red men and white viewed him with suspicion.

Jordan pulled up alongside Free and motioned for him to ride away from the column and out onto the arid plain several yards from the troops. Mickey complied, puzzled by Jordan's behavior. Still, the chief of scouts must have his reasons for wanting to speak out of earshot of Buell's command.

The two had drifted about seventy yards from the column when Jordan pulled up sharply and, turning in the saddle, confronted Mickey Free, a revolver suddenly materializing in the older man's hand. Mickey stared down the barrel and then back up into Jordan's eyes. Free calmly took a drink from his canteen, rinsed his mouth, and spat in the dirt underfoot. Then he slung the canteen back over the pommel of his saddle and waited for an explanation.

"I'm sorry, Kid, but I'll take your belly gun." Jordan walked his mount in close and, reaching over, removed Free's revolver from its holster.

"*Heii-ya*, Reverend . . . what the hell?"

"It's for your own good, Kid. I don't want you to go and do something that'll get you killed."

Mickey looked past Reverend Doctor Jordan and watched, dumbfounded, as the other Apache scouts were disarmed by the troops and placed under guard. Had Buell taken leave of his senses? Jordan might have read the young man's puzzled thoughts, for he immediately offered an explanation.

"The orders came from General Miles himself. There's nothing Buell can do about it."

"What are you saying?"

"That Geronimo and all the male Apaches of fighting age are to be removed from San Carlos and sent to Florida. Even the army scouts. There's been too many Apaches who've turned renegade and then returned to the reservation when it suited them. Relocation to Fort Pickens is the only way the settlers in the territory will feel safe." Jordan sighed and wagged his head. "All the men from San Carlos have already been rounded up and are being held in a stockade north of the fort. Geronimo and the rest will join them and be put on a train headed east right soon, I suspect."

Mickey shook his head and scowled. "No . . ." he muttered. The enormity of such a betrayal overwhelmed. It wasn't right. He'd given his word that only Geronimo would be taken away from the ancestral mountains. Now it was the rest of Geronimo's braves and, worse still, the scouts and every *tame* Apache at the agency.

"Come along, Mickey. I'll take you back to McDunn's. There is nothing to be gained by staying here."

"I gave my word," growled Free, cold fury in his eyes. His hands began to clench and unclench. His muscles tensed.

"It's the way things are. Ride away from it, Kid. Let it be."

"No."

"You got to."

"I can't. I gave my word."

"You got no choice, Kid."

"There is always a choice!"

Mickey Free dug his heels into his mount. The animal leaped away. Mickey lashed him with the reins until the Appaloosa broke into a gallop and charged the troopers. Any second Mickey half-expected the bellow of a six-gun to sound behind him and a slug to knock him from the saddle. And yet some inner voice, a gut feeling, told him the chief of scouts would hesitate at the last second. Free leaned low over the Appaloosa's neck. He was one with the charging beast, one with the rage coursing through his veins like fire in the blood.

Jordan's finger tightened on the trigger as he struggled to bring his gun to bear. For a moment he had Free in his gun sight. But he couldn't bring himself to shoot. "Gawd-dammit!" the chief of scouts muttered. The move had caught him by surprise. His own mount was no match for the Appaloosa but would have to do.

"Come on, you mean-tempered cuss." He raked the animal's flanks with his spurs. "Kid!" Jordan shouted, too late to stop the younger man. "Hell's hinges!" The stallion leaped forward and galloped off in pursuit.

Mickey Free caught hold of the Yellowboy and slipped it from the saddle scabbard as he leaned low over the Appaloosa's neck. The startled troops, the anxious faces of the former army scouts, the dusky features of the prisoners, all became a blur as he stormed past, his fierce gaze focused on only one man, Major James Buell.

The distance melted away. All that remained was the heat rising from the arid landscape, the bright sunlight, the gleam of Mickey's rifle's brass casing, the slick lever action as he chambered a round. Mickey heard voices calling out to him, heard the warnings shouted, the alarm given, as he bore down on the head of the column. Buell noticed him now, wide-eyed, startled, like game, knowing, sensing you've come for the kill.

Perhaps General Miles had given the orders. But Miles was elsewhere. Buell had given his word that only Geronimo would be sent away. James Buell had betrayed him. So Buell had to answer for it. Flame spat from the Winchester. The Yellowboy bucked in Mickey's grasp at the same instant as a bullet tore through the Appaloosa's heart. The animal dropped and ruined Mickey's aim. As he leapt to safety, Free saw the blood spurt from the major's arm. Buell's horse reared and tossed him.

Mickey struck the ground and rolled with the impact, and allowed the momentum to carry him to his feet. He glanced over his shoulder and saw it was Reverend Doctor Jordan who had shot the Appaloosa in pursuit.

Free turned and charged the fallen major, ignoring the leveled rifles and revolvers of the troopers who were about to open fire and cut him to ribbons. Mickey loosed a war cry and tried to work the lever action of his Yellowboy. Jordan galloped up behind Free and, wielding his own rifle, clubbed Mickey and sent him sprawling head over heels.

Free came to rest flat on his belly. He tried to push himself off the ground, spat out a mouthful of sand. His blood spattered the earth. Mickey's head felt as if it were about to split open. His limbs were leaden. Pain blinded him. He heard, as if from far off, Jordan telling him this was for his own good, that he had saved Free's life. *For what?*

Mickey laughed. The sound made grown men shiver.

"Better finish me off," someone growled. Mickey dimly recognized the sound of his own voice.

Before the others could agree, his arms lost their strength, the world went black, and he sank back, allowing the earth to draw him into its desolate embrace.

Chapter 13

Chato hunched in the shade of the limestone battlement and watched the Colorados, Mexican soldiers in dusty red leggings and light brown coats, toss a thickly knotted hemp rope over the stoutest branch of a cottonwood and adjust the hangman's noose so that their intended victim would swing free and clear. It wouldn't do to have a man like Julio Lopez dragging his boot heels along the ground. Let that happen and the little killer was just selfish enough to take all day to strangle and waste everyone's time. No . . . there was a correct way to hang a man. It must be done right or not at all.

"Idiotas. Watch what you are doing!" Chato heard one of the men complain in a loud voice that reverberated among the rocks. The Apache understood Spanish. He'd raided south of the border on several occasions. Geronimo's renegades were as feared here in Sonora as in Arizona Territory. But over the course of the past year the Colorados had waged a relentless war against the Apache and had hounded them back into the United States.

First the Colorados and then Major Buell and the cavalry . . . and don't forget Mickey Free. No, never forget him. Chato was still chafing from the trap the army had sprung on the legendary war chief. *He should have known better than to hole up in the canyon,* Chato thought. *Geronimo should have known better; he was too old to lead us. He should have listened to the counsel of the younger men like . . . me.*

He wiped the sweat from his eyes, ignored the sting of perspiration, and attempted to clear his thoughts. But the image of his foster brother standing over Gray Willow's lifeless body was always lurking just below the surface of his thoughts. *It wasn't my fault. Mickey Free poisoned her thinking and turned her against her own people.* After ten years of walking around with the horror of his misdeed branded on his soul, Chato had come to believe his own delusions. Except for pulling the trigger, the blame was entirely Mickey Free's. And one day ... yes ... there would come a day when the two must meet again. *And I will write his name in blood.*

He stared at the Mexican soldiers. Soldiers' uniforms were interchangeable as far as Chato was concerned. He had hidden in the rocks and watched Geronimo's surrender from afar, and ever since, the renegade Apache had been hunted like an animal. The raid was ended and the war. . . . He was alone, and there was nothing for him to do but run and hide and, seething with anger, travel by the light of the moon until he crossed into Mexico. Now fate had provided him the opportunity to take revenge.

The Apache licked his forefinger and thumb and moistened the gun sight, then cradled the stock against his cheek and bided his time. The three soldiers continued to argue about the rope length. Then the youngest of the three men, a corporal and from the looks of him hardly dry behind the ears when it came to soldiering, ordered the two under his command to present the prisoner. The two soldiers scowled and stalked back to the campfire where Julio Lopez awaited his fate. The bandit was a slim-hipped, wiry man, dressed in stolen finery: a sweat-stained ruffled cotton shirt, chestnut-colored trousers, and knee-high boots. His curly black hair was matted with dust; his black eyebrows were dark and thick and gave him a brooding quality. He stood as the soldiers approached. It was an act of defiance, though his ribs and thighs were bruised from an assortment of savage kicks and his jaw was discolored beneath the salt-and-pepper stubble of his beard.

"Since you won't tell us where the rest of your men are holed up, then it is time to answer for your sins," another of the Colorados bellowed. "Make your peace with God, *bandido*, but prepare to meet El Diablo."

Lopez spat at the soldiers and kicked one of them in the kneecap. The man yelped and launched a series of punishing blows that drove the bandit to his knees. But despite his lean physique, the bandit rose again, albeit unsteadily, laughed through his swollen lips, and spat blood in the direction of his captors. Two of the soldiers cursed him then and rushed forward to catch him by the arms and drag him to the noose.

The corporal provided the *bandido*'s horse, a hammerhead roan, rebellious as his rider, with little regard for authority. But today the animal had been blindfolded, a trick the corporal used to ensure the animal's cooperation. The roan sensed trouble and, even unable to see, strained against the reins and the unseen hand holding his head down.

Lopez was forced up onto the saddle. His boots found the stirrups. The corporal slid the noose over the prisoner's head. Lopez continued to berate his executioners. He cursed their lineage, every aspect of their conception, saying that they were the offspring of wild dogs, that they copulated with javelinas. The Colorados endured the man's tirade secure in the knowledge that they were about to have the last laugh.

"Hey, *pachuco*!" one of the privates called out. "Don't worry. We will stop by Magdalena and tell your mother how you died begging and pissing in your pants, eh? And maybe we'll give her some of this." He grabbed at his crotch.

Chato cursed and lifted his gaze toward the walls of the canyon that had been carved out of limestone and bedrock by the winding ribbon of water that flowed down from the high sierras. It was just his dumb luck these three Colorados had been returning to their main camp at Pitiquito after a week spent running whores down in Caborca. Lopez had grown careless and had finished half a bottle of mescal, fallen off his horse, and passed out here by the banks of the Rio Magdalena where the Colorados had discovered him. The three had nothing to show for their liberty but empty pockets, hard hangovers, and one had a slow burn deep in his groin. Apprehending Julio Lopez, the notorious defiler of women, desecrater of churches, and merciless assassin, was a gift from God. They promptly helped themselves to the stolen baubles and the stolen trinkets discovered in the bandit's saddlebags. Now it was time to ensure the outlaw would not incriminate them. Dead men told no tales.

"I reckon me and El Diablo will be seeing you bastards before too long," Lopez said. The outlaw spied a glimmer of sunlight off the length of a rifle barrel. Was one of his men up above the creek bed, back in the rocks? If so, who? No matter, he decided to stall for time. He lifted his eyes to heaven. "Hombre, I've committed just about every sin there is. Seeing as how I am about to come to the end of my rope, I just want to set some things right."

One of the soldiers doffed his hat as the outlaw began to pray. His companions scowled at him but to no effect. The corporal picked up a wooden switch and placed himself behind the horse.

"Well, kind sir, I reckon I'm about to swing from this rope. And I deserve it, I know." Lopez lifted his voice and continued to bellow forth his prayer. "But if you could see clear to sending me an angel to help me out of this fix, why, I'd side with him and he would never have a truer *compañero.* I'd ride the trail with him no matter where it led. Down here in Sonora a man can use all the friends he can get."

"The hell with this!" the corporal exclaimed, and raised his arm to swat the horse. A rifle cracked. The corporal staggered backward and dropped the wooden switch before he could strike the rump of Julio's stallion. His legs buckled, and he sat down in the dirt and stared with mute amazement as his belly sprang a leak and blood seeped into his clutched hands. He would die sitting upright and full of regrets.

The other two men rushed for the rifles they had left in their saddle scabbards. The Winchester on the ridge spoke a half a dozen times in rapid succession. One of the Colorados reached his rifle, but a slug tore through his side and flung him to the ground. The last man made a run for it and climbed into the saddle. A slug dusted the front of his coat; his horse bolted off, dragging the man to his death. The killing stopped as quickly as it had begun. Now there was nothing but the heat, the fading echoes, and buzzing flies.

The roan started forward despite the bandit's protests. The animal halted just as the rope went taut. Julio was forced to lean back in the saddle, crane his neck, while gritting his teeth as the noose dug into his throat. He heard the sound of an approaching horse as it splashed through the shallow creek. "Hey, *ángel!* You better hurry, eh?" the bandit managed to croak. He saw the rider's shadow before he spied his benefactor in the flesh. "*Bueno,* my friend. You come just in time. You . . ." Julio's eyes widened in amazement. The outlaw was shocked to discover his benefactor was an Apache.

The two men stared at each other. Of course Chato had all the time in the world. It wasn't his face turning blue.

"Hey, hombre, you could get hurt hanging from trees like that," Chato said. "What are you doing there?"

"I am testing this rope," the bandit replied through gritted teeth. "*Sí*, it seems strong enough to suit me. Now that I am satisfied this is a good rope perhaps you will be so kind as to cut me loose, *por favor*."

"Why should I do that?"

"Because I am Julio Lopez, the scourge of Sonora. Grown men tremble at my name; children cling to their mothers when I ride past."

"Tsaaa!" Chato stretched out his hands. "But I am not trembling. Then again, I am Chiricahua."

"*Sí*, I can tell you are a brave man. I, too, have courage. Better yet, I am a river to my friends. And in these mountains, it is good to have a friend."

"I ride alone."

"Then you won't ride far. The days of the great Apache *rancherias* are over. Your people have been driven from their land. But I can always use a man who knows these mountains." A fly circled the outlaw's head and landed on his sweat-streaked cheek. Vultures, already attracted by the blood in the sand, began to cut their lazy spirals in the sky. "Well then, amigo, do we ride together?"

Chato considered his options. The Old Ways were dying. Like the coyote, he must adapt to survive. The renegade slid his Winchester into the saddle boot, snatched a knife from his belt, and slit the noose and the coarse ropes binding the bandit's wrists. Lopez righted himself and grabbed the blindfold from the roan's eyes. He dismounted and retrieved a small-caliber pearl-handled Colt revolver, his Winchester and *bandolera*, and in the process gave the corporal's corpse a brutal kick that flattened the dead man onto his back. Lopez swaggered back to his roan and remounted.

"Come along, *mi amigo*. It is back to the mountains for us. Ride, hombre, ride!" Lopez swung his sombrero in the air and then slapped the roan across the rump and galloped off in a cloud of dust.

The Apache wasn't all that certain he could trust the bandit, a man whose loyalties were for sale. Then again, the outlaw's allegiance had been bought and paid for in blood. It was the only currency some men understood.

Chapter 14

"Kid, you left me no choice," Jordan said, peering through the iron bars separating him from the man on the cot. His breath formed on the chilled night air as he spoke. From within, only silence.

"Damn, why couldn't you ride away from it?" Jordan dug his hands deep in his coat. "You hear me, Kid? They were fixing to shoot you dead. And killing Buell would not have helped nothing. Orders have a way of getting carried out." Jordan shoved his hands in his coat pocket. He could feel the prisoner was watching him. Something in the hushed dark made his flesh crawl. "You in there writing my epitaph, eh? Well, I won't go under so easy." Jordan shrugged and lost some of his belligerence. "See here, I know rounding up all the fighting men ain't right. But there's not a family in the territory, Mex or white, who hasn't buried a friend or one of their own over the past ten years. You can't blame folks for being afraid." The raw-boned old Indian fighter spat a stream of tobacco in the dirt. "Colleen's out here. Maybe you'll talk to her."

Again silence.

"Damn," Jordan grumbled, and turned on his heels and walked off across the compound. But the woman standing at his side refused to leave with him. Colleen stepped up onto an empty rifle box and placed herself level with the window and held onto the cold iron bars. She waited until the chief of scouts had left before speaking. The guard out-

side the jail was around by the door, struggling to stay
awake.

"Mickey, Reverend Doctor was only trying to save your
life."

Free eased his legs onto the floor. The stockade was a
single narrow adobe hut with a heavy oaken door at one
end, the barred window at the other, and a row of cots
placed against one wall. It stank of perspiration and cigar
smoke. Colleen didn't care. Crossing to the window,
Mickey gingerly repositioned the bandage the Fort
Apache's resident physician had wrapped around his skull.
After a single attempt to get the damned thing to feel right,
Free discarded it completely and tossed it on the earthen
floor.

"He's got a funny way of showing it," he muttered.
"Maybe I'll get a chance to 'save' his life sometime."

Colleen didn't like the sound of that. She shifted her
stance on the box she was using to place herself near the
window. In the moonlight, her fine blond hair looked like
spun silver, her features silken and unblemished, her lips
full and dark. She glimpsed movement. It was like standing
too close to a caged panther. For a moment the woman was
tempted to retreat a step as the prisoner inside approached;
then she felt ashamed for even thinking Mickey might mean
her harm. Free's face appeared in the window, framed by
the weathered adobe bricks holding the bars in place. He
reached out and his hands found hers. Instantly there was
a connection, familiarity and warmth and perhaps even a
stirring of unsettling urges.

The voices of nearly a hundred warriors hung upon the
night air. No one was sleeping this night. Under guard by
nearly half the troops, the Apache, behind a stockade of
wire and wood, were singing for what was to come, songs
of power, of misgiving, of loss. Mickey Free knew all the

chants by heart. He lowered his head to their entwined hands.

"I thought I was bringing peace, by bringing in the renegades. It's what my mother wanted; it's what she died for." He looked up; the shadows masked his features. But moonlight glinted off his eyes, left them cold as crusted ice on a drowning pool. "What will you tell the children when they ask you about their fathers?"

"I don't know," Colleen said in a soft voice. "First I have to think about a way to save your life. James doesn't want you to hang; I know it. Even if you did assault him."

"James? Ah, Major Buell . . ."

"We are . . . close. Oh, Mickey, this is all so awful. James will be mustering out soon. He intends to settle here and grow with the territory. One day Arizona will be a state. There is no telling what a man like him can achieve." Colleen could feel his fingers slip away from hers. "And I wanted you to be there with us. You're like a *brother* to me. . . ." She tried to reestablish contact, but his hand suddenly dropped away and all that remained was the sense of him, in the darkness, and that colder-than-death gaze that chilled her to the bone. What had she said to bring such a response?

"You have friends," she pressed on. "My father is already meeting with James—Major Buell. We will find a way out of this." She reached in through the bars, but he was already out of reach. "Mickey . . . I know what's happening with your people, I mean the Apaches, is wrong. And we will try everything to correct it; I promise."

Silence.

"Remember when we were young, that first year, after Gray Willow's . . . death. I taught you to read. By the end of the year you were working your way through Father's library. We sat at the kitchen table on winter nights and you would read to me from Shakespeare." She gently laughed, an image coming to mind. "A boy, more Apache than white, reading: 'To be or not to be, that is the question,' and we would drink strong coffee and eat fry bread. You loved the stories and the sound of the words."

Nothing.

She drew her arm back, realizing he was beyond the reach of her words. She climbed down from the box, then glanced up at the window and pressed her cheek against the adobe wall. "Don't hate me, Mickey; please don't hate me."

Within the jail, Mickey Free stood with his back to the wall. He could hear her footsteps recede into the night. He closed his eyes, slowly exhaled. *Hate you?*

" 'Shall I compare thee to a summer's day?' " he whispered, his thoughts reaching deep within for written words of a time past that spoke what he lacked the courage to say. " 'Thou art more lovely and more temperate.' " Yes, he had read those very words to her once upon a time, and she had listened. But she had not heard his heart.

Now the chanting in the night increased in volume until it seemed to swell to deafening proportions. The prisoner shook his head, tried to remember the rest of the words, tried to fix on a memory as if he were a drowning man reaching for an outstretched hand.

Mickey Free. The Apache Kid.

Coyote, where are you now? Long ago you abandoned me. And now I am lost.

He covered his ears and sank to the floor, his legs drawn up tight. Free sagged forward and lowered his head to his knees while the emotions raged like thunder, while the chanting railed and worlds collided in his heart.

* * *

"I should have him hung. General Miles will insist on it when he returns," Buell said, pacing the commandant's office, a room that had suddenly become much too confining the longer he endured Colleen's stern stare. It was warm here within the adobe walls, for a fire crackled in the hearth to ward off the desert's chill. Firelight mingled with the sallow glow from the oil lamps on the desk and a nearby bookshelf.

Angus McDunn and his daughter sat upon two ladder-backed chairs in front of a hand-hewed pine desk whose surface was littered with official-looking documents. The walls were festooned with an assortment of maps, a woven blanket, and a pair of chromolithographs—one depicting English gentlemen riding to the hounds; the other, landed gentry promenading with their ladies along a flowering creek bank.

"James does have a point, my dear," Angus interjected, coming to the officer's defense. But then the two men were in a position to help each other out. Buell was preparing to resign his commission and muster out of the army to devote himself to building up his ranch. With the accolades the major had already begun to receive for bringing in Geronimo, Buell sensed an opportunity to become involved in the political workings of the territorial government.

Angus was anxious to see his daughter married to a man like James Buell, who came from a good family of considerable wealth. The Indian agent believed the major was destined for greatness. Angus placed his hand on his daughter's shoulder. "The army cannot allow the attempt on an officer's life by one of his own men to go unpunished."

Colleen glanced down at her folded hands, slender fingers entwined; her shadow flickered across the woven rug underfoot. The chanting from the Apache compound drifted in through the cracks in the shuttered windows. She could also hear one of the troopers in front of his company's barracks playing a lonesome melody on his harmonica. Any other night the sound would have been relaxing.

But not with so many soldiers posting guard duty at the makeshift compound. Despite the fact that the Apache braves had been paired up and shackled together, Buell was still concerned they might attempt an escape. He chose to err on the side of caution and keep a heavy contingent of soldiers on duty. Colleen wanted to blame him, but she knew him well enough that he found the situation distasteful. But he would do his duty and see it through. It was a quality of character she found both admirable and exasperating.

A pair of flying beetles had made their way through a crack in the shutters and frantically circled overhead, searching among the crossbeams for a place to alight before being lured to the oil lamps and their eventual date with death. Steam drifted from the spout of the blue enameled coffeepot set before her on the desk. The men were taking a measure of brandy in theirs. By God if Colleen didn't think she needed a shot to ward off the evening chill. It seemed to take all her strength to fill her cup with coffee and add the brandy. An inexorable gloom had settled over her and robbed the young woman of her energy.

Buell's left arm moved stiffly. His shoulder was heavily bandaged beneath his blue woolen shirt and unbuttoned coat. His boot heels rapped a steady cadence upon the wooden floor as he paced. "There is a principle here. My course is quite clear in this. I must see it through."

"It wasn't his fault," Colleen said, looking up at him.

"He came charging at me like a banshee and nearly blew my head off!"

"Mickey couldn't help himself. Don't you see?" Colleen rose and crossed to the officer and took his hands in her own. She looked into his eyes, her gaze pleading. "Try to understand. It was the Apache him."

"The Apache . . ." Buell repeated, frowning. He started to reply, then halted, waited a moment, gathered his thoughts. "Then let him join *his* people."

Chapter 15

The Southern Pacific locomotive, crouched like a beast on its tracks in the early morning, breathed steam in terrible rasping whispers while a fireman stoked its great heart of flame and iron. The beast was impatient, so it huffed and growled and clanked. The iron rails shuddered beneath the locomotive's weight. Smoke drifted from its stack and trailed across the coal box like a shroud.

Colleen and her father waited in their carriage. She was wrapped in a lemon-yellow shawl and her breath clouded the air. Angus touched his daughter's arm and gestured toward the wheel-rutted road that wound off from the spur toward Fort Apache. To the west, along the tracks, a scattering of lamplit windows and the coal oil streetlights of Rio Seco flickered against a velvet black backdrop of distant hills.

They were four miles from the outskirts of town, safe from the intruding curiosity of the inhabitants who might have ventured forth to watch the Southern Pacific take on its load of prisoners. Buell had chosen to load his prisoners aboard the train in the wee hours of the morning to prevent further confrontation. Under his steadfast gaze, wagon after wagon deposited their dejected burden and then started back toward the fort. Flanked by mounted troopers and escorted by a well-armed infantry, the Chiricahua filed forlornly into the boxcars.

Angus and his daughter waited and watched throughout the long, sad procession. Several families had left the San

Carlos reservation in hopes of catching a final glimpse of
their husbands, fathers, sons, brothers. Families cautiously
approached the carriage, braving the ranks of cavalry drawn
up to secure the area and guard against any last-minute
insurrection on the part of the Chiricahua.

The pleas of the old ones touched Colleen's heart. Her
eyes welled with tears while Angus told them he was powerless to stop this injustice but vowed to see it corrected
and the tame Apache returned to home and hearth. Until
the men returned, the women, the children, and the village
elders would have to tend the crops and see to the cattle.
Angus's words did little to raise the spirits of his charges,
but at least they were something. So the McDunns returned
to the train and kept their vigil while the Apache men, both
warriors and farmers, marched up the ramps and into the
railroad cars without incident, their silence all the more
unnerving. The chanting had ceased now, and the Apache
moved as men already dead, with lowered heads and eyes
fixed upon a world beyond the kin of the long knives.

As fortune would have it, one of the last wagons brought
Geronimo and his band of renegades along with the former
scouts, many of whom had already received harsh treatment
from those they had hunted. The army's former allies were
bruised and bloodied from frequent attacks by the recently
surrendered renegades. For now an uneasy truce kept them
apart. The two disparate factions made their way into the
last boxcar without any further trouble. But then they were
under the gun, and the soldiers had been ordered to execute
any troublemakers outright.

Geronimo was the last of the Apache to climb the ramp.
He paused at the entrance to the boxcar, took in a lungful
of the dry, cool air, and turned to face the east where morning's first light kissed the underside of clouds and etched
them in gold. Then one of the soldiers nudged him with
the barrel of his Springfield, finding courage in the fact that

the notorious war chief was shackled and unarmed. Geronimo glanced down at the soldier and, with his wise, sad eyes, dismissed the youth with a shake of his head. Then he eased through the entrance.

Major Buell and Reverend Doctor Jordan rode up out of the dark and flanked the carriage. Buell touched the brim of his hat. "You shouldn't be here, Colleen."

"You're wrong," she replied. "My place is here. I want to remember this day for a long, long time."

"I fear we shall rue it," Jordan glumly added, echoing her sentiments. "Here is the last of them, coming along."

A solitary wagon emerged from the twilight. A lone figure stood in the center of the wagon bed, his legs slightly bent. He seemed to anticipate every lurch, adjusting to the sway and shudder of the wagon as it progressed along the road.

Looks like I'm the center of attraction, Mickey Free silently observed. Indeed, all eyes were upon him. He glanced at the driver, a sour-looking enlisted man hunched forward on the wagon seat. The man kept checking over his shoulder as if he expected Mickey to attack him. But that was the furthest thing from the prisoner's mind. His flagging spirit held him bound, more so than the chains at his wrists or the eight mounted troopers riding in the wagon's dust.

Take it all in now. Breathe deep. The desert air must sustain you, the way the earth loses its heat, the golden blush of sunrise, the air so clear a man could see forever. Hear the faint stirring breeze and the sound the wind makes as it creeps out of the distance like a stalking panther, pauses to brush your cheek as it passes and vanishes into the howling wilderness.

Take it all in, hold it in your heart, Mickey Free, for these are the final days of a people who will continue to live but will never be the same, for better or ill, never the same. Something is lost today.

The wagon rolled to a stop alongside a crude-looking ramp leading up to the boxcar into which Geronimo had disappeared. Buell and Jordan started forward and the carriage near them also followed.

Look at them. Your friends, your betrayers. They cost you your honor, the future you saw for yourself. Feel the pain in your chest, your heart wounded as if from a knife thrust. See her, with her yellow hair and her sad face. Does she weep? Weep for yourself.

Mickey Free stepped down from the wagon bed and proceeded up the ramp, and when he reached the gaping entrance to the boxcar he turned and confronted the soldiers and Buell with his arm in a sling against his chest. There was the Indian agent and Colleen. Jordan, astride his nervous mount, reached up and touched the brim of his hat.

Jordan, McDunn, Buell . . . Weep for all of them, Colleen. Because it shall not end here.

He backed into the boxcar, and as the door slid shut an army of hands reached up for him out of the dark interior and roughly dragged him to the floor. He jabbed a thumb into someone's throat, bit the hand of another assailant. But there were too many; the weight was crushing. He was pinned and a set of wrist shackles stretched across his windpipe and tightened.

"You hunted us," one of the Apache snapped.

"Better we died like men than believe your words," another of his attackers said in a voice trembling with rage.

"Zi-hil-zee. I will kill him!!"

The pressure around his throat grew unbearable. Free struggled as best he could. He clawed at the chain cutting into his flesh, kicked and squirmed while the pinpricks of light exploded before his eyes and his lungs screamed for air.

And then the chain loosened and he rolled over on his belly and retched and afterward gasped for one precious breath at a time, his sides heaving, heart pounding. And when he finally managed to lift his head he looked up and discovered the reason he was still alive. The Chiricahua warriors had drawn back as Geronimo approached from the opposite side of the boxcar.

"No more," said the crafty old warrior shaman. He squatted in front of Free. His weathered features looked carved from ancient stone. There was wisdom in his eyes and a sad, strangely centering calm in his voice that disarmed the hatred within the boxcar walls. "We are Apache." Geronimo's gaze swept across the faces of the prisoners, silently studying the war-hardened features of the men he had fought beside, had led into battle, the men from the reservation whom he had fought for even though they had not wished him to do so. "We do not make war upon our own."

He took Free by the arm and helped him stand even as the train lurched forward. Mickey lifted his head and looked at the man who had just saved his life. My God, what had he done? Gray Willow's legacy had brought him to ruin and imprisonment. How could her dream of peace have been so wrong, unless it was not the dream but the time itself and the wild country that shaped the lives of those who lived here?

Geronimo stepped past Free and walked to the door the soldiers had slid in place and bolted from the outside. Still, through the cracks, he could glimpse the land and the sky; he could make his connection with the source of his strength. Mickey joined him there, to peer through the gaps in the boxcar's wooden walls, to catch a scent of sage and distant pine, but all too soon the soot from the smokestack fouled the air and the drone of the powerful engine drowned out the call of the wild.

"We . . . are . . . Apache," Geronimo repeated, but his voice cracked.

"All of us," said Mickey Free, glimpsing a truth he had never fully realized until now. Several of the other Apache men joined them. And so they stood shoulder to shoulder and watched the desert sweep past as the locomotive gathered speed carrying them all into the land of the dead.

Part II

Chapter 16

December 1886
Christmas Eve at the San Carlos Agency was a still, cool
afternoon with the sky overhead layered with high, thin
streaks of cloud and the Chiricahua Mountains in the distance a patchwork horizon of purple and gray and dark
sienna. Christmas Eve was a dinner of wild game and roasting hens stuffed with piñon nut and corn bread dressing,
onions and potatoes and a fiery beef broth laced with *chipotle* peppers. There was strong coffee, smooth brandy, and
apple tarts for dessert. Christmas Eve was a time for the
fellowship between Angus McDunn and his daughter and
their honored guest, the soldier who had *captured* Geronimo, James Buell. This heroic mantle had been thrust upon
Buell by a relieved populace eager to show their gratitude.
The plaudits had made him uncomfortable at first, but glory
had its uses.

"Well, Major, I daresay you were never fed like that
while you were in uniform," Angus said, easing back in his
chair and loosening his belt. He took a sip of coffee and
then dabbed at his bushy mustache. He gave the tips a twirl
to keep them curled. His eyes darted from his daughter to
Buell and back again. *Don't they make a handsome couple?
And high time she found someone.*

"No, sir, nor did I ever enjoy such charming company,"
Buell said, his eyes flashing as his gaze drifted to Colleen,
who blushed and shook her head. He cut a handsome figure
in his frock coat and black string tie. He had allowed his
goatee to grow into a full beard that he trimmed close to

his jaw. His brown hair was brushed back from his head and parted in the middle. He carried himself ramrod-straight, as befitted a man of breeding. Arizona was rough country and Lord only knew the territory needed all the refinement it could get.

"And I shall clear the table and allow you men your cigars. Shall you take them on the front porch?" the woman asked.

"Why don't you let me tend to that, my dear?" Angus spoke up. "Take our guest out for a breath of air. There never has been a prettier day." The air was cool but not intemperate, a far cry from the miserable fate of a Christmas back east with its sleet and freezing temperatures.

Colleen frowned at her father's peculiar behavior. What were these men up to? Angus would prefer a snake bite to clearing tables and washing dishes. Still, she didn't mind keeping company with Buell. True, he could be quite self-centered, but she had also glimpsed an inner core of decency in him. In the months that followed the removal of the men from San Carlos, Buell had written letters of protest that, unfortunately, had gone unheeded by General Miles and the Congress. And indeed, there had been some call for the trial and execution of Mickey Free for assaulting his commanding officer. Buell's swift punishment and Free's removal had placated the ones who made those demands.

"I would enjoy that." Buell rose and offered the woman his arm. The house smelled of sage and freshly baked bread and roasted fowl, and yet he was eager to leave, eager to ask a question and hear her answer. "I shall take that walk outside, ma'am."

Colleen took his proffered arm and allowed the man to escort her onto the porch. There was a chill wind and Buell immediately doffed his coat and placed it around her shoulders. "I can get a shawl," she protested.

"Please, Colleen, you do me honor by wearing my coat."

"There is no honor in catching pneumonia."

"I am not cold. See, I am even sweating." Buell followed her to the corner of the porch and stood at her side. They looked out across the semi-arid landscape, the bridge and dry wash, the dusty houses and jacals of San Carlos where the elders worked side by side with the younger women and the children, tilling their hardscrabble gardens of corn and mending fences, weaving baskets, and moving the livestock before they overgrazed so close to the village. It was a tranquil tableau yet disturbing, in its own quiet way, for the absence of young men.

"The children have begun to return to school. I shall have all ten back before too much longer. Twelve if Iron Bear allows his son and daughter to come to me." Colleen lifted her gaze to the adobe schoolhouse local laborers had built alongside the Agency House. A brass school bell hung in its carriage over the front door.

"What would they do without you?" Buell observed. A couple of the children waved to her. Then they recognized Buell standing with her on the porch and ran off. "I see my popularity is undiminished."

"They'll forgive you. It's only a matter of time before they learn the truth within your heart. I have."

"Then I am twice blessed," Buell said. "And if you know my truth, then you know what I have come to ask you."

Color crept to Colleen's cheeks. A smile flirted with the corners of her mouth, but she feigned ignorance.

"Well, madam, you leave me very little choice but to place myself at your mercy."

He reached out and touched her arm. She turned to look at him, seeing past the demeanor he projected to the world to the man she knew him to be. She held her breath as he searched for the proper words. To Colleen's relief, Buell found them.

"Miss McDunn, I pray that you will do me the honor of consenting to be my wife."

"Why, James . . . you are a lulu."

Buell fumbled for a reply. "Does that mean . . ."

"Yes. It means yes."

"Ahh . . ." said Buell. He started to speak, then held his tongue. What more was there to say? It was going to be a merry Christmas after all.

Chapter 17

December 1886

The rain knew him by name. The thunder raged, as did his spirit, but the wailing wind called him to freedom, tormented him with freedom dreams. *I am Mickey Free, one of the dead who walk, who live, but you cannot see me. You Bluecoats are the living and you hide from the thunder. The lightning blinds you in these hours before dawn.*

He had to hurry. The storm would subside. And the soldiers would come at first light to bury the dead. They would be anxious to return to their whiskey-soaked Christmas celebration. What was that noise? Had they come already?

He froze.

Then in the gloom the Apache Kid spied a scuttling rat The rodent made its way beneath the longhouses. *Wise old scavenger, I'll follow.* Mickey crawled through puddles that sucked at his tattered clothes and lean torso. The mud wanted to draw him under and turn him into worm food. *Not yet, not tonight.* He worked his way beneath the infirmary with its empty beds. Cap Broadus, the old sot of an army doctor who liked his ration of hard cider, would be asleep upon one of those spare cots.

Mickey searched by touch, his fingertips probing the underside of the floor until they found the loose board he had noticed last week. He pried the wood apart with his makeshift knife, a jagged piece of saw blade wrapped with dried strips of leather. He reached up, caught hold, and lifted himself up through the floor and into the darkness. Lying prone on the floor, he waited, listening, searching every corner of silence and storm sounds until he was certain he heard the doctor snoring in the other room. *I'm alone . . . no . . . not quite. Another is near.*

Nacori.

And though Nacori knew the foundling by name and bore Mickey Free only ill will, the old renegade was beyond calling out. He was beyond forgiving Free, who had hunted him down and handed the irascible renegade over to the Bluecoats. Mickey tiptoed across the room, his sodden clothes spattering the floorboards with every step. Would the grave diggers notice? Perhaps not. Some things had to be left to chance.

He found the table in the center of the room. A burlap-shrouded figure rested quiet in the timeless sleep of death. It was Nacori, or what remained of him upon the earth. Mickey worked quickly with the knife, cutting the seam that held the corpse in its rough burial shroud. He peeled back the flaps and tried to avoid peering into that grim gray visage. Mickey maneuvered the body from its wrappings and lifted it off the table, dragged stiff old Nacori across the room to the hole in the floor and lowered him down into the darkness, into the mud, where with any luck the dead man would not be found until Free had made good his escape.

Before Mickey could return the loose planking, a second pair of arms rose up out of the gloom. Free gasped and rocked back on his heels and reached for his knife, then relaxed as he recognized Geronimo, who worked his squat, solid torso through the opening and lifted himself into the room.

"Tsaaa!"

Geronimo wiped a forearm across his features. "Nacori waits below. I must not remain here for too long or he might return."

"I think I am safe from him."

"Then you do not know him. He had a powerful hate for you."

"I may answer to him, but I do not think it will be today," Mickey replied.

Geronimo shrugged and laughed softly. "You did not know him as well as I. Had you ever walked in his moccasins it would be different." The tired-looking old warrior walked over to the table and stared down at the burlap bag that had once contained Nacori's corpse. The mud below and a grave outside the walls were both the same to the deceased.

"Lie here. The bag must be stitched from the outside. One of the soldiers might notice. I will make it right." Geronimo found the coarse iron needle Mickey had intended to use to sew himself back into the corpse bag.

"You should take my place," said Free. "Father . . ." There. The word was spoken. The warrior shaman had been his father. And was still, and always would be.

"No," Geronimo told him. He crossed the room to stand by one of the shuttered windows and peered out at the gray downpour, the somber walls of the prison huts, the tall fences surrounding the prison yard, and the rain-battered cypress trees looming at the edge of the bayou, their moss-laden limbs driven low by the storm. "I no longer can walk such a path, my son." The silence that followed was an unbroken chain binding their final moments together, to memory and legend.

He returned to the table. "Hurry. It will be light soon enough and I will be missed." Suddenly, without warning, the aged warrior was wracked by a violent spasm of coughing, which he managed to stifle with a hand clamped across his mouth. His skin was dark as rusted iron. His eyes, too, were hard and black. But his voice seemed to come from a far-off place ruled by resignation and defeat. "My war is ended."

Mickey did as he was told, quietly crossing the room. He stretched himself upon the table within the folds of the burlap bag and gripped the makeshift knife before him in his folded hands. Geronimo immediately began to seal the flaps. He worked quickly with all the skill of a man who had repaired his own moccasins, shirt, and cartridge belt. He kept the stitches shallow in order to make them easier to tear apart. Mickey Free watched him as he worked until the last few inches of cloth were all that remained.

"It was you who kept me alive all these months. Your words were my shield. Why do you not hate me?"

The warrior shaman merely shook his head. "Shall I hate the wind when it stings my eyes with sand? There was a time you heard the Coyote speak. But you have lost your way."

"Yes," said Mickey Free. "How can I find it again?"

"Look among the bones of the rain."

The warrior shaman finished sewing the last few inches of the seam, then tucked the needle into the pouch dangling from his belt. He crossed the room, his gait awkward and stiff from the arthritis that had begun to plague him. He hesitated, squatting at the edge of the opening in the floor, then took the loose board in hand, lowered himself down with care, and gave the room a final inspection. Glancing over at the lifeless-looking form on the table, he chuckled softly, a gentle, melancholy laugh.

"*Tsaaa*, Mickey Free. How have you suffered?"

The Run of the Arrow . . .

"What have you learned?"

And those were the last words Geronimo ever said to Mickey Free.

Chapter 18

How much longer? My back hurts. Ignore the leg cramp. I cannot afford to move. What of the stitches? Perhaps Geronimo left the seam too tight. The burlap has the smell of death. What if the grave diggers notice me breathing? Maybe if they're tired and anxious to complete their task . . .

The cloth is cold to the touch. It's wet and clinging to my face, covering my mouth, choking me. Ahhh . . . ! Swallow the scream, the horror. Fight the panic.

What if . . . ? No.

And what if . . . ? Stop it!

If I take too long to free myself it will mean a bullet to the head.

Then, either way, I'll have escaped. Mustn't lose my resolve. Turn my head and breathe, just breathe. Draw the terror into my lungs and exhale it back into the world. Quiet now.

Where's the knife? . . . Ah . . . there, now start to work. Slice through a stitch at a time. Blast this wagon, lurching side to side. I almost groaned. Damn wagon is jarring my backbone loose. And the wet burlap is pressing against my face. I won't be able to breathe soon. Careful now, slice another strand, and another, now another. Soon I'll be free. One way or the other . . . free.

* * *

"It's a fine way to spend Christmas," Private Noah Tallman complained, tilting his pockmarked features to Florida's rain-drenched sky. Fine beads of moisture spattered his grizzled chin, his pouched eyes, and the white ridges of year-old scar tissue on his forehead. The scar was the puckered legacy of a drunken argument that his best friend, Regal Beulah, had settled by cracking Tallman across the skull with a three-legged stool.

Unlike Tallman, who harbored a grudge toward the deceased in the body bag and the officers who had ordered the burial detail out into the elements, Private Beulah had already come to terms with their situation. The dead Apache had begun to ripen. Beulah was determined to accomplish the task at hand with minimal trouble or effort. He tossed a pebble at the team of horses as his raw-boned companion seated beside him on the bench seat flicked the reins and applied the whip.

For Regal Beulah, a twenty-two-year-old recruit of average height and build, the army was a place to draw his pay and bide his time while waiting for the rest of his life to happen. He seldom made plans but rather accepted his lot with a casual, noncommittal air that served him well in the gambling halls and brothels nestled among the bayous that flourished in the vicinity of the prison.

While Tallman chafed at being assigned to Fort Pickens, Private Beulah took the duty in stride. Guarding a bunch of Apache renegades imprisoned here at the edge of the swamps certainly beat marching across some dusty badlands getting shot at by bloodthirsty savages. After more than half a year within the barbed wire–enclosed compound of Fort Pickens, their health ravaged by swamp fever and malaria, Geronimo and his bunch were about as fearsome as a church choir.

"A minor discomfort." Beulah grinned, turning his features to the rain. He opened his mouth and drank in the rain, then lowered his head and allowed the droplets to roll off the brim of his hat. "Pity the poor bastards out west who have to hunt these renegades down." The soldier reached around and patted the corpse in the burlap bag lying supine on the wagon bed. "Now here's my kind of Redstick. Ain't nothing for us to do but dig a hole for the ol' sonuvabitch and plant him."

"He picked a sorry time to die. Seems the colonel might have let the old bastard season till after Christmas. I hear they're serving turtle soup in the mess. The lads will be resting with full bellies while we're up to our butts in mud and gators." Tallman spat off to one side and dug deeper into his slicker while a trickle of cold water worked its way down past his collar and found the back of his neck.

The horses plodded on with lowered heads. They knew the way to the burial ground and kept to the wheel-rutted path that wound beneath the moss-draped cypress trees and weeping willows with their swaying branches brushing the moist earth like emerald curtains in the gray downpour. Thunder rumbled from afar, the sound muffled by the thicket. Raindrops spattered the surface of the bayou, mud puddles formed on the path and filled the trenches left by the iron-rimmed wheels. Beulah produced a slender brown bottle from his coat pocket and uncorked the vessel and tilted it to his lips. Tallman glanced aside at the bottle and brightened.

"Bless my soul, Regal, if you ain't Father Christmas after all!"

Beulah pretended to hide the bottle beneath his slicker. The expression on Noah Tallman's homely face was ample reward. Beulah grinned and feigned surprise.

"Oh . . . did you want a taste? It's only sour mash and not anything like the silk-smooth taste of real sipping whiskey you're accustomed to."

"I'll make an allowance for it in this case," Tallman said, licking his lips. He made a grab for the bottle. The front wheel rolled over a length of rotten log half-submerged in the mud. The wagon lurched from side to side and the bottle went spinning from Noah's grasp. "Nooo!" He dropped the reins and leaped down from the bench seat as the wagon veered to the left and continued to roll forward along the cemetery road. Tallman landed in the mud on all fours and began to frantically search for the whiskey bottle. The soldier slogged along the path, his boots sinking ankle-deep, his eyes wild as he examined the area alongside the wagon. Suddenly he heard a distinctive crack as one of the slow-stepping mares in harness stepped on the brown glass bottle; the vessel shattered beneath one of the animal's iron-shod hooves, spilling the sour mash into the mud.

"Ahhhh!" Tallman groaned, and began to curse the mare. He shook his fists at the lowering gunmetal clouds that seemed to brush the very treetops. That was it. He couldn't take any more. He was wet and tired and no *goddamn dead Injun* was worth this ordeal. "We've come far enough. Stop here!"

"The cemetery is up yonder!" Regal shouted back, gesturing to a patch of rain-drenched shadows up ahead.

"Brake this damn wagon or I'll drop the nag where she stands!" Tallman shouted. He drew his pistol and scrambled forward to place the barrel against the mare's head. Regal hauled back on the reins he had only just retrieved.

"We'll dump him in the bayou and be done with it. Let the gators have him. Ain't no one gonna know if you keep your trap shut and your wits about you."

Tallman crossed around to the back of the wagon bed and reached in to catch the corpse by the ankles. It was only then he noticed the peculiar-looking saw blade poking through the burlap bag. The makeshift knife made quick work of the loose, uneven stitches, opening the length of the bag. A thunderclap boomed close by; lightning flashed; then the dead began to rise.

Tallman's plain, homely face went pale. He staggered back, his mouth framing a silent scream. Mickey kicked him and sent the soldier sprawling. Regal Beulah swung about, hesitated in surprise, then brought a forearm across Mickey's throat.

"What the devil? This bastard has some life in him." This close to Free, the soldier recognized him. "It's him. Noah; it's the white Apache." The forearm crushed against the prisoner's windpipe. "We come here to bury a dead man. Reckon you'll have to do," he muttered.

Mickey jabbed the makeshift knife into the forearm locked beneath his chin. Private Beulah howled with pain and loosened his grip. Mickey Free spied Tallman standing in the middle of the muddy road. The soldier leveled his revolver, a Navy Colt .36-caliber. Flame spewed from the muzzle. Mickey dived face-forward into the wagon as Tallman fired. The bullet meant for the prisoner struck Private Beulah in the abdomen. The soldier gasped, ignoring the superficial slash below his elbow, and clawed at his belly as he rolled off the wagon seat and landed in the mud.

"Noah . . . you've done me in." Regal Beulah sank to his knees as he made a grab for the side of the wagon, for the brake, for the wheel rim. "Oh, sweet Jesus, just one more day. Let me see the sun." But he was dying in the rain and there was nothing to be done but whisper a prayer, the only one he could remember, something his mama used to say over their meager meals. "Lord, we thank Thee for the food set before us, to the nourishment of our bodies . . ." The words drifted from his lips, became fainter and fainter until as inconsequential as his sigh. He slumped forward in the mud.

Tallman watched, shocked, then tried to bring the pistol to bear as Mickey leaped over the side of the wagon and charged him; three quick strides and he was in striking range. Mickey batted the gun aside. Tallman fired into the air. Mickey knocked him down, twisted the Navy Colt from the soldier's hand, then stood, his chest heaving as he gulped in a lungful of air. Tallman looked up into the maw of that gun barrel. It looked as big as a cavern or like the dark opening of a grave.

His grave.

Thunder rumbled; lightning crackled; rain near blinded the soldier. He held his hands up to his face. "No. Please, oh, Mother of Mercy, don't do it. Don't."

Mickey thumbed the hammer back and took aim as the man cringed. All he had to do was squeeze the trigger, and not squeeze very hard, either. What did he owe this soldier or any soldier? He had ridden with the soldiers, hunted his adopted people, and been betrayed and locked away. They called him Apache Kid; well, now he would show them, show them all. But despite all the reasons he had to pull the trigger, Mickey couldn't bring himself to finish off the soldier. All he could do was sigh and slip the Navy Colt into his belt. Then he knelt by the grave digger, stripped him of his holster and ammunition. Mickey's wild rust-red mane was plastered to his skull now. Rain dripped from his craggy features, ran along his neck, soaked into his coarse shirt. In the lightning's glare, his own ice-blue eyes flickered with iridescent fire. If death had a face, this was it.

"You tell them, I let you live. You tell the soldiers how this happened, who shot the other man, how it was an accident by your hand?"

"Yes." Tallman nodded, his hands trembling. "I swear on my mother's grave. I'll tell them how it played out, that it was me shot him by accident." He wiped the moisture from his eyes, blinked, glanced about.

He was alone in the mud.

* * *

Mickey released both horses from the singletree and, without looking back at the man whose life he had spared, leapt astride one of the mares and led the other off through the storm. The tempest swallowed him up as if the white Apache were one of its own, another seething mix of fire, thunder, and primitive force about to be unleashed.

Chapter 19

James Buell wanted to dream of the woman he was planning to marry. He wanted to dream of spun-gold hair and buttermilk skin and a smile that made him glad to be alive, to fantasize a future of moonlit rides and warm embraces amid desert flowers in bloom and hungry kisses and unquenchable desire. He wanted to dream of Colleen Mc-Dunn.

But a cold north wind in February moaned outside the window and rattled the glass in its pane and conjured nightmares as it prowled about the walls of the Larkspur Hotel. The blue norther, rebuffed by the hotel's foot-thick adobe walls, eased its chill around the shutters and wormed beneath ill-fitting window frames, until it roused the former officer from his troubled rest and he sat upright in bed and glanced about the darkened room and wiped the sleep from his eyes. The last vestiges of his nightmare receded like fraying strands of a web that sleep had draped across his face.

Tattered hills and howling coyotes and feral eyes seemed to be watching him from shadows. His mind was clouded with illusions and an overwhelming sense of loss and guilt. Images of disturbing clarity, the faces of the Apache men as they were led to the boxcars, lingered for a brief moment, then lost their intensity as he became fully awake.

He shivered, glanced about him in quiet appraisal of the hotel room. Juan Mendoza, the owner and a native of Tucson, prided himself in offering the cleanest rooms and the most comfortable beds in all of Rio Seco. A kitchen out back with a single long-board table for the guests served up the best damn *cabrito,* chili *rellenos,* and chicken *molé* in the territory. And a thirsty man had easy access through the lobby to the Reveille Saloon for those moments when a more *robust* nourishment was required.

"Damn," Buell muttered, wiping a forearm across his eyes. He crawled out from beneath his woolen blanket, pulled on his trousers and boots, and tucked in his nightshirt. In another couple of weeks his hacienda outside of town would be ready, he mused, and he could leave these temporary headquarters behind.

Headquarters, catching the slip as it entered his mind. Those days were gone. Buell had resigned his commission from the army with honors, garnering praise and notoriety throughout Arizona for having commanded the expedition that punished the Apache renegades and brought in Geronimo.

He was the talk and the pride of Arizona, Major James Buell of Philadelphia, a blueblood whose wealthy family had sired a real warrior, a man determined to achieve his own success. Sure, he had more money then just about anyone between the Staked Plains and the Golden Gate. But more important than money was his ambition. The man was going places. Now he was Mr. James K. Buell, monied cattle buyer, novice rancher, and a leading candidate to become the next territorial governor, not to mention the future husband of Colleen McDunn, the prettiest girl in all of Arizona.

He crossed to the window overlooking the street where several new buildings had been erected along Main Street over the past six months. His breath clouded the already-opaque window as the norther renewed its protestations. Buell squinted, thought he spied a horseman ride past along the empty street, but it was difficult to be certain.

"Rio Seco," Buell muttered. Well, a man had to begin somewhere. And there were worse towns. At least he was known here. And the town was growing. With its connection to the Southern Pacific railhead, Rio Seco was becoming a center for cattle buyers out from California. And the town continued to be nourished by its trade with the army. Save for the occasional raid by outlaws from across the border, Arizona Territory was enjoying its first lengthy peace since the cessation of the Apache Wars.

Buell was only too happy to take credit for pacifying the San Carlos renegades. If ever a monster deserved his fate it was Geronimo. It was just too bad the war chief had brought so much ruination down on the tribe itself and entrapped the innocent with the guilty.

All the blame rested with Geronimo; that was profoundly clear, Buell told himself, repeating an inner dialogue that had plagued his rest for months now. Perhaps when his hacienda was completed and he was residing with his new bride within his own adobe walls, maybe then he could rest. Until then, Buell knew one sure remedy for a troubled sleep.

He pulled on his frock coat, maneuvered around a bed stand, the night table, a chair, and a chest of his personal possessions, crossed the room to the door, and entered the dimly lit hallway. With his shadow silently gliding over the wall at his side, Buell made his way to the top of the stairs where the light was better. He fumbled in his pocket and found his timepiece, a gold-embossed pocket watch that had belonged to an uncle who had been shot dead by a Rebel sniper four days after Lee's surrender at Appomattox. Some said the watch was cursed for that. Buell said it was damn nice workmanship and he'd take gold any day, cursed or not.

"One twenty-eight," he said softly, reading the time aloud. There was no one to hear him, save a moth fluttering around the glass chimney of the closest table lamp. Sooner or later the insect would be lured to its demise by the golden promise of unreachable flame.

Buell descended to the front lobby with its scattering of high-backed chairs, serape wall hangings, a table and settee by the front window. He walked past the front desk where Heck Boone, the night clerk, sat upon a stool, his upper torso sprawled across the counter. Boone used the register for a pillow; his brown hair parted in the middle and combed close to the skull was showing a tad more scalp these days. Buell prodded the man with the nib of the fountain pen placed by the registry book for the convenience of the patrons.

"Straighten up, Mr. Boone. I cannot abide a man who sleeps at his post."

Boone snorted and sat upright, wiping his face and blinking his eyes as he looked wildly about, struggling to adjust to the waking world after being startled from his dreams. The lamp in the lobby had been turned low so as to be conducive to the clerk's rest. "See here, Mr. Buell. I ain't no sentry. And there ain't no war."

"Indeed, but vigilance is the price of our victory," Buell gravely replied. "None of us should forget that."

He looked over at the side door leading off into the saloon. It offered a bit more life and light. Buell took the bait, admonishing poor Boone about the value of work and then heading off through the entrance into the Reveille Saloon.

Behind the bar, a swarthy broad-shouldered man in a cotton shirt with rolled-up sleeves, brown brocaded vest, and black woolen trousers buttoned just below his protruding belly and held to his frame by a pair of black suspenders already had a bottle of his best rye and a clean glass waiting for Buell.

"Evening, Major. In for a final round?"

"Hello, Sergeant. Have I become so predictable?"

"Like clockwork." The bartender grinned. Sam Nance had served with Buell, mustered out a few weeks before the officer, and taken a job in the Reveille, the very place he had spent most of his leave while stationed at Fort Apache.

Buell ambled over to the bar, leaned his elbows on the walnut surface, inspected the glass and found it suitable, then poured an inch of the tea-colored liquid and threw back a shot that was anything but tea. The liquor hit the back of his throat and didn't stop burning until it found the pit of his stomach.

"It's got a bit of edge," Nance remarked, nonchalantly wiping another glass clean. He peered out from beneath an eyebrow that scrawled in a continuous bushy line above both eyes. The faint hint of a smile touched his lips.

"Not hardly," Buell gasped. He poured another drink and turned his back to the bar to survey the saloon's rustic interior, a space he was more than intimately acquainted with. He found solace in familiarity. Oak beams ran along the ceiling of the room. Tables and chairs were haphazardly arranged for the patrons, most of whom had departed for the evening for the comfort of their homes and hearth. One man, a dark-skinned bronc buster, perhaps descended of Zulu kings, lay across a tabletop, snoring, his head pillowed on his folded arms, his ebony features turned toward the back wall. A pair of old-timers, both prospectors, sat in the corner, nursing the last of a shared bottle of "Who hit John" as they talked of gold strikes and fabled riches that always seemed just out of reach.

Another of the late-night patrons kept a lonely vigil with a deck of cards and a game of solitaire. The gambler, of Mexican descent, was slender, almost rail thin, with long, tapered fingers that made the deck of cards dance every time he reshuffled. He appeared to be a man of some means, for he wore a handsome frock coat, chestnut trousers cut to fit close to his wiry frame, a ruffled shirt, and a black satin vest. His curly black hair glistened as if he had wet it with rosewater. The play of lamplight and shadows deepened the harsh brown planes of his high cheekbones and deep-set eyes. Where the gambler's coat fell open, Buell could just glimpse the pearl handle of a small-caliber pocket pistol. The gambler nodded; the former officer returned the gesture. The gambler waved a hand toward the cards, inviting Buell to take a seat and try his luck.

Buell raised his glass in salute but declined the offer. The Mexican shrugged, taking no offense, and continued his game. It appeared the inclement weather had cut into his earnings for the night. But there would be other times and other opportunities. Patience and a sense of observation were a gambler's only allies.

"You hungry, Major? The pickled eggs are fittin'. And there's some corn dodgers I snitched from the kitchen."

"This will do."

"And . . . uh . . . Carlotta and Chinese Mary are alone in their cabins out back. . . ."

"This will do," Buell pointedly repeated. The third drink didn't burn as hot as the first two, but then he figured his throat was numb by now. Embers popped and crackled in the wood-burning stove that commanded a space at the other end of the bar. Nance wandered over and began to stoke the fire and feed some fresh wood to the hungry flames. The stove helped, but there was a quality to the keening wind that made a man shiver and turned his thoughts to mortal things, to regret for those things left undone, to the lies a man must cling to, or go mad.

* * *

A couple of hours later, Buell made his way to the bottom of the stairway, glanced over his shoulder at the desk clerk asleep yet again behind the counter. A Seth Thomas clock on a shelf behind the slumbering clerk tolled a quarter past three. Buell assessed his chances of ascending the stairway and making his way to his room without falling flat on his face and didn't like them. But he was determined to make the attempt. Now that he could sleep, he by God was not about to make his bed on the stairway. A man had to have his pride.

He kept a tight hold on the balustrade and pulled himself up the stairs, willing one step after another, and used the same technique on the hallway, only this time he braced himself against one wall and guided himself to his room. He felt in his pocket for the bottle he had been nursing, then remembered he had left it on the bar. He stifled a yawn. Forget the bottle; he didn't need it.

* * *

The gambler, Julio Lopez, watched Buell depart from the saloon, then slid his chair back from the table and approached the bar. Sam Nance waited until Buell had started up the stairs before helping himself to a drink from the ex-major's bottle. He noticed Lopez watching him, filled another glass and slid it over toward the man he took to be a gambler.

"Gracias, señor."

"Por nada," Nance replied. "The son of a bitch won't notice."

Lopez took his drink slowly, savoring the fiery brew. "Your friend has good taste in whiskey."

"He can afford it," Nance said, his tone of voice revealing the bartender's true feelings toward officers.

"Porqué?"

"Don't you know who that is?"

"I am new to Rio Seco, my friend."

"That was none other than Major James Buell. I mean, he ain't a major no more. Mustered out, he did, with full honors. Got himself a fine ranch, a real future. Not like me, stuck behind this bar wiping out glasses till the day I get planted. Course it beats breaking horses like Mose Woodard over yonder." Nance nodded toward the black man asleep on the table. "That'll age a man faster than a fifty-cent whore."

Lopez emptied the contents of the whiskey glass down his gullot and slammed the glass down on the countertop. "The name is familiar. This major, he is of some notoriety."

"Where have you been? Why, he's just about the most popular man in the territory!" Nance exclaimed. "He's the man who captured Geronimo. And that's the reason you were able to ride up from . . . uh . . . where did you say you hail from?"

"Tucson."

"Right," Nance agreed. The bartender had a full head of steam now and needed no prodding. He gave a blustery account of the campaign against the Apache and how Sergeant Sam Nance helped Major James Buell bring down the most notorious renegade to ever plague the frontier. ". . . And once we had 'em all in chains we shipped them red heathens off to Florida so we wouldn't have to chase 'em all over again when they decided to break out from the reservation and loot and murder some more innocent folks."

Lopez placed a silver dollar on the counter. "My friend, it would be an honor to buy a drink for such a hero as yourself."

Nance grunted in satisfaction. "About time someone noticed that rich bastard wasn't alone when he took the measure of the damn savages." He pocketed the Mexican's change, then placed the major's bottle on a shelf beneath the bar and brought out his own personal brew. "I appreciate it, amigo. You know, for a Mescan you ain't half-bad."

"Neither are you, my friend. Neither are you."

Nance tried and failed to make sense of the gambler's reply. But he laughed anyway and filled the man's glass to the brim with tequila. Lopez lifted the drink in salute and tossed it back and slammed the glass down once more. "And what of Major Buell? I would be proud to buy him a drink."

"The sonuvabitch can buy his own, believe me. The man owns most of the land to the south of town. His ranch borders the reservation all the way to the Chiricahua Mountains. He's a blueblood all right. Born and reared in Philadelphia, got more money than God." Nance helped himself to a glass of tequila, closed his eyes and relished every drop, then braced for the heady aftereffect, a rush of well-being that rose from his heels to his scalp. "But he's come out here to make his mark. Mind you, a man could do worse. Wouldn't surprise me to see Buell become territorial governor. And from there, why, we might have us the future president of these United States staying right here at the Larkspur." The bartender could not keep the bitterness from his voice.

"I envy such a man—wealth, influence, a fine ranch, such good fortune. All he needs is a beautiful señorita to share it with."

"Got him one, a right pretty yellow-haired gal. Colleen McDunn, the daughter of the Indian agent. The major dotes on her, too. There ain't nothing he wouldn't do for her, not a damn thing. I can't see carrying on like that over a woman, but then, I reckon one man's poke is another's princess."

"*Sí*, to a man in love," Lopez replied, his mind working. Thanks to the talkative sergeant he had discovered all he needed to know about James Buell. He grinned and wiped the back of his hand across his mouth, then gathered his cards and tucked them away in his coat pocket. Nance spied the Mexican's pearl-handled pocket pistol.

"Best be careful about carrying that hideout gun."

"Oh?"

"They say Julio Lopez carries one just like it, pearl-handled an' all. That bastard's been causing grief on both sides of the border."

"Now, señor, you frighten me. I've heard that name and want no part of him. Carlos Gonzales is a humble gambler and wishes no trouble with anyone."

"That's why I warned you."

"Again I am in your debt, *mi amigo*." Lopez bought a bottle of tequila to help him ward off the chill of night and started toward the back door of the saloon. His boot heels rapped against the floor; his California spurs jangled with each step.

"Chinese Mary's got her a guest. But I think Carlotta is all by her lonesome," Nance quipped.

"Not for long, eh?" Lopez grinned and patted the bottle. He continued past the stove and down a narrow hall to a door that opened onto the alley and a wooden walkway that led from the rear of the hotel to a pair of one-room cabins set side by side and beyond them an empty corral with a pair of freight wagons barely visible against the black of night. Lopez pulled his coat around him and walked along the length of the hotel until he reached the corner. And then, unnoticed, he made his way to Main Street and hurried along the boardwalk to the livery stable where he had left his horse. Sooner or later someone was going to recognize him. A man had to know when to leave. And he was anxious to rejoin Chato back in the foothills. With his mind racing, Lopez reached the stable and marched straight to his horse. By the time the roan was saddled and ready to travel, the bandit had already devised a plan, one he knew Chato would agree to, one that would make them both rich, powerful men.

*   *   *

Buell opened the door to his room. The faint illumination from the hall cut a swath through the room's dark interior and played across the corner of the bed, the bed stand and washbasin, and the shadowy outline of a man seated in the chair by the window. Buell recoiled in surprise, momentarily lost his balance, and staggered back through the doorway, striking his head against the doorsill. He slid to a sitting position and caught himself from toppling over.

"Damn!" he exclaimed through clenched teeth.

A rough-skinned hand that looked as big as a country ham dangled before his eyes. He reacted as if about to be struck, then relaxed at the sound of a familiar voice. Buell looked up past the hand to the plug-ugly features of Reverend Doctor Jordan. The scout wore a deputy U.S. marshal's badge now. The chief of scouts had been the first to retire from the military, turning in his papers on the very day the train left carrying the Apache into captivity in Florida.

"Relax, Mr. Buell; it's only me. You won't have to worry about *him* for a while yet."

The big man hauled Buell to his feet, dusted him off, and pulled him into the hotel room. Jordan lit a lamp and then took a seat by the window. James Buell crossed to the night table and splashed some water from the basin onto his neck, wiping the back of his neck with a damp cloth. Then he sat on the side of the bed, the wooden slats creaking beneath his weight, and studied his uninvited guest.

Jordan seemed even larger in his greatcoat; his huge bulk strained the chair. It looked as if any moment it might collapse. The former chief of scouts removed his hat; wisps of gray hair sprouted from his sunburned scalp like an afterthought. Lamplight glinted off the deputy marshal's badge pinned to his vest. He scratched his bent nose, then fished in his pocket for a flask, found what he was looking for, and took a drink, finishing off what remained. He made a mental note to have Sam Nance refill the flask with his cheapest rattlesnake juice.

The deputy marshal returned the flask to his inside pocket. The movement caused his coat flaps to fall open, revealing the heavy leather gun belt buckled tight against his impressive girth, and the Colt revolver that was holstered on his left side, worn walnut grip jutting forward for a cross draw. He dabbed his grizzled mouth with the faded red bandanna that he kept loosely knotted at his neck.

Buell hadn't seen the man for months, ever since word reached him from the capitol in Prescott that Jordan had been hired on as the territorial deputy marshal. The appointment seemed to suit the Indian fighter. He was leather-tough and crafty as an old curly wolf. Still the man's sudden appearance, looming up in the room like that, had given Buell quite a start. His heart was still racing.

"Who?"

Jordan gave the former major a quizzical look.

"You said, *I won't have to worry about him yet.* Who?"

Jordan handed the man a wanted poster. Buell turned up the wick on the lamp by his bed. He gazed down at the bill in his hand and sucked in his breath then as he read aloud, " 'Wanted for murder committed during an escape from Fort Pickens Military Prison. Mickey Free . . .' "

"They're offering seven hundred dollars for him, dead or alive," Jordan said.

"I don't see what this has to do with me."

"You . . . me . . . we turned our backs on him. We sent him off to prison with the same renegades he helped to capture."

"He shot me, Mr. Jordan; have you forgotten?"

"You deserved it. Hell, we both did. We used Free and then betrayed him and every peaceful Apache on the reservation."

"I had my orders. There was nothing I could do."

"There is always *something* a man can do. And I'd think you've enough of a decent streak in you to know I'm right." Jordan folded his arms across his barrel chest. "I hear you don't sleep so good, Major. A conscience is a troublesome thing; yessirree, it can be a sure-enough nuisance."

"Mr. Jordan, I appreciate the visit. I've seen this wanted poster. Is there anything else you feel the need to share? If not, then perhaps you'll be so kind as to leave me to my rest."

"Only this: He's on his way. Mickey Free is coming back here."

Buell stood and crumpled up the poster and tossed it aside, then crossed around his bed and stood before the room's only other window. It also faced the street. Maybe it was the whiskey, but he had no fear. Feel guilty? Why should he? An officer follows orders.

"Then let him come. Arizona is my home now. Will I be driven away by some white Apache? I think not. My future is here, my bride-to-be, my fortune . . ." He pulled back the curtains. And as he stood there it seemed as if he defied his own inner demons and the bleak elements of this winter's night. "I took no pride in following those orders. I have promised Colleen to do everything in my power to undo this injustice. But damn if I will run from Mickey Free."

Jordan watched him in silence. Buell was the territorial hero, the man who supposedly had brought in Geronimo. *By heaven, the fool's begun to believe his own lies.* The wind moaned like a lost soul and the moon peering from behind a cloud cast a pale, ghostly light that turned Buell's features an ashen gray, like a man already dead but walking and planning and dreaming. There was nothing he could not accomplish, nothing he could not achieve. Let his enemies beware.

"Take heed, sir. The man who captured Geronimo casts a tall shadow," Buell said.

To which Jordan replied in a dire tone of voice, "That's what I'm afraid of."

Chapter 20

Out of sand and distance and broken hills, out of the shimmering dry air and billowing battlements of clouds resting on the serrated skyline, a man comes riding. The great swamplands are behind him, also the drums of the Deep South and the bayous where he hid and gathered strength and waited out his pursuers who wrongly assumed he would immediately head west. Behind him are miles of black land and king cotton and the Father of Waters. He has foraged when needed, taken a horse or rifle or clothes and raided root cellars and smokehouses for sustenance. He has not kept count of the days, but it has been a long, lonely trail across the Staked Plains and rolling hills and up into the dry country and across the rugged backbone of the world. And now, after so many days, he has come to trade the lupine meadows of the high country for the lowlands with their spring blooms of paintbrush and tufts of milkweed and the spiny welcome of the ocotillo and prickly pear topped with its own butter-colored petals. But he cannot hear earth's brown heartbeat or the siren call of the whispering wind.

Ba-ts-otse the Trickster has followed the lone rider down through stands of mountain pine where the hawks nest, down where white-winged doves and thrashers dart among the ironweed and hyacinth, down along a dry wash whose eroded banks are blanketed with pink and orange fairy dusters. Hummingbirds and cardinals scold him, Horseman pass by. Then they see Ba-ts-otse shadowing the intruder

*and fall silent, for the Trickster is old and wise and the
spirit of an ancient one still glimmers in his eyes.*

*Who is the man and why does he disturb the way of
things? There is trouble behind him, trouble before him,
trouble under his feet. The Coyote does not call him by
name. He knows this man will not hear. Perhaps one day,
once again, but not now.*

Vengeance is deaf.

* * *

Colleen McDunn tied back her hair with a length of blue
ribbon. With a pair of shiny gold ringlets firmly tucked
away, the woman wiped her hands on her apron as she
instructed two of her pupils, Kutli, a twelve-year-old boy,
and Prairie Star, his nine-year-old sister, to gather the slate
tablets and pieces of chalk from the wooden desks and stack
the primers on a corner table. Outside, their companions,
ten children ranging in age from six to eleven, were amus-
ing themselves in the play yard. It was good to hear their
laughter and squeals of enjoyment as they raced about with
their hoops and sticks and short bows. The children's trust
had been a long time in the earning. Colleen took pride in
her accomplishments.

The woman glanced around the one-room schoolhouse
she had filled with love and learning. Colleen sighed, sur-
veying her domain as if for the last time. Then scolded
herself. No, it would only be for a few weeks and then she
would be back. Her husband's hacienda was a substantial
ride from the reservation school, but that didn't matter. She
was willing to endure any ordeal if it meant keeping the
school open. If the Apache were ever to have a chance at
a good and decent life, then the children must be educated.
And who better than the one person who had been their
champion, even to the point of her ostracism from the local
community?

"Miss Colleen, you want us to wipe clean the slates?" the boy asked. It was plain as the nose on his coppery face that Kutli did not approve of the woman's impending departure. After she nodded, he handed a rag to his sister, a doe-eyed little girl with a dark sweet face brown as burnt sugar, and fell to work alongside her.

"Who will teach us our letters and cyphering, Miss Colleen?" said Prairie Star in a trembling voice, her eyes glistening with tears.

"Why, I will, of course," Colleen replied, crossing to the girl and wrapping her arms about the child's chunky little frame. "I'll be back. I promise. Nothing will change. Except I shall have a husband."

"Major Buell," Kutli added in a derogatory tone of voice. "The one who sent our father away."

"James is a good man. But there were orders he had to follow even though he did not want to." Colleen studied their faces and knew they did not understand. Nor did she feel like defending the indefensible. "Your father shall be returned. Mr. Buell has promised to make this happen. And so do I." She could not tell whether they believed her, but her words seemed to assuage their concern. They resumed cleaning the slates and stacking the primers while pausing every few minutes to chance an over-the-shoulder glance in the direction of Colleen's desk, on which she had arranged a feast for her students.

The front door opened. The noise of the school yard rode in on the rays of sunlight that flooded the interior of the schoolhouse. Dust motes like flecks of golden ore swirled and spiraled in the air.

"A fine way for a spring bride to spend her last afternoon of freedom," her father dryly observed from the doorway. Angus McDunn took a few steps into the schoolhouse and glanced about him at the drawings, the maps, the lines of grammar written in both the Apache dialect and English on the slate board that covered one wall, the simple arithmetic equations laboriously transcribed by his daughter for her students to copy on their chalk tablets. He counted twelve chairs behind the desks. That meant she had gained two students since his last visit to the classroom.

Colleen patted the wrinkles from the white cotton apron that kept the dust off her faded blue calico dress. Perspiration dotted her upper lip. She wore a look of consternation that mingled with the joy she knew she was supposed to be feeling. And indeed she was happy. But the children's attitude only mirrored the opinion rampant throughout San Carlos toward James Buell, the same opinion that was directed toward Angus McDunn, although to a lesser degree. But both men were held responsible for the deportation of the Apache men.

In truth, she did hold her father responsible by his inaction. As for her husband-to-be, James was handsome and proud and pretended not to care. But Colleen knew he possessed a conscience and that he saw full well that the removal of the San Carlos Apache men to Florida, and punishing them for the actions of the renegades was a despicable betrayal, and that the authorities must be called to task. Now that Buell's fate was no longer tied to the military, he had become more vocal in attempting to right this wrong. His opinions, because of the esteem in which he was held throughout the territory, carried more weight and had helped to call attention to the plight of the people of San Carlos.

As for Angus, well, despite everything, he was her father and she loved him. Colleen smiled at the Indian agent, then shooed young Kutli and Prairie Star from the schoolhouse with orders for them to play with their friends until she rang the bell to bring them all inside.

Alone with her father, she sighed and took a seat behind her desk, folding her hands upon the oak surface. Angus remained standing, shifting his stance, looking for all the world like one of her pupils who had been caught misbehaving.

"You certainly won't leave them hungry," Angus observed.

Before his daughter was an array of delicacies piled high upon wooden platters and china plates. She had prepared fry bread, flapjacks, flour tortillas rolled around strips of *cabrito* and chilies, and *huevos con nopalitos*, a mixture of beaten eggs and cactus pad. For dessert, Colleen had dug into the agency larder and opened two tins of peaches and baked a cobbler, something the children were unaccustomed to having. The fruit would be a special treat for them.

"No," she replied. "But their hearts starve as well as their bellies. When their fathers and older brothers return—"

"Always that."

"Of course."

"What can I say to make things right with you?"

Colleen shook her head and leaned back in the chair and closed her eyes for a moment, then exhaled slowly, softly, "It's not what you say; it's what you didn't say. You should have spoken for them. They might have stopped the train for you."

"We don't know that."

"Because you didn't try."

"Tomorrow you will be married. Things will look different."

"Oh. Do you think I'll go blind the moment James puts the ring on my finger? That I will not see the truth? I love you, Papa. But you should have tried to make things better for these people. And for Mickey Free."

Angus frowned. He had heard just about enough from this young woman. "I cannot name one family in Rio Seco who hasn't lost a child or parent or cousin, not one family who hasn't buried a neighbor or friend, because of the Apache. Hatred doesn't get buried that easily. But the source can be removed; there can be a time of healing. That's what I bought by the forced removal. I bought time for healing, for peace to take root."

Colleen's father realized he had begun to pace. His boots drummed upon the wooden floor; his cheeks were flushed. He blinked and wiped a hand across his mouth. "It is a decision I am prepared to live with." He pulled out a pocket watch and checked the hour. "I have a meeting in town with a cattle merchant." He returned the watch to his vest pocket.

Angus tried to think of something else to say. But he was sick to death of this argument. "See here . . . I don't expect you to understand. You sit in this room with these children, with your books and maps and such, safe within these walls." Angus noticed she seemed to have lost interest in the conversation. Damn, and he was about to make a keen observation. "As I was saying—"

"Shhh," Colleen hissed.

"What?"

She held up her hand, motioning for him to be silent. And when he ceased to argue, even the Indian agent could tell something was amiss. The play yard was strangely silent where before there had been shouting and squeals of laughter and the raucous banter of children. Angus appeared puzzled. It was oddly quiet. He turned on his heels and made his way down the aisle between the rows of desks and opened the school door and stepped outside, leaving it ajar.

Colleen shooed a fly away from the cobbler, slowly rose, untied her apron and placed it over the food, then started after her father. She only went a few steps when a shot rang out, startling her. Then her father stumbled through the doorway, clutching his side. Blood dripped from his pockmarked nose. His eyes were wide with alarm. He reached out for her and collapsed as she hurried forward to break his fall.

"Papa!"

Her hands beneath him came away crimson. *My God, what was happening?* Angus tried to speak to her, but his voice was a groan of agony. He pointed toward the doorway. A name suddenly formed in Colleen's mind. Reverend Doctor Jordan had shown her the wanted posters and cautioned the father and daughter to be on their guard. Wanted for escape and murder. Mickey Free had killed and would probably kill again. And he was coming . . . or was he already here?

A shadow fell across the woman as a familiar figure filled the doorway, blocking the sun, splitting the rays so they flooded around him and the smoke curling from his rifle. Colleen shaded her eyes and peered into the glare, her heart racing as her father's attacker advanced into the schoolroom.

One . . .

Two . . .

A few steps and she recognized him. A shudder of fear coursed through her. The woman's hand rose to her mouth to stifle any exclamation. What was the point? Her father appeared to be dying. Colleen was alone. And there was no one to hear her scream.

Chapter 21

Kutli hurled a stone that missed Mickey Free's head by inches. The Apache Kid ducked despite himself and swung his horse about to confront the pack of boys who were challenging his passage through San Carlos. He hadn't expected this kind of reception. After all, these were his people.

He touched his boot heels to the gelding's sides and the animal lunged forward. The children scattered like prairie chickens spooked from their nest. Kutli and a pair of older boys hung back and continued to pelt the intruder with rocks they'd gathered from the dry wash.

But as Mickey Free bore down on them, their courage failed and the boys ran for the relative safety of their homes, a dusty brown collection of adobe cabins. The horseman could sense the scrutiny he was receiving from behind the shuttered windows.

"Bicha-digah!" someone shouted. "Get out."

Mickey Free twisted in the saddle to locate the source of the outburst. His hand dropped to his belly gun, a Colt .45. He spied a number of the elders and half a dozen younger women peering at him from the paths among the houses and their fenced-off gardens. He didn't need to ask about the men; he knew only too well their fate.

He walked his mount up to the well in the center of the settlement and eased off on the reins to allow the thirsty animal a drink. He sat easy in the saddle, studying the houses and the newly planted gardens, the occasional rack bearing a stretched wolf pelt, mule deer, or mountain lion, and waited for one of the villagers to approach him.

Had he changed so much? He'd discarded the stolen army uniform in Florida and stolen a change of clothes off a farmhouse clothesline. In Alabama, he'd "exchanged" his army mounts for the sturdy little bay gelding he'd found grazing the lower meadow of a plantation. Crossing into Texas, he'd paid a nightly visit to a mercantile in Washington on the Brazos and come away with his woolen pants, *botas*, the half-leggings made of sturdy buckskin, a faded woolen shirt, and the first pair of leather boots that fit since his escape. And so it had gone, living off the land, living by his wits, tightening his belt when necessary, and letting the anger in his belly provide him the fuel he needed to keep going.

And so he was home . . . ?

Then again, perhaps not. The Apache kept their distance. Mickey sensed an unspoken warning that he should not approach or there would be more than rocks coming his way. Perhaps they associated him with all the misfortunes that had befallen them. It saddened him to see this once-proud tribe, his adopted people, not just tame, but broken in spirit. He had no words to offer them. He was a man caught in the middle, in a clash between two worlds. This was the hand he had been dealt, and he would have to play the cards as best he could. He looked around, spied the graveyard, pulled the horse away from the water, and pointed the gelding toward the row of weathered wooden crosses. No one made a move to stop him as he walked his mount past upturned coppery faces. He brought the horse to rest before Gray Willow's grave.

"Little Mother," he whispered. "I'm here. What now?"

He heard the voice of a coyote in the distance, wild and mournful.

Gray Willow had spoken of Ba-ts-otse, the Coyote Spirit, lulled him to sleep with stories of the Trickster, left her white Apache child with dreams to grow into, taught him to listen for that which was beyond hearing, to see beyond sight. *If he calls you by name, my son, then some say you are dead. But others say . . . you never will be.*

"Where is the truth?"

The dry wind ruffled the wildflowers someone, Colleen, had left on his mother's grave. The voice of the coyote faded in the distance. Had it even really sounded? Or did it matter? The answer to that was as elusive as the dust in the wind. He tugged on the reins, turned the bay, and headed for the Indian agency on the opposite side of the dry wash that separated McDunn's house from the main settlement. Mickey noticed the one-room school and wondered why Kutli and the other rock throwers weren't at their desks.

He rode up to the schoolhouse, the hooves of his horse leaving miniature plumes of dust in his wake. Mickey slid his Winchester from its saddle scabbard and walked his mount close enough to the front door, within a barrel length, and nudged it open with the rifle sight. The door creaked on its hinges and swung ajar to reveal a shadowy interior, a swarm of buzzing flies, an ominous emptiness. Mickey walked his mount in a circle, around a solitary post that held the large brass bell with which Colleen summoned her charges to class.

Colleen McDunn.

Mickey had tried to hate her, tried as hard as a man could try, but he couldn't twist his heart like that. But it wasn't about to make him change his mind. He would do what he had to do. He heard a horse whinny from behind the agency. Angus had to have seen him by now. Good, he wanted the agent to know what was coming.

Mickey Free halted his mount in front of the Agency House, feeling more alone than ever, a stranger caught between the San Carlos settlement and McDunn's . . . the red road and the white, and at home in neither. Mickey squinted against the glare—sweat matted the shaggy red mane that he'd tied back with a length of cloth; he made himself a promise to steal a hat when he was finished here—then he called out, "Angus McDunn!"

Reverend Doctor Jordan emerged from the house and stepped out onto the porch. The deputy cradled a Winchester 66 in the crook of his arm. A dry gust of wind lifted the flaps of his black frock coat. The flat-crowned hat he wore further shaded his punch-ugly features. His thick jaw sported a week's growth of silver stubble.

"A line rider spied you snaking down from the Santa Ritas and rode into Rio Seco to bring me the news. I lit a shuck for here, figuring this would be your first stop. Looks like prison made you careless, Kid."

"It made me a lot of things."

"Including a murderer."

"The only thing I killed between here and that damn prison was a horse I rode to death the first night I broke out."

"That's not what the army says."

"That guard got killed by one of his own, and by accident. I let the other man live so he would tell how it was." Mickey cleared his throat and spat in the dust. "He lied." Mickey casually maneuvered the bay to put the sun off to his right and behind him. "But I've been lied to before by the army, as I recall."

"That's far enough, Kid. You leave that horse sit where he is and quit trying to put me looking into the sun."

"That's an old rifle, Jordan. Do you think it still works?"

"Don't you worry," the lawman replied. "If it don't, well, these others are bound to."

The shutters to either side of the door swung open, and another pair of rifles poked through the open windows. Mickey recognized Sergeant Nance, although the man was dressed as a civilian. And in the other window, another townsman who had the look of an Indian fighter about him.

Mickey Free raised his rifle. The tension instantly became palpable. "Angus McDunn!"

Jordan brought his rifle to bear, three against one, damn near point-blank, and blast it all but if that still didn't seem like good-enough odds against a man like Free. The deputy thumbed the hammer back. But he cautioned Nance and the other man to hold their fire. "You're too late."

Mickey obviously didn't understand.

"Angus is recuperating at Jim Buell's hacienda. He was shot down in cold blood by bandits. And on the eve of his daughter's wedding day."

Mickey Free was listening intently now, ignoring the rifles trained on him. *Wedding?*

"But they didn't want him dead," Jordan continued. "They left him at Buell's ranch, rode in under cover of night and left the poor bastard more dead than alive. But he delivered the terms."

"Where is Colleen? What has happened to her?" Mickey lowered the rifle in his hands.

Jordan glanced to either side. "Sam . . . you and Mose head on out the back. I can handle things here from now on."

"You sure about this?" Nance said, aching to squeeze the trigger. Free was a fugitive, a killer, and with a price on his head. But Nance wasn't about to cross Jordan, at least to his face. Mose Woodard eased his finger off the trigger. His ebony features registered his displeasure.

"We can take him right now. That's what we come out here for, ain't it?"

"You'll die," Mickey growled. He made no gesture; indeed, his Winchester was lowered. Yet the certainty in his voice was unmistakable. "Two of you, and I'll put a bullet in the third before I go under."

"Listen to him crow," said Sam Nance.

"No brag. Just fact," Free calmly replied.

"Goddammit, my word is law here! You boys back off or I just might stand aside and let Free carve you up for brisket." Jordan's outburst served its purpose. The rifles disappeared from the windows. He waited until he heard the back door open and then two horses gallop away.

"Where is Colleen?" Mickey said, steeling himself for the worst.

The deputy marshal ambled forward to the edge of the porch. He still held his rifle pointed at Free's chest. "The bandits took her with them back into Mexico. If Buell ever wants to see her alive he has to bring a hundred thousand dollars and meet them down in Huachaca. They'll swap him the girl for the gold." Jordan gnawed the inside of his cheek a moment as if considering what else to reveal.

"He can raise that much money?" Mickey asked.

"And more, from what I hear tell. The hard part wasn't raising the ransom; it'll be transporting it to Huachaca, with every tinhorn and desperado itching to try for the gold and the hell with the poor girl."

"Buell's got a problem he cannot lie his way around."

"It's your problem, too, since you're going with us."

"Go with you? You want me to help Major James Buell?" Mickey Free laughed aloud; his voice rang out on the desiccating breeze. "Why would I do that?"

Jordan lowered his rifle and shrugged, glanced to the right and left, then answered, keeping his voice low, "Because you are in love with Colleen McDunn." His reply had the desired effect. Mickey stiffened as if struck. Jordan pressed his advantage. "And because Chato has her!"

Chapter 22

The sun was setting behind a bank of gold-etched clouds. The dying day washed the sky with bold strokes of azure and vermillion, and in the fading light for a few brief moments the harsh, dry landscape of cholla cactus and chino grass, of spiny arroyos and broken hills, seemed to glow as if beneath its hard surface all of creation seethed, waiting to pour out and transform the land into another Eden. But here creation wore a formidable face. The land would take the measure of a man before revealing its stark beauty.

They came to the hacienda at dusk. Mickey saw that the outbuildings were still under construction, but the main house looked complete, a large single-story adobe structure with a red tile roof, another long bunkhouse for the vaqueros, a corral and barn, and a smokehouse, all of which were surrounded by a low whitewashed wall. A freight wagon had been left under guard directly in front of the house. A pair of dogs trotted out and announced the arrival of the four riders as they approached the gate. Within the walls the front of the hacienda and the adjoining outbuildings and a number of long, solid-looking tables set out for the invited guests had been gaily decorated with streamers and lanterns, the preparations for a wedding feast and shivaree so cruelly interrupted. Everything was as it had been, but weathered and tattered now and naught but a melancholy reminder of tragic events and a desperate situation.

Several rough-looking men lounged about the wagon, and as Mickey drew near he could see right off that the center of attention was the large black iron-reinforced trunk on the wagon bed. The men guarding it all carried Winchester rifles. Most of the ranch hands were strangers to Free, but he recognized the type. The vaqueros had no use for Apache, especially a white Apache. They wore their animosity like an aura that existed as a permanent warning for Free to keep his distance. But this night he had business here. So the hell with them.

"Ride easy," Jordan muttered to Mickey Free as James Buell strode purposefully through the front door and out onto the veranda. Buell continued out into the compound and past the freight wagon and waited by the singletree while Sam Nance and Mose Woodard dismounted.

"We brought him in, just like you told us," Woodard said, mopping his bald black scalp with a bandanna that he'd dunked in the horse trough. The man was hot-natured and would continue to sweat until the chill of the desert night had firmly settled on the land.

"Brought nothing," Jordan interjected loud enough for every man in the compound to hear. "Mickey Free come here on his own. He's under my charge and a hand lifted against him is lifted against us both unless I call otherwise." He turned toward Free. "That doesn't mean I'm forgetting you're a wanted man or the fact I'm wearing this badge."

Mickey nodded. "If there is any gunplay it will not begin by my hand. However, when it commences I shall do my part." He discarded the serape he wore to ward off the chill, draping it across the pommel of his saddle, revealing in the process the gun belt around his waist, the holstered long-barreled Colt revolver, and the second army-issue revolver tucked in his belt.

His gaze met Buell's. If Mickey was surprised by the former officer's civilian garb he did not show it. "Evening, Major. How's the shoulder?"

Buell frowned, recalling earlier events and Free's attempt on his life. "It's stiff, and now and then it hurts like blazes."

"Good," Mickey replied, and dismounted.

Jordan sighed and wagged his head. Brother, if this night didn't end in a bloodbath it would be a miracle, he thought.

"Where's McDunn?" Mickey asked.

"Inside. He's still fighting a fever," Buell told him. "Now see here, Free. Before we talk we need to get a few things straight between us. . . ."

Mickey stepped around him, continued up the steps and into the house. Jordan dismounted and hurried after the fugitive. Buell caught him by the arm.

"Did you tell him?"

"I haven't told him a blasted thing except she's gone," Jordan snapped, brushing past the former officer. He bounded up the steps, showing uncommon grace for a man his size, and vanished into the hacienda. "Kid! You wait up. You hear?" His call went unanswered.

* * *

"Colleen!" Angus sat up from his pillows, supported himself on his elbows. He trembled; his voice belonged to a frightened old man beset by a nightmare that he could not awaken from. "Colleen . . ." He shook his head and eased back against the bedding. The wick in the lamp alongside his bed flickered and snapped as the flame consumed it. *My daughter . . . my daughter . . . please God.*

The bandages on Angus's side needed changing. Buell's housekeeper would see to that and dress his wounds. But his wounded soul was another matter entirely. *Send her a savior. She is an innocent lamb.* The agent's hair was matted with sweat. He wiped a forearm across his mouth and then turned his head aside and gasped when he saw the figure in the corner of the room, watching him. Angus recognized the man.

"Free . . . here?"

"Yes."

"Are you a ghost?"

"Yes," Mickey said, stepping forward into the light. "Look for me in your sleep."

Angus brought his hand to his mouth and gnawed at his knuckle. He closed his eyes as if willing Mickey Free into dissolution. But this was no specter. And when he looked again, Mickey Free was standing by his bed, leaning on one of its four posts.

"That's enough, Kid; you've seen him. Now let the poor bastard be," Jordan said from the bedroom's doorway.

"Damn you," Angus blurted out.

"Thanks for the *blessing*," said Mickey Free. Ignoring Jordan's admonishment, Free stepped in close and leaned over the agent. "I'll find Colleen and have her for myself." He touched his finger to his lips, instructing the wounded man to be silent. McDunn's eyes widened. "Shhh."

"You go to hell," the agent gasped.

"Yessir, I'm on my way."

Jordan dropped a big calloused hand on Mickey's shoulder. "Free, I said—"

"I heard you," Mickey cut him off. He sauntered out of the room and followed the lamplit hall into the main room of the house, where James Buell continued to pace the floor. Worry lines had aged his once-youthful appearance. His brown corduroy pants and faded blue pullover woolen shirt looked slept in.

Some of the vaqueros from outside lounged about the room waiting for orders, although they had made it clear riding for the brand did not include crossing the border into bandit country to save a girl they either did not know or, frankly, did not care that much about. And besides, if Julio Lopez or Chato had her prisoner then the girl was as good as dead. The vaqueros were clearly curious about Mickey

Free. They had all heard of the notorious Apache Kid, how he had scouted for the army and then at the end turned renegade and tried to kill his commanding officer. They expected just about anything to happen and wanted to be around when the violence erupted while at the same time out of harm's way.

Sam Nance and Mose Woodard had just stepped inside for a pot of coffee and were returning to the walled courtyard in front of the hacienda when Free entered the room. The two men paused to stare at him, determined to save face and demonstrate for all concerned that they were not going to be cowed in the presence of the Apache Kid.

"Sam, you and Mose stay close to the wagon," Buell said, interrupting their reverie. The black man nudged the bartender, but the ex-sergeant hesitated.

"What about him?" Nance asked, indicating Free. "We might oughta lock him in the smokehouse." He hooked his thumbs in his suspenders. His large, round belly made a tempting target. The man was broad as Jordan but lacked the deputy's height and, yes, his presence. But he was not afraid of crossing the border, and that was all anyone could ask for.

"Mickey Free is none of your concern," Buell reminded him.

Nance looked as if he might dispute the former officer's decision but thought better of it at the last minute. "C'mon, Mose; we got a job to do." The two men proceeded outside while the remaining vaqueros lingered in the main room, awaiting their orders.

Buell suddenly stopped his pacing and glared at his underlings. "What are you doing here? I told you to patrol the walls, three men on and three off; switch every couple of hours until I drive the wagon out the gate."

The remaining men filed out into the compound where the wagon with its fortune in gold and greenbacks waited.

The iron-embossed trunk on the bed was securely pad-locked and impervious to the curiosity of the men sent to guard it through the night.

Nance stepped off the porch and leaned against the wagon and ran his hand lovingly over the stout sides of the trunk. He wondered aloud what a hundred thousand dollars looked like. "I'd sure like to take a gander at what I'm about to die for."

"Ain't for our eyes, amigo," Mose said.

"Any man has a right to a dream," Nance grumbled. He winked at his compadre and lit the stub of a cigar he had fished from his vest pocket. "Any man . . ."

* * *

Alone in the main room, James Buell, Reverend Doctor Jordan, and Mickey Free quietly appraised one another in silence. Their shadows flickered on the whitewashed walls. The hand-hewed tables and chairs, the great hearth with its massive mantle, the brightly woven blankets and curtains on the windows all bespoke refinement and a rustic opu-lence that most men could aspire to and Buell had achieved. But at what price?

"By rights I am supposed to slap the irons on you and bring you to the nearest army post," Jordan began. He un-rolled a map across the closest table and held the corners down with a bottle, knife, and revolver.

"Or die trying," Mickey said.

"Don't take me lightly, Kid." His gaze narrowed. And Mickey nodded that he understood, but there still was the faintest bemusement to his expression that got under Jor-dan's skin like a burr under a saddle blanket. "But the rea-son I'm not arresting you is because of the Major here . . . and Colleen."

Mickey's expression changed again. The gravity of the situation was not lost on him. Indeed, for most of the ride out from San Carlos he had been unable to think of anything but her, at the mercy of such a man as Chato. The man was wild and dangerous as a cornered cougar, full of hatred and thirsting for vengeance. *A man like you.* Mickey glanced around, wondering who had made that last remark. He stared at Buell, who seemed a bit unsettled by the fugitive's behavior. Mickey returned his attention to the map. It depicted an artist's dated attempt to show the lay of the mountain country to the south.

"I am to bring the money chest to Huachaca, right here in Sonora." Buell tapped a finger against the map. "From town, one of the locals will send word to Chato and Julio Lopez to bring Colleen in to hand her over."

"The bandits are probably hiding out up in the Apache *rancheria,* in the mountains to the west."

Buell and Jordan exchanged glances. "Then you know the country?" Buell asked.

"I've been there, with Geronimo, long ago."

"Then if something were to happen, if we had to, do you think you could find their encampment?"

Mickey shrugged. "There is a valley, up in the high country. I think I'd remember the way."

"We have to deliver the money before April or the girl dies. If someone else takes the money from us there will be no second chances; Miss Colleen dies," Jordan stated.

"Come with us," Buell blurted out.

"Or you'll hand me over to the soldiers so they can finish what you started a year ago," Mickey said, folding his arms across his chest. He looked up from the map. The heavy ceiling with its crossbeams seemed to be weighing down on him. Yes, he could find the Apache *rancheria.* But this was not going to be a church picnic and he was going to need all the help he could get. He did not know Julio Lopez, but Chato would be wary and watchful. And he would be merciless. "I'll go with you."

For the first time Jordan and Buell seemed to relax.

Buell walked over to a table by the wall and uncorked a bottle of bourbon and poured himself a drink. He stared absently into space for moment while the warmth of the liquor spread to his limbs. "I love her. From the first day I ever set eyes on her, I loved her. But I suppose a man like you wouldn't understand that. I mean living with the Apaches as long as you did. It's different for them."

Mickey Free did not respond.

Buell looked at him. "So then . . . why did you come back? You had escaped. Why here?"

Mickey Free casually slipped the army revolver from his belt. "I came here to kill you."

The movement was so unexpected it caught both Jordan and Buell completely unaware . . . and unprepared to defend themselves. Buell dropped the glass in his hand. It shattered on the clay tile, its contents spreading out like a bloodstain on the floor. Jordan glanced uselessly at his own holstered weapon.

"But I can wait," said Free.

Chapter 23

The column of soldiers that arrived at the hacienda on the morning of departure looked relieved that their duties kept them in Arizona. News of the kidnapping had spread throughout the territory, quick as a prairie fire; and likewise, Buell's response. Capt. Kenneth Kania, a windburned young officer newly assigned to Fort Apache, even had a copy of the *Rio Seco Telegraph* tucked away in his dispatch case; the newspaper's front page blazoned:

James Buell to Pay a King's Ransom for Stolen Bride

Kania's patrol, a dozen men in dusty blue uniforms and sweat stained campaign hats, continued across the compound to a long, low trough where a hand pump pulled water from an aquifer deep beneath the dry earth. While his men saw to the needs of their thirsty mounts, Kania alighted from horseback and walked up onto the veranda, where the wide, deep roof provided plenty of cooling shade. Buell was standing in the front door. He made no move to welcome the officer inside. Time was precious to James Buell, and he would brook no delay from the military despite his former rank.

"Cool here in the shade," Kania observed, stating the obvious. He dabbed his forearm across his sunburned features. He was Minnesota-born and -raised, and his fair complexion was better suited to the northern climes and suffered from exposure to the sun. Even the flesh beneath his thin blond mustache was pink and beginning to crack. "I swear if the devil had a choice he'd rent out hell and live in Arizona." Kania grinned, then coughed nervously, realizing his humor was out of place at such a moment. He grew serious then, determined to put up a bold front, and saluted from force of habit. "Compliments of Major Allen."

Buell was well aware that Fort Apache had a new commandant, a man older than himself, dyspeptic, with an affinity for brandy and an acute distaste for his latest appointment, where he would forever be under the shadow of his predecessor, the officer who had captured Geronimo. "My compliments to the major." Buell returned the salute out of habit. It was a bright, clear morning with the sun like an amulet of molten gold displayed against a sapphire sky. "I assume you bear a request from the commandant?"

"Yes, sir," Kania continued. "The major has requested that you return with me to the fort. He would like to discuss in greater detail your . . . uh . . . dilemma and what might be the best response."

"My dilemma is that my fiancée has been taken by a cutthroat named Julio Lopez. My response is that I will do whatever needs to be done, pay whatever price, to return her safe and unharmed."

"Yes, sir, I can appreciate that. However, the major is concerned that paying such an enormous ransom might only lead to more depredations, this time by a well-armed force of these murderous rogues." Kania glanced around as more of Buell's vaqueros drifted over toward the wagon. He was keenly aware that his force was outnumbered and outgunned. However, violence was the furthest thing from his mind. "But if you will meet with him . . . Major Allen feels certain you both can reach an accord. Entreaties have already been extended to the Mexican authorities and they have assured the major that every effort is being made to apprehend this man Lopez and rescue Miss McDunn."

Buell hooked his thumbs in his belt, the flaps of his frock coat parted to reveal his side arm, a Navy Colt, holstered high on his right hip. "That news is most welcome and I shall take some comfort from it. Convey to the major that by his leave I will meet with him tomorrow. I have some pressing matters to attend to today, involving the purchase of some cattle, that require my immediate attention."

Relief flashed across Kania's features. "Tomorrow will do nicely. Major Allen will be pleased to hear that." Kania's gaze swept across the faces of the men gathering around the wagon. He recognized Sam Nance and Mose Woodard, for both men had ridden beneath a guidon in the past, although Kania knew them from town. The barrel-chested brawler lounging by the wagon was easier to identify. "Is that you, Marshal Jordan?"

"Deputy Marshal," Jordan corrected, standing alongside the freight wagon. He slouched forward, leaning on an iron wheel rim, his thickly muscled arms folded before him. But Kania was already looking past the peace officer, his attention drawn to the vaquero standing in the big man's shadow.

"You there."

Mickey Free peered up at the man from beneath his sombrero. The señora who ran the house and cooked the meals had taken a scissors to his shoulder-length red hair and trimmed his mane close to the nape of his neck. He had discarded any clothing that even remotely resembled something favored by the Apache and instead wore faded brown nankeen pants, a calico workshirt and rawhide vest, his *botas* to protect his legs from the thorny underbrush, and worn leather boots. A pale yellow kerchief circled his neck and trailed in the breeze that tugged at their hat brims and set the columbine and larkspur blossoms shuddering to the caress of the wind's invisible hand.

"Me?"

"Do I know you?" Kania frowned. Damn but the man's face was familiar. "Where are you from?"

Mickey pointed south. "Sonora."

"Buell hired him a few days back. His name is Jesus Montoya. You might say he still has the bark on," Jordan interjected.

"The man does what he's told to do and doesn't have much to say about himself," Buell added, trying to swallow and coax spit from a mouth as dry as sandpaper. He had visited the fort and seen the wanted circulars touting the reward for the Apache Kid . . . Dead or Alive. But Free's likeness depicted a man with a shaggy mane of hair, a scowl on his face, and a bandanna tied about his head. "And I don't ask."

"I know ·you, Montoya. Maybe from Rio Seco, yes, that's it. How long were you there?"

"Long enough to run out of money, señor."

"Hmm," Kania replied. "Yours is not a unique story, Mr. Montoya." Kania was suspicious of the man; after all, he hailed from Sonora. Then again, Buell could hire whomever he chose to; it was none of his business. Kania glanced in Buell's direction, touched the brim of his hat, and then spun on his heels and sauntered over to his horse and eased astride the gelding he had chosen from a herd of quarrelsome beasts. "Until tomorrow." He tugged on the reins, eventually got his mount's attention, and pointed the animal back toward the arched entrance to the compound. A sergeant barked an order for the troop to move out and fall in behind the officer from Minnesota. Buell waved and remained smiling until the last of the soldiers had filed out through the walls.

"He's gonna get back to Fort Apache this afternoon, take a gander at one of them wanted posters, and come charging back here with half the damn garrison ready to storm the walls."

"Let him come," Buell snapped. "Get ready to ride." He stamped back into the hacienda for his hat and his rifle.

"Brother, that was close," Jordan remarked, glancing aside at Free as they walked toward the corral. "So what do you think, Kid? Is she alive?"

Mickey Free paused and gazed toward the distant mountains beyond which lay the wild country of the last great Apache *rancheria* and the broken hills where a man's life could be measured in the crack of a Winchester or the slap of leather and a flash of blue lightning from the muzzle of a Colt .44. She was alive. He knew it. Colleen McDunn was alive. But for how long was anyone's guess. Rescuing her was going to be mean, hard, dangerous work and would require a mean, hard, dangerous man to bring her safely home.

* * *

Los Pilares was a place of stark beauty, a valley nestled on the dry side of the Huachaca Mountains, a fertile high-country plateau surrounded by a maze of barrancas whose granite battlements had been eroded by wind and rain and shaking earth until they resembled jagged rows of teeth. Entering the valley was like riding into some enormous maw, a forbidding foray into the mouth of a beast. Until now, only the Apache had known of this place. From this Apache *rancheria* the Chiricahua had conducted their raids with impunity and continued a reign of terror until the plains ran red with blood.

But for the Apache, Los Pilares had been a seasonal retreat. The harsh winters at this elevation continually forced the tribe to abandon the Apache *rancheria* for gentler climes down in the desert country of Arizona, where growing ranches and fattening herds of cattle waited to be plundered.

But those days were gone. And where the hogans of the Chiricahua once stood, Julio Lopez had built a formidable blockhouse of logs and slabs of granite for himself. It was the kind of dwelling more befitting a governor then a bandit. But then Lopez was a man of vision. Other lesser dwellings were scattered about the valley floor in close proximity to the blockhouse so that what had once been a rough encampment now resembled something akin to a feudal estate.

His force of renegades and cutthroats had grown to thirteen men. But this was only the beginning. He expected the dispossessed peons from the surrounding lowlands to come with their families. The poor had a burning desire for power and land, always land, and that was what Julio promised them, the power that comes with fear, the land that comes with victory.

He no longer saw himself as merely an outlaw. No, a man like him should aspire to something bigger, grander. Sonora was far removed from the authority of the president in Mexico City. On this far-flung frontier, anything was possible, if Lopez was careful and played his cards right, and if he had enough men to back his play.

Men with guns, Julio reflected, lounging on the porch that ran the length of the blockhouse facing south. Clovia Madrigal, a hot-tempered vixen he had liberated from her parents' dirt farm and taken to his bed, emerged from the shadowy interior of the blockhouse and handed her lover a bottle of mescal. She looked no older than sixteen, a dark and sensuous creature whose beauty was marred only by an inch-long scar on her forehead where the spiny limbs of an ocotillo cactus had slashed her flesh during her childhood years. She knelt by the bandit and rested her head on his thigh, her black hair spilling forward to partly conceal her features. Clovia was dressed in a loose-fitting white blouse and a simple cotton dress of scarlet, and her ample bosom was crisscrossed by a pair of bandoliers. She carried a short-barreled Navy Colt holstered at her narrow waist.

Half a dozen men galloped past, racing their horses for gold and bragging rights. They were showing off for a trio of señoritas Lopez had brought from Huachaca to serve the carnal needs of his *compañeros*. But Clovia was his and his alone. Lopez stroked the young woman's raven hair as he casually appraised the saw-toothed ridge where his sentries were posted. The men were prepared to sound a warning should any strangers enter the Apache *rancheria*. The sentries had been handpicked by Chato, who chose them for their keen sense of observation and their ability to memorize every twist and turn of the approach. The Apache wanted them to know the terrain whatever the time of day, by sunlight or the dark of the moon.

"In another few months I will have enough men," Lopez purred, his hand coming to rest on the sixteen-year-old's soft brown neck. Then he looked aside at Colleen, seated across from him on a wooden bench. "Bring drink for the *gringa*."

Clovia frowned as she stood. She glared at their captive. "I am a *soldado*," she declared. Clovia grabbed the nearly empty bottle of mescal from the small table near Julio and tossed it into the air. Her hand swept down, then reappeared with the Navy Colt in her hand. She snapped off a shot, and the bottle exploded in midair, showering the ground with fragments of fired clay. Clovia proudly holstered her gun. "I will not be her servant."

"You will do as I say," Lopez snapped. Then he tilted his head back, laughed heartily, and gave the girl a pat on her rounded derriere and sent her on her way. He returned his attention to his reluctant . . . guest. "Now what was I saying . . . ? Ah . . . soon I will have enough men, *sí*. But guns are another matter. They will cost a fortune. Yet I need rifles for my *soldados* when they arrive. And they will come. Once I have something more than machetes for them to fight with. You see, that is my problem." Julio Lopez glanced across the porch at the yellow-haired woman he and his men had kidnapped from the schoolhouse. He glanced toward the front door, scowled, then sipped his drink and briefly gave an angry glance to the shattered clay bottle. "A shame to waste mescal. Clovia has a temper. A jealous little *puta*. And a crack shot, now there is a dangerous combination."

"And one you would do well not to underestimate . . . her . . . and me," Colleen said.

"You are both women," Julio flippantly replied. "You come when I say come, leave when I say to, lift your skirts when I want you. This is all I need know of women." The bandit brushed a hand through his dark curls, then tossed his silver-embroidered sombrero aside, leaned over, and, with lust in his eyes, attempted to pass the remnants of his cup to Colleen McDunn. "Here, drink. I left you some. You will feel better."

"No," Colleen said, ignoring the gesture. "I shoot snakes, not drink with them."

Lopez exploded with laughter. He slapped his leg and almost choked on the mescal. "Suit yourself. More for me. You are a proud woman. I like that. But don't be too proud. Maybe you and I will become good friends, eh? You had better pray we do." He glanced around at no one in particular. "Look at her. Yellow hair, smooth skin like a newborn calf." He spied Chato standing by the corner of the porch watching them both. Another man, a hard-looking thief and cutthroat, Esteban Emilio y Perez Garza, lounged in the shadow of the porch alongside the Apache. Garza kept a wary eye on Chato, for it was not in his nature to trust a savage whose very name, Apache, meant enemy. "Chato, Esteban, mi amigos." Lopez waved for both men to approach.

Garza was not a big man. He stood about five-foot-two. But his shoulders were sloped and muscled, he was long-armed and slightly bow-legged, and his round, solid belly strained the fabric of his woolen shirt. A wide-brimmed sombrero shaded his thick, jowly features. His upper lip was delineated by the thin scrawl of a mustache. He appeared to be a man at home in a world of highbinders and fallen women. A brace of pistols jutted from a sash that circled his waist.

"*Jefe,* how may I serve you?"

"Esteban, my good and trusted friend. I want you to ride to Señor Buell's ranch, wait for our benefactor to start out with the ransom. Be their shadow. See that no one interferes with their progress and that my money comes to no harm. Bring them in to Huachaca and then come and tell me."

A wide smile split the bandit's features, revealing a row of yellow teeth. But his eyes twinkled with a merry light, as if receiving an order from Lopez gave purpose to his life. "*Sí, Jefe,* it will be as you say." He touched the brim of his hat and started off.

"Esteban!" Lopez called out, halting the man, who glanced around. "See that you be careful. We have ridden many trails together, *compañero.* I would have you at my side."

"*No tenga ningún miedo,*" Garza replied. "Have no fear. I am like the rocks. I remain." He sauntered off in search of a horse. He rode a different mount every day, no matter who the owner, and no one ever protested. Garza was a bad man with a vicious temper. It was rumored he had singlehandedly burned out an entire village during a drunken brawl. Whether or not it happened, the story's possibility bought him a wide berth among the rough-hewn rabble who had flocked to Lopez's standard.

Chato ambled toward them, his dark eyes revealing nothing of his thoughts. His short, powerful physique was concealed beneath a faded scarlet-and-black serape. A pair of bandoliers crisscrossed his chest. He kept a revolver tucked in the waistband of his cotton trousers. A knife hilt jutted from the top of one of his knee-length moccasins.

"Did you hear the way she talks?" Lopez grinned. "What do you think of our guest?"

Chato rounded the house and paused to lean against one of the poles supporting the roof of the porch. He took a dipper from the olla suspended from one of the beams overhead and took a drink of cool spring water, then tossed aside what remained in the cup. The few droplets of water leached into the trampled earth. "I think there will come a time when she will beg for a cup and drink plenty, pulque, mescal . . . and welcome every drop."

"I know you, Chato," Colleen coldly told him. "Your own mother's blood is on your hands."

He recoiled from her remarks as if from a cauldron of coals hurled in his face. Lopez heard the man snarl like some wounded beast. Then Chato's hand swept down to his leg and came up with his knife. The naked blade stopped at her throat.

Colleen winced at the kiss of the steel edge. A thin line of crimson oozed from a superficial cut. She went pale despite herself. For a moment she thought he had killed her. Lopez shared her fear. His hand shot out. Before he could speak, Chato straightened. But he held the knife pointed at her. He nodded and his fierce eyes blazed with the promise that next time . . . *next time* . . .

"Madre de Dios!" Lopez exclaimed, and shook his head.

"This is not San Carlos. Your father cannot save you. And I am no tame Apache," Chato snarled as he wiped the blood from the blade on his serape, then returned the knife to its sheath.

"I thought I was going to have to shoot you, my friend," Lopez said.

"You owe me your life," Chato reminded him.

"Sí. It would have broken my heart." Lopez grinned.

Chato took the man at his word. "One of us would have died; that is for certain."

Lopez reached out and clapped the Apache on the shoulder. "Listen to us. What kind of talk is this among friends, eh? All this nonsense about killing." Lopez tugged on his silk brocaded vest. Something had triggered Chato's behavior, and Lopez was determined to discover the cause. "We must be careful, my friend. Remember, we need guns. But where to get the money for them? Now that is the question." Lopez fixed the woman with his taunting gaze. "And she is the answer."

Chapter 24

Mickey Free crossed into Old Mexico on a bright spring day. With a cloudless sky above him and dreams of love and retribution to lead the way, the Apache Kid returned to Sonora, following the path that in a long-ago time his adopted people had used until the tracks of their travois were worn into the hard earth.

Ba-ts-otse, Coyote Spirit, I have come home. Are you watching me from your proud, sad height? Hear me now. Heal me now. Mickey Free studied the hills and beyond them the purple mountains where the dry wind moaned and eagles soared, where a winding trail would take them up and over the escarpment, to the broken ridges and barrancas so deep that the Apache name for them was Bichagosh-oh, the Shadowlands.

He watched the hills and listened in his heart, but he heard no reply, felt no icy stirring as he had, once upon a time, when he thought he would surely perish during the Run of the Arrow. He had seen the beast, recognized in its blazing eyes and raging heart a kinship, a oneness that bound him to the land and the spirit country that lay beyond the realized senses. For an instant the hawk circling overhead hung poised in mid-flight; the breeze held its breath; heart stopped; the sun, the radiant heat, scuttling tarantula, and loping horse, all ceased and then began again. Time was out of joint and then resumed, yet in that pause lay hidden the power of the one. He had glimpsed it, as a youth . . . and now? What now?

Damn, he chided himself, and willed himself back to reality, breaking the bonds of reverie and reflection. Let the Coyote take care of itself. Mickey had been young then and driven near crazy from the heat and thirst. Better to concentrate on the present. A man could think too much and catch a bullet in the back for his trouble.

He glanced over his shoulder at the freight wagon lurching across the scarred terrain. Mose Woodard and Sam Nance rode on the bench seat, Nance with the reins and Mose cradling a twelve-gauge scattergun, a Parker, whose Damascus steel gun barrel had been sawed off to half its normal length. Mickey Free had no use for those two. They had hungry eyes. Nor did the pair make any attempt to hide their opinion of the Apache Kid.

James Buell rode a bold-looking chestnut stallion that wanted to forge ahead and draw abreast of the bay. But riding point had fallen to Mickey Free. He knew the country, remembering it from the days before the Apache had settled at San Carlos, when they were the masters of the howling wilderness and even the bravest men who came to settle the frontier trembled to hear the war drums talk. That left Reverend Doctor Jordan to eat the trail dust. The deputy, to keep from swallowing more than his fill, kept well back of the wagon, allowing some of the gritty air to dissipate.

They all had their reasons for coming. Mickey Free knew his. He was well aware of what he had to do. If Julio Lopez had men watching them from the hills, they would see five men, all of them vaqueros. No one would recognize Mickey Free. Nor would any of the bandits realize there was one man who knew his way into the Apache *rancheria*. And that's where they had to be, if Chato was with them.

Free pulled his brim lower out of habit. The bay had an easy gait, a crisp, steady walk that he could hold for hours on end, his blaze face bobbing with every step. The fugitive returned his attention to the trail, studying the lay of the land, struggling to focus on the here and now, and yet memories kept coming, unbidden. The quest that had begun at Buell's hacienda was carrying Mickey Free south to yesterday.

* * *

Geronimo crouched down beside the eight-year-old foundling he had rescued long ago, delivered from the tragic fate that had befallen his parents. Geronimo had saved his life by making him one of the People. The war chief placed a hand on the boy's bronze shoulder. "Tell me, Dabin-ik-eh, what do you see?"

Mickey Free studied the terrain ahead. The war chief had taken him apart from the others, had brought him out of the Apache rancheria *where the Chiricahua spent the spring and summer. Mickey knelt here just below a line of stunted pines that looked as if the wind had twisted the tree trunks as they sprouted from the rocky face of the escarpment. He watched a hawk trace lazy circles in the sky before swooping down to an unusually fertile rift in the jagged ridge where the pines grew thick along a narrow, winding spring-fed rivulet.*

"Do you see a place for us?"

"There's water down there, because of the trees," the young boy observed. He checked the slabs of stone behind them. "See the claw marks in the rocks there? Cougars have hid right here and watched the same trees and wondered if it was safe, just like us, Bik-eh." Mickey addressed the shaman warrior as teacher. His respect was no pretense. Like the other boys of the village, he looked upon Geronimo with a mixture of fear and reverence.

"And is it?"

"Yes . . . no, wait!" Even as Mickey spoke he saw the hawk dart down toward a rabbit among the trees only to swerve at the last second and rise into the air, abandoning

its intended prey. "Something scared it away from the trees.
There is someone there."

Geronimo smiled, pleased with the boy's answer.
"Watch our brothers—the hawk, the coyote, the cougar.
They will warn you and keep you safe as long as you walk
the warrior's path. Come."

Mickey Free followed the war chief as he scrambled
down the hillside and led the boy into a maze of boulders
strewn about a dry wash by flash floods. Geronimo placed
his ear to the ground. Mickey mirrored his actions. He
listened to the Warm, closing his eyes, waited, wondered.
"I don't hear anything."

"Listen. Hear beyond what you think can be heard,"
Geronimo whispered.

Mickey tried. He tried until sweat beaded his forehead
and his skull ached. He tried until he thought he would
have to stand up and scream and dance about to get the
feeling to return to his legs. He listened until he wanted to
cry, until he quit thinking about listening and the fatigue
drifted away and the youngster became impervious as stone
to the thirst and the aching, and only then did he hear . . .
the scrape of shod hooves upon stone, the pulse of the
earth, the infusion of life and the oneness with the ancient
land that bridged the seen and unseen. It was the sound of
shadows, the smell of lost pines, the call of the wild imprisoned in layers of limestone. And for a moment he was
no longer apart, no longer a boy, but instead part of the
landscape, and there was only the earth and the wind and
the afternoon sun and a picture in his mind of Mexican
troops riding in a column through the stand of trees and
then along the dry wash where they passed within a stone's
throw of the boy and the man. And yet the Colorados did
not see them. Mickey held no fear; he was a rock after all.
The boy was aware of the presence of the troops and yet
removed from them at the same time. He was not merely

hiding among the dry wash. Mickey was as much a part of it as the weathered boulders and broken trunks of trees, the drifting shadows and rising heat.

And after the soldiers had passed, he came to life once more and stood alongside the shaman chief who sensed in the foundling things the youth might never be aware of. Mickey learned that day what it was to be the hunter and to use all his skills, to listen and watch and wait. It was only the first lesson with Geronimo. There would be others until their paths separated and the boy called Dabin-ik-eh became Mickey Free, the Apache Kid.

* * *

Buell gave the stallion his lead and the animal trotted ahead and drew up alongside the bay. They were three days out of Rio Seco and continued to push their mounts. "Think we can reach the mountains by tonight?"

"We could. But then one of our horses or perhaps all of them might pull up lame." Mickey gestured toward a line of hills that resembled a man lying on his back. "The Sleeping Giant. There is a farm at the base of the hills. If the old woman is still alive we will have water and food."

"The Apaches didn't burn her out long ago?" Buell replied, somewhat taken aback. "I find that difficult to believe."

"Her name is Hester Alvarado. Many an Apache child has been nourished by the milk from her goats." Mickey Free wagged his head and sighed. "Not everyone is our enemy, James Buell."

Buell was obviously skeptical. But he would learn. Now that he had traded his military uniform for the casual attire of a gentleman rancher and hacendado, his mind was open. The former officer wiped a kerchief across the back of his neck. He had discarded his coat long ago.

The two men rode in silence for a while; then Buell cleared his throat. "I say, Free, did you mean what you said back there at the ranch . . . about coming to kill me?"

"I always mean what I say. It is men like you who break their word."

"Let it be," warned Buell. "I won't go under as easy as you think. I might surprise even you."

"You already did," Free replied. "Once."

"And I tried to undo it; as God is my judge, I tried to bring the men from San Carlos back home. If I become territorial governor, I'll try again, and this time maybe my words will carry some weight in Washington."

"And if we weren't bound for Mexico, you would have handed me over to Captain Kania, eh?"

"In the blink of an eye," said Buell. "You're wanted for murder now. But I love Colleen McDunn and I will have her for my wife, and woe to the bastard who tries to keep us apart. I would make a pact with the devil himself to bring her home. And in this case the devil is you."

"Now you speak straight," Mickey chuckled.

"Then we know where we stand," Buell said, his gaze narrowing.

"It is good to know where to stand," Free icily observed. Then a bemused expression drifted across his face. "And when."

* * *

Geronimo turned to the eight-year-old. "You did well. But not all those who would harm you will be so easy to spot. A cautious man must guard against not only his enemies, but also his friends."

* * *

"We'll take them tomorrow morning, early, before we strike camp," Nance muttered.

"I've little stomach for it," said Mose Woodard. He glanced over his shoulder at the money chest he was guarding. "But a hundred thousand dollars can buy one helluva lot of conscience. Still, can't we just take the horses? Do we have to kill them all?"

Nance spewed a stream of tobacco off to the side, spattering the wheel, steadying himself as the wagon found another patch of broken sandstone. The ex-trooper curled his fingers through the reins and cursed the pair of deep-chested horses pulling them deeper into Mexico as if the animals were responsible for his discomfort. But it was his own misgivings that plagued him.

Every day that he and Mose delayed acting on their plan brought them ever closer to a rendezvous with Lopez and his bandits, or any other pack of gold-hungry breeds driven to make a try for Buell's fortune. Better he and Mose should have it. Where was the harm? What was the point of risking their necks for a woman Lopez and his desperados had probably killed already? The bandits would do the same to Buell and anyone foolish enough to follow him into Huachaca.

"Take the horses, you say, Lord have mercy!" Nance muttered, aping the black man at his side. "And spend the rest of our lives watching our back trail. Buell might have some quit in him, and maybe Reverend Doctor Jordan 'cause of his age, but the Kid . . ." The bartender scratched at his enormous belly riding over his belt like a bay window. But his sloping shoulders were thick with muscle. He might not have much wind, but there was strength in the man. Mose looked just as seasoned, though his hands could no longer hide the tremble left by too little sleep, too much cheap whiskey, and a nettlesome fever he seemed to have picked up from one of the whores in town.

"The Apache Kid won't ever rest till he's lifted our hair," Nance concluded.

"Then it's settled," Mose replied, caressing the scattergun with its load of buckshot. "Mickey Free will be the first to die."

Chapter 25

Hester Joy Alvarado and her goats lived in the shadow of a sleeping giant, a great range of hills that resembled a massive human form reclining on its back. There was the *head* of pink granite capped by a prominent *nose* of eroded stone, a rounded *belly* fringed with scrub oaks and mesquite, and lesser hills that made up the *legs* and *feet*. To the Chiricahua Apache the formation was an ancient warrior, one of the grandfathers of creation, who would endure for as long as the winds blew and the rains fell.

Beyond the reclining ridge, like a bad dream looming over the sleeper, were the Huachaca Mountains, a jagged skyline of saw-toothed ridges and forbidding canyons slashed out of solid rock where nature had tortured and twisted the landscape into a maze that few men other than the Apache could master. Here were the old places, the primal haunts, where only the valiant prevailed. The first people in the long-ago time had sprung forth from the fissured terrain, or so it was whispered and so it was sung.

Mickey Free, Buell, and the rest reached the goatherd's shelter near sundown. Although the old woman's jacal and hardscrabble garden were pretty much like all the others they had seen around Rio Seco, what made the homestead remarkable was the presence of a large spring-fed pond, a *posas* that bubbled out of the desert floor and covered at least a couple of acres of land. The pool was surrounded by cattails and long grassy rushes that the goats like to keep trimmed back with their constant grazing. As the day lost its heat, a diaphanous mist drifted over the placid surface of the pool. Bats and night birds dipped low to glance off the water and come away with a prize catch, some wriggling morsel of miniature fish or wriggling insect.

Come evening, the men enjoyed the old woman's hospitality; they filled their bellies with corn tortillas and frijoles and nourishing platters of stew made from squash, corn, and cuts of meat from a recently butchered goat. Normally, Hester Alvarado kept her flock for their milk and for shearing, but occasionally one of the animals would become too old or injure itself beyond healing. Such unfortunate beasts were destined for the cook pot, and no matter how tough or stringy the *cabrito*, it only took boiling in spring water seasoned with dried *chipotle* peppers from her garden to tenderize the meat.

The men ate their fill at a hand-hewed table Hester had placed beneath a cabana outside the thick adobe walls of her cabin. With a wide view of the cooling plain that lay to the north and the ominous destination that awaited them, the five ate in relative silence, each man facing his own mortal fears. Mickey Free studied the moon-tipped range and gauged the odds of coming out of those silver mountains alive. Then he scolded himself. This was his home as much as Chato's, and he did not intend to die among those lost and lonely places. Colleen was up there, frightened and alone and at the mercy of bandits and Mickey's own implacable foster brother. Julio Lopez might have the reputation, but Chato was the man to be feared. Then again, the same could be said of Mickey Free.

The "white Apache" turned and quietly appraised his companions. Mose and Nance made him uneasy. They tended to pair by themselves, and there was something disquieting in the way they kept their own counsel, as if they hoped to keep others from overhearing what they had to say. Jordan hadn't seemed to notice their odd behavior. But then, the deputy was getting along in years and not as sharp as he used to be, although he was certainly the man to side with in a fight. Mickey found it difficult to hate the man for what had happened at San Carlos. He and Jordan had history together.

Not like James Buell. Mickey glanced in the direction of the former officer, a blue-blooded easterner. The man's lineage counted for nothing out here. In the back country of Sonora only one thing mattered: survival. Money might buy a man like Buell a little time, but it wouldn't get him back to Arizona alive.

A long, meandering road led off from the old woman's jacal toward the Huachacas, where it snaked along the base of the ridge, then climbed over a desolate pass before descending into the town that bore the same name as the mountain range. It was upon this road, bathed in the cold light of a full moon, that Mickey spied the horseman, riding toward the jacal. He had suspected this man had been following their progress since crossing the border.

"Fill another plate, Señora Alvarado," said Free. "We've got company."

"Who is it?" Buell asked, reaching for his carbine.

"I'd guess he rides for Lopez. He's probably been watching us since we crossed the border, or maybe since we left the hacienda."

"The hacienda . . . !" Buell gave Jordan a look of consternation.

The deputy shrugged and shook his head in reaction to the news. "Damn, Kid, you could have mentioned it," the lawman remarked.

Nance and Mose looked visibly upset and drifted back to quietly argue between themselves.

"I didn't know for sure. Just kind of sensed him. But it's what I'd do."

"What's bringing him in now?" Mose asked, checking the loads on his shotgun. Buell and the others quickly armed themselves. Rifles appeared in their hands. Jordan and Buell took up a defensive position by the wagon. Mickey noted that Nance and Mose grudgingly surrendered their place by the money box. The bartender stepped inside the jacal and could be heard levering a round into the chamber. Mose, cradling his shotgun in his arm, crouched by the corral fence. The goats immediately protested his presence.

Mickey Free eased out of the glare of the lantern light and drifted out of sight. The desert night was like a velvet cloak to him. He knew how to walk with the shadows. As for Hester Alvarado, the gray-haired woman decided the best place for her old bones was safe within the stout adobe walls of her cabin.

"I will see what he has to say and then send him on his way," Buell announced, placing himself alongside the wagon and squarely in the entrance to Hester's front yard.

The next few minutes crawled by slow as molasses in winter. After what seemed like an interminable amount of time, a horse whinnied in the night. The threat of violence made the silence ominous and the sudden brief sound startling as a crashing drum.

"Hombre, I do not come looking for trouble!" a voice called out. His voice had a hollow ring to it.

"We have no place for strangers here this night!" Buell shouted back.

"But Esteban Emilio Garza is no stranger to the old woman. Ask her."

Buell glanced over his shoulder toward the woman who peered around the edge of the window. She revealed more of her features, eased into view, and nodded when she saw the former officer looking at her. "Lopez runs him," she said. "I've filled his belly more than a few times."

"*Sí . . . sí*, Julio Lopez sent me." The man rode into the firelight, astride a big brown stallion and bearing a flag of truce, a white scarf tied to the barrel of his Spencer carbine. Garza removed his sombrero and looped its chin string across the saddle pommel and dismounted; the large rowels of his California spurs gleamed in the amber glare. The bandit was dressed for the desert night with a woolen shirt, leather *botas* similar to those worn by Mickey Free, and a waist-length cinnamon-colored jacket embroidered with silver thread and frayed at the wrists. He sported a pair of Colt revolvers tucked inside a faded yellow sash that circled his waist. He removed the white scarf and tied it around his neck. "See?" He patted the scarf. "I come in peace."

Hester Alvarado emerged from her cabin and hurried over to her cook fire, where she proceeded to ladle some food onto a stoneware plate and pour another cup of coffee. She set the food and drink upon the table under the thatch roof where the others had taken their meal.

"*El Jefe* feared for your safety," Garza continued, the fingers of his right hand fidgeting with his mustache. "So much gold, it turns a man's common sense inside out, yes, just thinking of it. Maybe it even makes some men do very foolish things, gives them just enough courage to make a big mistake and interfere with *El Jefe*'s plans. But as long as I am riding with you, there will be no problem." The bandit ran a hand through his shoulder-length thick black hair, then wiped it on the front of his jacket and smacked his lips at the sight of the food. But he wasn't about to forget his purpose for being here.

He held out his hand. "We will be *compadres*, you and I, all of us. Eh?" Finding no takers on a handshake, he stretched out his long arms in a magnanimous display of brotherhood that, again, no one rushed to join. Garza glared at the faces surrounding him, then shrugged. He could read the animosity in Buell's expression. "I know, I know, you'd like nothing better than to shoot Esteban Garza like a dog. Do it!" He laughed in a voice smooth as silk being draped across a saw blade. "Go on! Be brave, eh? No." He wagged his finger at the former officer. "Smart man, Señor Buell. If you arrive in Huachaca and I am not with you, the woman will die. Mmmm. I tell you, such a woman like that could spark a flash in wet powder. My *compañeros* will have much use for her before they slit her throat."

"You son of a bitch," Buell replied through clenched teeth, struggling to restrain himself. The effort brought tears to his eyes. But there was no getting around the fact that to harm this brigand would mean Colleen's death.

"But why talk of unpleasantness? Your woman is safe. When we reach Huachaca, you can rest in town and I will ride on and bring word to Julio Lopez. Then *El Jefe* and I will bring the girl to you. And take the money in return. Everyone will be happy, *sí*?" Garza's eyes darted to Jordan, then to Nance and Mose. It was obvious he realized there was one of their number missing. He looked about, his quick jerky movements betraying a sudden loss of nerve. At long last he noticed movement in the night; then Mickey Free stepped out from the shadow of a mesquite tree. He held his Winchester across his chest, his finger curled around the trigger.

Now there were five, Garza thought. Something about this fifth man troubled him. The bandit sauntered over toward Free and stood before him, searching the redheaded stranger's expression. "Hombre, do I know you?"

Free did not answer.

"Maybe it is in the eyes. I have seen those eyes before, but in another face. Who are you?"

A coyote howled in the night, a mournful wail like that of some lost and lonely spirit doomed to haunt the barrancas. Mickey Free leaned forward and spoke in a whisper that only the outlaw could understand. "I am your death."

Garza frowned, squinting, confused at first, caught off guard, then recovering his composure, a half-smile revealing crooked teeth. His breath reeked of tobacco and mescal. The bandit retreated a step, then slapped his thigh and roared with laughter that sounded forced as he swaggered back to the wagon.

He returned his attention to the strongbox on the flatbed. "Maybe you will show me the contents of the money chest? I have never seen a hundred thousand dollars."

"Sure thing. I'll open it up just as soon as I have Colleen McDunn at my side and not a minute before," Buell flatly stated.

"I just want a quick look."

"Buy it," said Buell.

Garza's expression grew mottled. He was accustomed to having his own way. He turned to check on the whereabouts of Free. The man was gone again. Damn. Now where was he? Oh, there, off to the left. The bandit did not like the way this one moved, how he seemed to linger on the periphery of the night, like that damn Apache, Chato, whom Lopez had befriended.

"Now I eat," Garza said, slouching past the wagon and seating himself at the table. "Pulque!" he called out, and brushed the coffee aside. He grabbed a spoon, wiped it on his shirt, and began to wolf down his food.

The old woman emerged from the jacal, her silver hair pulled back in a tight bun. Her coarsely woven skirt and cotton blouse gleamed white in the moonlight. She shuffled along, her brown feet in sandals she had made of rawhide and hemp. She shot a curious glance in Mickey's direction, then set down a jug of pulque and enough clay cups for all her visitors. Hester Alvarado had been a beauty once, dark and willful, but lost love and age had taken their toll. Still there was a sense of peace that seemed to emanate from the woman. It permeated her homestead. She had a way of looking through a man that made some of the travelers uneasy. Buell no longer wondered how a woman could survive alone out in the desert country. She was part of the land, and it protected her in ways he could sense but never fathom.

Jordan climbed down from the wagon and took a place alongside Buell. "The bastard may be right. Looks like I didn't figure on how wide a shadow Lopez throws down here. Everyone knows the money you carry belongs to Julio. With this man Garza along to keep an eye on things, no one will dare touch that money chest and risk having Lopez hunt 'em down. No, our problems will begin in Huachaca, I think, when Lopez opens that chest." He licked his lips, watching as Garza tossed back a shot of pulque.

Jordan quietly recounted the stories he had heard, of how Huachaca had once been a sleepy little village in the heart of the Apache *rancheria,* until Lopez made the area his base of operations. Over the past few months the village had acquired a more notorious reputation as a place where cantinas and bordellos catered to the lawless elements, all within a stone's throw of the local mission, La Iglesia de San Miguel. The deputy marshal had forgotten how a man's voice, or any sound, carried on the cool clear desert air until Hester Alvarado approached them with cups of pulque.

"When I was younger I used to live in Huachaca, where I sold the milk from my goats." She shrugged. "Now I am content to stay here, most of the time. It is too far for a woman to walk. And the talk of villagers bores me . . . It is too dry . . . too wet . . . a wife has been seen with another man . . . another child will be born to work the cornfields . . . when will a padre come to visit the mission? . . . always the same conversation. I prefer my goats. They don't bother me unless it is very important."

"Yes, ma'am." Buell nodded as if to humor the old woman, uncertain what to make of her. He eyed the pulque, debating whether or not to chance a sip of the milky-looking liquor made from the fermented pulp of the agave cactus. Damn, but he needed a drink. Finally he got up the courage and tilted the cup to his lips. It was slightly sour, not unlike a cheap wine. He coldly appraised the bandit who was still leaning over his plate of food. Garza belligerently ordered the old woman to be more attentive.

Jordan acknowledged her generosity. "If there is anything you need, ma'am, we will be more than happy to repay you for your hospitality."

Garza looked up from his plate of food and frowned in the big deputy's direction, then laughed aloud. Half-chewed meat and squash spilled from his mouth. He swiped his forearm across his chin.

"Well, the wood needs splitting," Hester suggested.

Buell and Jordan returned to the table where the deputy motioned for Sam Nance and Mose Woodard to join them. "You boys get on it then," the lawman matter-of-factly stated. "I'll tend the horses and see they're watered and fed. As for you, Free . . ." He glanced around, realizing Mickey Free had vanished yet again, this time skirting the perimeter of lantern light. Garza shifted uncomfortably as he and the other men searched the night in vain.

"What is he up to?" Buell asked, looking in the direction of the deputy.

"That's anybody's guess."

"What if he turns against us?"

"He won't do anything to endanger Miss Colleen."

"I don't like that man," Garza interjected, shoving the plate aside and fishing a cigarillo from his vest. "Who is he?"

"Just a man," Buell gruffly said.

"A dangerous man, I think. He rides for you, yes?"

"He is with us."

"Maybe. Maybe not. This is a deadly companion. He troubles me. I am thinking you have made a pact with the devil, Señor Buell."

Something about Mickey Free had unnerved the renegade after all. Buell took satisfaction in that. He filled his cup with pulque, scooped a dead moth off the milky surface like a trooper, tossed the insect aside, then drained the stoneware cup, slammed it down on the table in front of the bandit, and leaned forward until he was right in Garza's face.

"Then I suggest you walk soft . . . a-mi-go . . . and give the devil his due."

Chapter 26

"I know you," Hester said. Her voice drifted to him on the murmuring breeze while above the raging moon draping its diaphanous mantle of clouds posed against a backdrop of deep blue velvet and starlight. The goatkeeper found Mickey Free standing alone beyond the glare of the lanterns and the earshot of her many uninvited guests. He had skirted the *posas* and avoided the mud that had formed so uncharacteristically on the arid landscape and walked out upon the desert to find a place of solitude where he might confront his troubling memories.

"The others are strangers, well, except for Garza," she continued. "I have no use for him. Not like Geronimo and the Chiricahuas. They came to rest, to slaughter some goats and have milk for the little ones. I showed them no fear and cared for the injured. And so I remained and lived. I was no threat. I had made my peace." The woman drew closer to him, feeling his eyes upon her, studying her. "I remember there was a young boy, with red hair, many times he came with the Apache and stayed here and drank the milk from my goats. And then one day he came no more, only Geronimo and a handful of warriors. And always fewer in number. Then no more. But I remember the boy, a white Apache. Grown now, I think he would still know of the secret places and be one of the few men able to make his way into the Apache *rancheria* there in the mountains. He would know how to find Julio Lopez."

"Perhaps you are an old woman whose mind wanders."

"I am that. I am all you say." She laughed. "And if I spoke my memories of this white Apache to Esteban Garza?"

"Then I fear you would come to a bad end."

Hester Alvarado sniffed and cleared her throat and drew herself erect. "Do not mistake my age for helplessness," she said, drawing attention to a "pepperbox" percussion pistol tucked in the pocket beneath the serape she had draped across her shoulders. It was a devilish little six-barreled gun, as dangerous to the person who fired it as the unfortunate victim in front of the gun barrels. "I know you." Hester indicated the jagged skyline where the black-and-silver mountains loomed beneath the few feathery wisps of clouds. "Listen. The mountains call you by name." The old woman stood at his side, reached out to touch his cheek, her wrinkled flesh burned dark by the sun, thick veins scrawled across the back of her hands like blue ropes.

"Lopez stopped here on his way to Huachaca. He had a yellow-haired woman with him; her hands were bound."

"Buell's . . . intended bride," Mickey said, struggling to get around the words. "Lopez has taken her for ransom."

"There was an Apache with him."

"Chato," Free said.

"It is you then." Hester smiled, encouraged that her memory was still sharp. "Yes, I remembered your brother. I asked him about you and Gray Willow, his mother . . . your mother. She was always kind to me. But Chato cursed me and brushed me away."

"Sounds like him." Mickey's gaze narrowed. "He hasn't been the same since."

"Since what?"

"Since he killed her."

Hester's eyes widened in horror and she blessed herself with the sign of the cross. "Madre de Dios!"

Mickey left her side and continued out onto the plain until he was well away from prying eyes. Time passed. He let it and made no attempt to number the minutes, this ripening force that bows all men and yet means nothing when confronted with the infinite expanse of ageless light. He had not measured his steps, only knew he was alone with the wind and stars and spindrift moon, alone . . . and then not alone. Shadows shifted, stirred, parted, and Geronimo was there, not as he was, in prison, sick in spirit. No. Here his spirit was strong. It emanated from him like heat from a wildfire.

"Bik-eh? Teacher?"

But the vision did not speak. Geronimo knelt and motioned with his hand. Two boys approached him. Mickey recognized himself and the older boy, Chato, from a time when they were truly brothers, so long ago that it seemed like the memory of a stranger. Mickey cautiously moved in closer, the hairs on the back of his neck tingling, his own breath coming hard and fast, his flesh ice-cold.

Mickey watched as Geronimo shoved his hand deep into the soil, scooping up a handful of rock and sand and clay. Then again, deeper now, the shaman warrior dug his fingers into the earth and brought them up again, and to Mickey's horror this time his hands were full of blood, thick and old; it spattered the ground as it slipped through Geronimo's fingers. The blood spread out upon the earth, the puddle widening, becoming a miniature rivulet that flowed out in two directions, toward each of the boys.

Mickey willed his younger self to stand, to back away from the horrible course and escape, but the boys knelt there, transfixed by the blood as it moved like a crimson snake upon the earth. When it reached the knees of both boys it began to curl up their legs, past their waists, until the blood reached their arms and spread to their fingertips, both youths, their hands as gruesomely marked as Geron-imo's.

"Bik-eh, what is the meaning?"

But Geronimo was gone before he could answer and the images of the boys were gone and in their place a pair of glowing eyes, in their place hot feral breath and silent paws and great heart beating at one with the wild. Coyote . . . Trickster.

My blood is your blood.

Mickey blinked and rubbed his eyes, realized for the first time he no longer held his rifle, that he was kneeling upon the earth and had been that way long enough for his legs to be nearly numb from the effort.

My spirit in you, and both of us Free.

Mickey shook his head; the world began to reel before him; he brought a hand to his face, felt the sticky moisture smear across his features, and jerked his hand back to find it covered with coagulating blood. He gasped and shoved it into the sand to clean it, scraping at it until the flesh was raw. He glared at the animal watching him, sitting on its haunches. Mickey gingerly examined his hand and features. They were dry. Clean.

Hear beyond hearing. See beyond seeing.

"Damn you," Mickey cursed, and picked up a stone and drew his arm back as if to hurl it in the animal's direction. Coyote continued to watch him, unmoved by the threat. Eyes locked, beast and man, staring into the heart and soul of each other. Then Mickey lowered the rock and let it drop and slumped forward; his cheek struck the very stone he had been about to throw. A jagged edge slit his cheek. The pain felt real and Mickey clung to that, the pain and the sensation of a single droplet of blood oozing out of his wounded cheek and mingling in the earth, joining him in sacred covenant to the land and the truth of things he could not understand but at long last accept.

*Who are you? Hero ... renegade ... man of vengeance
... shadow warrior ... who?*

"I don't know," he muttered to the beast, but the Trickster had vanished, leaving his questions in the dust. Mickey Free stared into the darkness and for a brief moment saw beyond seeing. And his ice-blue eyes grew bold and his expression filled with resolve. "Tsaaa! But I will walk the path, *my* path, and find out."

Chapter 27

His head nodded; his shoulders slumped forward. His neck popped, waking him instantly. . . .

Deputy Marshal Reverend Doctor Jordan clutched his coat around his barrel chest and shivered as a wind gust blew out of the dry distance and found him, propped against a wagon wheel in the wee hours of the morning. He estimated another three hours before sunup. Well and good. He'd welcome the sun, though not what it might bring. He sighed and sipped his coffee, decided the old goatherd must have strained it with a horseshoe, and fished a flat brown bottle from his coat pocket and added a healthy dash of rye whiskey to the contents in his cup to cut the "mud." He tossed back a shot for good measure from the bottle and damn near purred as the warmth spread throughout his belly and chest.

Fortified, he was able to contemplate his situation and the madness that had come over him and tricked him into taking part in this suicidal venture. A man had to be a dad-blamed fool to risk his life down here in Sonora. Lost causes were better left to young bucks, not some old buffalo like himself. And like it or not, Jordan wasn't getting any younger.

Tired, tired, tired. How could the night take so long? Hurry, sunrise. He yawned, started to drift off, caught himself in time.

Then again, maybe that was the reason he had joined Buell. Jordan didn't want to end his days some stove-up old lawman down-at-the-heels and scraping by. Better to go out while he could still make a stand. And yet getting killed wasn't going to help Miss Colleen. And he did not want to admit it, but she was in a bad way and there was little hope of rescuing her. Jordan would give it his all. But he had grave doubts. Her only real chance of surviving lay with the Apache Kid.

That was the cold, cruel fact. And there was another, something he had tried not to dwell on, but here it came rising up like war smoke from the recesses of his mind. They needed Mickey Free.

But he didn't need them. . . .

His eyelids were leaden, impossible to support. "I'll just close them for a second," he promised himself. "I'm still listening. Listening. Listen . . ."

* * *

"Drop the rifle, Deputy. Toss it in the wagon and stand aside."

Jordan stumbled forward, his eyes wide open now, as James Buell's voice roused him from his early-morning lethargy. What the hell!? How long had he been dozing? It was still dark. Drop his rifle? He turned and spied Buell and Garza walking toward him from the jacal; the men were backlit by the cook fire Hester had left burning beneath a cast-iron coffeepot. Jordan turned and brought up his Winchester, searching past the two men for some sign of a threat. As Buell and Garza glumly approached, they held their arms away from their sides. Garza had lost his serape and Buell wore only a shirt and trousers. Barefoot he gingerly picked his way across the broken earth. Behind the two men came Sam Nance and Mose Woodard.

The barkeep shoved forward and trained his rifle on Jordan while Mose kept the shotgun on Buell and Garza. Jordan stared at the men; it took several long moments for the deputy to comprehend what was happening. Back by the cabin, Hester Alvarado watched from the window. She wanted no part of what was transpiring.

"You heard the major," Nance said. "Toss the rifle in the wagon and stand aside, Reverend Doctor."

Jordan glared at Nance, then fixed his stare on the black man with the shotgun. "Mose, you are no cold-blooded killer. You haven't the heart for it. Lay the mare's leg down. And tell me what's going on."

"Sorry, Mr. Jordan, sir, but a hundred thousand dollars can buy me a whole passel of conscience. I been poor. It's time I tried rich. Me and Sam here aim to split the money. Now you best do as we say and we'll just take the horses and the wagon. That'll buy us plenty of time to git." Mose thumbed the twin hammers back on the sawed-off scattergun. Nance said there could be no witnesses. Mose didn't see it that way. Take the horses and leave the others afoot. By the time they were able to pursue Woodard and Nance, they would be long gone. Still, Nance had a forceful argument. Mose Woodard didn't much cotton to the idea of killing unarmed men, but there it was.

"Jordan, you toss aside the Winchester," Nance said, "or by heaven we'll settle this with lead."

The deputy tried to weigh his chances. He might put a slug into Nance. But Mose would cut the others down and Nance might get off a shot as well. Not that Jordan gave a damn about Garza, but they had to keep the bandit alive to ensure Colleen's safety. The deputy had to stall and hope the two would-be thieves made a mistake.

"Mose, let Buell have it," Nance snapped.

"Stand down!" Jordan exclaimed, and tossed the Winchester onto the wagon bed.

At a signal from the barkeep, Mose immediately hurried forward and leaped onto the wagon bed so he could cover all three men with the scattergun, freeing Nance to eventually bring the horses around from the corral and hitch them to the singletree. But first the barkeep was determined to account for the rest of the party. He glanced up at the black man. "You got them covered?"

"One wrong move and they'll be cutting their teeth on buckshot."

"That chest belongs to Julio Lopez, señor," Garza said. "It will not go well for you to think otherwise." Garza glanced at Jordan and Buell with disdain. "What are Buell and the deputy to men like us, who know the value of money, men who do not wish to take needless risks? Lopez will see you both are rewarded for bringing him his money."

"Do we look like rednecked peckerwoods?" Nance exclaimed. "By the time Señor Lopez finds out what's happened we will be back across the border and there will be nothing the bastard can do about it."

Garza scowled and glanced down at his empty holster and wondered how he was going to explain this to *El Jefe*. He rubbed the sleep from his bloodshot eyes and scratched his neck, feeling for the slender hilt of a throwing knife he kept in a scabbard. That might account for the one with the rifle, but the other man would blast them into doll rags on the spot. He lowered his hand, leaving the knife where it was.

"My God, think of what you two are doing. You are killing Colleen McDunn as sure as if you were pulling the trigger."

"Major, she's probably already dead, or at least in such a condition that no decent man would lie with her," Nance replied.

Buell cursed his former sergeant and lunged for the man, but Jordan grabbed him by the shoulder and hauled him back into line, saving his life, for Sam Nance would surely have shot him dead.

"About time you were taken down a peg, Major." Nance chuckled, then turned his attention toward the deputy. "All right . . . where is the Apache Kid?"

"How should I know?"

"You run him. Always have, since he was a pup."

"That was when you and I both wore blue," Jordan said. "You've fallen a long way, Sam."

"Don't bother. I ate my plate of beans and saluted yes, sir, and no, sir; no, it is my time. Where the devil is Free?"

"You're probably in his gun sights even as you speak," Jordan replied. Maybe it was a bluff, but it gave him pleasure to watch the lumbering turncoat twist and turn as he checked the shadows.

"Call him in!"

"He doesn't listen to me," Jordan said.

"Nance, I got a bad feeling," Mose cautioned. "Get the horses and let's take what we can." Nothing stirred in these early hours of the morning, not a coyote or bat, not a sidewinder or the smallest fly. The black man, unnerved by the quiet, began to think it wasn't such a good idea to be standing in the wagon bed. A man made a mighty fine target up here.

He was right.

Gunfire lit the dark. A tongue of flame stabbed toward him. Mose yelped and on reflex squeezed the trigger on the shotgun as he lurched sideways in pain. The scattergun emptied both barrels into the money chest, blasting apart the lid and filling the air with currency. Mose staggered forward through a flurry of paper as he toppled from the wagon. Buell and Garza dived for the ground as Nance loosed a warning shot in their direction. Behind him, Mose staggered to his feet, clawing the revolver from his belt. He stumbled toward the goat pen but only covered a few yards before collapsing.

Nance crouched behind the singletree and fired in the direction of the muzzle blast. He blazed away at the night, firing again and again, moving the rifle in an arc. Mose rose up on one arm and squeezed off a round from his revolver, more by accident than intent. He fired into the air.

"He's killed me, The Kid's gone and killed me!" Mose wailed, clasping his side.

"Take it like a man!" Nance growled.

"Goddamn you. I shouldn't have listened. I should never have listened. I ain't no killer." Mose glanced down at his bloodstained shirt. His left side felt numb. "It don't hurt, but I'm dying all the same." He stared down at the revolver in his black hand. He looked up and saw Jordan crawling over to him. The deputy grabbed for the dying man's revolver.

Nance glimpsed the deputy out of the corner of his eye. "No, you don't, Jordan!" He swung the rifle around to put the deputy under the gun. Jordan shifted and rolled to the side and missed by inches catching a bullet between the eyes. The heavy slug spattered him with dirt and shale.

Mose slumped forward, his mind reeling with images of high life and riches, of silk sheets and feather beds and fine women. Then he thought of his mother's blackberry cobbler and the taste of cool buttermilk when it's fresh from the churn and heard her calling him by name and he regretted more than ever the choice he had made. *Oh, God. . . . Oh, sweet Lord.*

"Kid! Show yourself. Where the hell are you?!" Nance roared. He searched the shadows, then checked Buell and Garza, who had crawled to a water trough and were crouched undercover, seeking what protection they could get. Nance glanced in the direction of the jacal and saw Hester's silhouette in the window. The money would be his. No gawddamn white Apache was gonna stop him from getting what he deserved. But of course, that is precisely what Mickey Free had in mind, giving the murderous bartender exactly what he deserved.

"Kid!" Nance bellowed, levering a fresh shell into the chamber.

"Right here."

Nance swung back toward the singletree and tried to get the front of the wagon between him and the threat. He fired, the rifle kicking in his grasp. Mickey answered, firing once, twice, the slugs lifting the larger man off his feet, forcing him back, ever back. A revolver sounded. It was Mose Woodard and his target was Nance. The bartender twisted and lost his hold on his rifle. He tried to catch it only to have the weapon fly from his hands. He spun and tripped over the singletree. One of his suspenders popped loose as he landed hard and lay still, his legs curled over the wooden post.

Mickey Free materialized out of the shadows, his rifle ready as Buell and the other two men scrambled to their feet. Jordan started to rush forward to slap the younger man on the shoulder, but the Kid raised the rifle and forced him back.

Then Free climbed onto the wagon bed and crouched by the large, iron-reinforced strongbox, reached in through the jagged hole Mose had inadvertently blasted in the box, found a layer of worthless newsprint and a firebrick, then several layers of dynamite. It was a miracle Mose Woodard's shotgun hadn't blown them to kingdom come. He scooped up a handful of the worthless notes from the wagon bed. Instead of greenbacks, Free clutched a pack of curled, blackened paper in his clenched fist. More of the singed scraps were scattered about the wagon and fluttered across the ground like fallen leaves.

Buell and Jordan seemed resigned to the fact that Free had discovered their little secret. Garza stood transfixed, unarmed but staring at the ruined front of the box. There wasn't a real note or bag of gold to be found from what he could see. Free leaped down from the wagon and confronted Buell. Garza knelt and picked up one of the slips of worthless paper that had blown against his boot.

"Señor, what is this!"

"Where's the money, Major?" Free asked.

"There is none. Never was," said Jordan. "I figured once we got the girl I'd light the fuse there underneath the box and blow Lopez and his sons of bitches sky-high. Granted it wasn't much of a plan, but it was all I could come up with at the time."

"No money. But your family? *El Jefe* heard the talk. You come from nobility, eh?" Garza exclaimed.

"One of the best in Philadelphia. And financially broke. My father lost it all, long ago, one foolish venture at a time. I borrowed money on my name to buy my ranch and hoped I could pay back the bank by selling my cattle when they'd fattened." Buell extended his hands palm outward. "So there it is."

"No money. This troubles me," the bandit growled. "What? Do you think to trick us? I swear Julio Lopez will not be amused. When he finds out—" Before he could continue his harangue he glanced at Mickey and didn't like what he saw in those cold eyes. "What are you thinking, señor?"

"I'm thinking Julio Lopez will be none the wiser. I am thinking you should have listened to me and kept traveling," Mickey said. "You were warned, remember? I am your death."

Garza's dark, ugly countenance suddenly paled. He noticed Free's Winchester was centered on his chest. "Now see here . . . Señor Kid, wait." He grabbed the scarf around his neck, the white flag of truce he had arrived under. "You see here. . . ." He started retreating, unarmed and wishing he could reach his guns inside the jacal.

"You won't be telling Julio Lopez a damned thing."

"No!" Garza's hand swept up and closed around the hilt of his throwing knife. Mickey shot him in mid-throw. The report was deafening. The knife sailed off into the shadows. The bullet struck the bandit dead center in the white scarf that covered his chest. Garza was blown backward into the dirt. He hit hard and skidded several feet along the ground.

Then the frightened goats began to bleat. A rooster crowed. The gunshot reverberated in the twilight, carrying to the far hills. But Garza heard nothing. Nor would he, ever again.

Buell charged in and swung a fist at Free, leveled a blow that Mickey blocked with his Winchester. Buell ignored the pain. "What have you done? You bloodthirsty savage! What about Colleen? Did you even for once stop to think of her?"

Saying her name seemed to bring him under control. The strength seemed to flow away from his arms; his legs went weak, Buell staggered toward the wagon and grabbed for the iron-rimmed wheel. His mind filled with horrible images, of the woman he loved defiled by these murderous renegades who had stormed into his life and left in their cursed wake the wreckage of his dreams. "Dear God, what now?"

It was the aftermath of death and the approach of morning. A nightmare had begun and there was no escape for the weary. They would have to make a stand, the three of them, guarded companions.

"Now we find Miss Colleen and bring her home," said Mickey. He walked across the dark and bloody ground and stood over Mose, who lowered his revolver. He half-expected the same treatment and steeled himself. Instead, Mickey knelt by him and checked his wound.

"Went clean through. Doesn't seem to have hit anything too vital. I reckon you'll live."

"It hurts like hell."

"Hurting's better 'n dying." Mickey glanced toward Buell and Jordan. "We'll be leaving shortly after sunup," he told them.

"What about me?" Mose asked, uncertain about his fate.

"The old woman can patch you up."

"And you have a horse," Jordan added, glaring at the man.

Mose sighed, reading between the lines. He had that coming and more. "Don't worry. You won't ever see me again." The others seemed to approve. The black man lay back upon the hard earth and slowly exhaled and closed his eyes as he rode out the pain. "Shot to hell for a box of worthless paper," he muttered.

Mickey stood and began to thumb cartridges into his Winchester.

"Where do we ride, Kid?" Jordan said. He was completely alert now, a note of readiness in the old lawman's voice. He was like a warhorse, an old wild breed that once up to speed would walk till it dropped.

"To hell, Reverend Doctor." Mickey Free surveyed the carnage. The smell of blood was in the air and the killing had only just begun. "To hell."

Chapter 28

"By heaven, you were right, Kid," Jordan muttered, eyeing the narrow gap between two jagged ridges whose steep walls and forbidding crest did indeed resemble the maw of some enormous beast about to have them for lunch. "It does look like the jaws of hell." The deputy shifted his great weight on the wagon seat and pushed back the brim of his hat to reveal his dust-caked features and stared through the trees at the ominous-looking passage. "So that's Los Pilares, the legendary Apache *rancheria*." He wore three days of grit and grime on his coat and chaps. His jaw was dark and stubbled. The last time he had trimmed his whiskers was at Hester Alvarado's, three days behind them.

Yesterday, the three had cut a winding narrow trail above Huachaca. The music of the cantinas and the aroma of whiskey, freshly made tortillas, and chili (that even from a distance smelled spicy enough to make them break sweat) had drifted up from the isolated settlement. Right then and there Jordan had suggested they might drift into town and stand a round of drinks at the local *pulqueria* and pick up a little of the local gossip.

But Mickey and Buell determined the risk outweighed any good that might come of it. James Buell, especially, had become a man with a single purpose and would allow no deviation from the reason they had come to Sonora. Reverend Doctor Jordan could drink a bellyful of cheap pulque and chase whores on his own time. And Mickey had agreed, much to his friend's chagrin.

All that afternoon and the following morning the three pressed on into the mountains, threading their way around and over ridges, some blanketed with piñon pine and others barren, the color of bleached bones, deeper still to where the skies were continually patrolled by vultures and winter hawks cutting lazy circles against an azure ceiling. Mickey wisely skirted the more forbidding looking barrancas; he rode on and let the land awaken his memories, rode on with the eyes of a youth trailing in the shadow Geronimo, and by late afternoon of the third day the ridges seemed to part before them.

Mickey brought them through a maze of increasingly steep escarpments and through a thick stand of scrub oaks nourished by a spring that bubbled out of the earth and spilled its moisture onto the parched soil at the upper end of the valley, and it was here they came to Los Pilares. The narrow, treacherous-looking passage seemed to open its jaws as they approached. Granted it was an illusion, but that didn't make Buell or Jordan feel any better about entering the shadow-shrouded pass.

Free halted their approach within the stand of trees and dismounted to rest the bay and water the animal at the spring. Jordan climbed down from the wagon and rubbed his backside while Buell dismounted and removed his coat and knelt by the spring and drank with the horses.

"Now we wait for dark," said Mickey. "We cannot chance a fire this close to the pass. But some rest will do us good, and cold beans, jerky, and yesterday's biscuits are better than nothing."

"Any other orders?" Buell curtly inquired, sounding a bit perturbed. He was bone-weary and deeply anxious about the task that lay before them.

"Not that I can think of, but I'll let you know," Free said, enjoying the former officer's discomfort. But he couldn't spare Buell too much of his time. He had to make some preparations before entering the narrow pass. While the bay drank his fill, Mickey retrieved several strips of cloth from his saddlebags and knelt by his mount. With infinite-seeming patience he laboriously wrapped each of the horse's hooves in a couple of layers of material until the sounds of those iron shoes would be sufficiently muffled for Mickey to be able to walk his mount into the Apache *rancheria*. The cloth might not remain in place should he need to gallop to safety, but if that were the case, sound would be the least of his worries.

Free ambled toward the edge of the timber to study the saw-toothed walls that defined the pass. He knew there would be men guarding the entrance, posted to sound a warning should anyone approach. But by the time the sentries sounded an alarm it would be too late. At least that was the plan. But if Mickey Free didn't have Colleen by then . . . he didn't want to consider the possibility. This had to work. Period.

Jordan chuckled as he watched Free move off through the thicket. The deputy walked around the wagon, relieved himself against the wheel, then looked around for a suitable place to pitch his bedroll. He looked across at Buell kneeling in the grasses that ringed the pool. A patch of sunlight working through the trees set the waters glimmering, mixing the reflection of the trees with golden flecks. Lazy dragonflies hovered over the cool, still waters, dipped and dived, drank, and now and then died in beauty, their needlelike bodies squirming to free themselves while their diaphanous wings grew sodden and heavy as they surrendered to their fate.

"Officers don't cotton to taking orders from mere scouts," Jordan said, joining Buell by the pool. The younger man had to grin despite himself.

"No. Not this officer."

"Only you're not an officer anymore."

"No, I am not," Buell conceded. "Thoughtful of you to remind me, Mr. Jordan."

"And Free isn't a scout."

"You are right again. He is an escaped prisoner."

"Yeah, and your only hope."

"A fact you keep reminding me of," Buell offhandedly observed.

"I'd hate for you to forget it." Jordan led Buell's mount away from the spring. He used his bandanna to hobble the animal, then turned his attention to carefully leading the team pulling the wagon and brought them over to the spring. He handed the reins to Buell.

"Mind you, they drink too much and they'll founder."

"Then maybe you—" Buell started to protest, but the deputy was already walking off after Free. "Damn. Everyone's giving orders except me." He glared at the beasts. The animals whinnied and shook their heads; he assumed they, too, were being insubordinate.

* * *

Mickey was checking the loads on his revolvers and studying the lay of the land as Jordan approached. The deputy waited in silence, allowing Free his moment to bond with his past. He knew that finding the Apache *rancheria* was more than the work of a keen memory. It was as if the land itself had whispered to him, led him farther into the mountains, guided him unerringly to this place. Each cave, each thicket, the spring, the jagged toothlike ridges all had a link to his past. In the days before the tribe had abandoned the path of war, the Apache *rancheria* had been an impregnable retreat, secluded, protected, a respite from pursuing troops of cavalry and *federales*.

He turned and looked at Jordan. The deputy touched the brim of his hat. He reached in one of his hip pockets and brought forth an oilcloth packet of beef jerky. He removed a couple of strips and tossed one to Free. "Eat up, Kid. It might be your last meal. Mine, too."

"Not you," Mickey said. "You're too mean and ornery to die."

"From your lips to God's ears," Jordan cracked. It took some work, but he managed to bite off a strip of the dried meat. "Too bad this isn't buffalo. I cannot remember the last time I sat down to a plate of roasted buffalo hump. There's nothing better, 'ceptin' maybe the sight of a big herd charging across the prairie, the ground shaking beneath their hooves. There was thunder on the land in those days." Jordan shook his head. "Gone. All gone."

Mickey Free breathed in, relishing the cooler air, the scent of water and green growing rushes. The birds had fallen silent, but there was a wind in the branches of the live oaks and the rustling leaves and clicking limbs brushing against one another. And in patches of ground where the sunlight worked through the canopy of trees tiny white and purple wildflowers sprang from the shallow topsoil. Everything was the same and none of it the same. The People were gone, the race of warriors who would not compromise and fought a losing battle that cost them all they possessed. "Things change."

"Faster than I like to think." Jordan glanced over his shoulder, saw that Buell was still occupied, and lowered his voice. "See here, Kid, I don't know how it is all gonna fall tomorrow, but if we pull this off and rescue Miss Colleen, maybe you better not come back with us. Stay here in Sonora where the army can't touch you."

"We'll see," said Free. "It is not entirely up to me."

"That's right; this isn't just about Miss Colleen, is it? There's Chato, too." If Chato escaped, then Jordan knew Mickey would follow him, no matter where, even back across the border and into more danger. But the chase had to end. And Gray Willow's son had to answer for her death.

Jordan scratched at his stubbled jaw with the strip of jerky, gave the future a bit of thought, then decided his course. "If it doesn't end here, Kid, then you can count on me to help you."

"*Gracias,* you old jehu," Mickey said, clapping him on the shoulder, "But that's a trail I have to ride alone."

Jordan nodded and turned to leave, paused to look off toward the saw-toothed ridge, then back at his companion. "Say, Mickey, what about me and Buell? You still aim to settle accounts?"

Mickey shrugged, removed one of the Colt revolvers from his belt and checked the loads in the cylinder, determined the action was smooth and free of grit. "What do you think?"

The deputy was not about to be cowed by the Kid's performance. He reached out and snatched the revolver from Mickey's grasp, spun it by the trigger guard, and then let it slap against the palm of his hand, the gun sight pressed against Free's belly. "I think . . ." He twirled the pistol yet again, spun it once, and then with amazing skill returned the weapon to its owner's belt. "I think things change."

Chapter 29

The shadows stole down the peaks of Los Pilares and for a few minutes at sunset the great spiked pillars turned blood red before the velvet night dimmed their brilliance and turned them into somber sentinels looming over the pass, ominous in their proximity. Buell felt hollow, as if all his life belonged to someone else, had been lived by someone else, until now. This was his moment; his destiny called him. No prestige, no power other than his own, that of his hands, that of his courage, would see him through. Unable to rest, to relax like Jordan with his back against a tree and catching a last few minutes of sleep, Buell stole away from the wagon and made his way through the thicket, attempting to make as little noise as possible.

Suddenly an unearthly howl filled the night and he froze in his tracks as something padded through the brush a few yards ahead. He had never heard such a horrid wail. It rose in timbre, drifted higher in pitch until it was all he could do not to scream himself.

"*Ndolkah* . . . cougar," said Mickey Free, whispering in Buell's ear. He gave a start. He had been oblivious to Free up until the moment he spoke. The Apache Kid had quite literally materialized out of the shadows. Buell could have sworn he had stepped through the space Free was now occupying.

"Cougar . . ." Buell repeated, unsure whether or not to take comfort from the fact that although he was not confronted by some supernatural beast, it was indeed a lethal creature, all fangs and claws and thoroughly ruthless, before him, blocking the path.

"Yes," Free told him. "He says this is his water hole and he wants us to leave."

"Says? Really now, Mr. Free," Buell countered.

"Ch'inkii!" Mickey hissed.

The animal retreated, footpads on the hard earth, a rustle of underbrush. Then silence.

"What did you say?"

"I told him to leave," Mickey replied with a shrug. "Lucky for us he did."

"Lucky for me at the least. He probably would have recognized you as one of his own." Buell regretted the way that sounded, but the words could not be recalled. 'What I mean is . . . is . . ."

"That you're a long way from home, that here in Sonora all your family history doesn't amount to spit, that tomorrow you may die."

"And you don't think about it."

"Yes," said Free, leaning against the trunk of a live oak, his eyes on the ridge, hoping to catch a glimpse of moonlight glinting off a gun barrel. "I don't know how many men Lopez has by now. But you can be sure it will be more than enough."

"Damn it, man, then what are we doing here, if we have no hope?!"

"I didn't say that," Mickey replied, caught off guard by the easterner's outburst.

"Then you think your plan will work?" Earlier, Buell and Jordan had listened intently while Mickey Free had outlined a desperate gambit that involved his entering alone into the heart of the Apache *rancheria* and bringing Colleen out from the den of renegades. While Free took his chances within the stronghold, Jordan and Buell would prepare a trap with Mickey Free as bait, provided he made good his escape from Lopez's camp.

"No," Free said.

Buell looked startled. Then he heard the fugitive softly laugh. "Damn," Buell muttered, knowing he had been set up.

"Nobody here but you, Major. You won't have any men to order about. Come morning, you'll have to do your own fighting . . . your own dying maybe."

"I'll stand," Buell told him. Sweat stole down the back of his neck despite the chill of night. "Hands moist . . . mouth dry. Is it like that with you?"

Mickey thought about lying, then decided any man willing to take a stand deserved the truth. "All the time." He raised his hand, extended it into a patch of moonlight so that James Buell could watch it trembling.

"You?"

Free nodded. The two men stood side by side, sharing an unspoken camaraderie neither had expected to find. Fireflies swirled through space, like living embers cast from celestial flames. Mickey studied the man and grudgingly giving him credit. Buell wasn't prepared for any of this, the close-in, personal, vicious business of life and death. But he was still here. And maybe he would do his share.

"I didn't know," Buell said. "I was jealous of you. Because she cared about you, even though she looked upon you as a brother, I still saw you as a rival. And it twisted my judgment. As God is my judge I am sorry for that."

"None of it matters now," Free said. His blue eyes hardened as he searched the skyline. He caught a glimpse of silver there near the mouth of the pass, high up on the battlement, moonlight glinting off a rifle barrel. Just as he suspected, a watcher in the dark. Chato's call, no doubt. Free picked up his rifle, chambered a shell, and then started back for his horse. It was time for him to go. Buell walked

with him, realizing the hour was at hand. Then Mickey
halted in his tracks and started at the underbrush on the
opposite side of the spring.

*Was that a woman in the shadows? Gray Willow? No,
impossible. She's dead.* The coyote stepped out from behind a patch of cattails and lifted its head to sniff the air.
You, Trickster. Always you. Mickey Free mopped his features on the sleeve of his linsey-woolsey shirt, then looked
up. The animal had soundlessly vanished. But then he had
expected nothing less from the ghosts who walked the
howling wilderness. He continued over to the bay gelding,
took the reins in one hand, and with the other slid the rifle
into the saddle boot. Jordan stood and rubbed his features,
stretched, and worked the stiffness out of his legs. He raised
a hand, a simple gesture of friendship.

"Be seeing you, Kid."

Mickey nodded. He drew a hand across his chest and
then extended it palm down toward the deputy, fingers extended and together. It was Apache sign talk for a safe
journey, wherever it might lead.

"Just a minute ago . . ." Buell nervously interjected.
"The way you stopped, as if . . . well, what was it? What
did you see?" He had sensed a change coming over the
man standing at his side.

"Nothing. Everything. Who can tell? Get some rest, Mr.
Buell."

"Rest. . . ." Buell grimaced. If only he could. . . .

Mickey stroked the bay, softly sang a gentling song he
had heard the Apache chant to their war ponies. It was
supposed to instill courage and stamina to their mounts,
enabling the beasts to charge through gunfire and never
waver. The animal's muffled hooves were virtually soundless as Mickey walked the animal toward the break in the
trees and prepared to ride into the bandit stronghold. He
glanced down at Buell, could barely make out the man's

worried expression, and tried to find the words to bolster his resolve. What was there left to tell him, that by mid-morning they might all be dead and have added their stories to the ancient hills'?

So be it. There were worse things.

"A man cannot escape his fate," Mickey added. "But he can rise to meet it."

Chapter 30

A man, a ghost, walks his mount into the jaws of the beast, into the realm of the killers, comes walking, soundless as the shadows, beneath the eyes of the watchers dozing when they should be alert instead of slouched against stone battlements, half-asleep, their stomachs gnawing on their backbones. A man, a ghost, follows the whispering breeze into the dark and deadly ground, allowing memory to be his guide, to blaze an old trail into the cold heart of the Apache rancheria.

Dabin-ik-eh, One Who Is Free, Mickey Free, Apache Kid . . . call him what you will, his own identity is a blur, two paths to walk and only one man to walk them both, or to go his own way. He is risking his life. That much is for sure. He has come for vengeance. He has come for love. Which will win the war in his heart? Free cannot say, but he knows this. He has come to finish what began long ago, lured here by destiny and the tricks of Old Coyote, the spirit of an elder god.

Once Geronimo took him aside, drawn to the lonely solitude of a foundling child, drawn to the power he sensed in the child, something ancient, yet untapped until the shaman warrior awakened the boy's connection with the same howling wilderness that had stolen his parents but left him a gift, the power of one.

You know the rest.

The boy listened and learned his lessons well. You will not hear him, you will not see him, because he is of the

*land now, he is stone and cholla, he is night hawk and
prowling cougar, he is the silence, and he is the wind.*

You will not hear him. . . .

You will not see him. . . .

* * *

She was the dancer in the firelight, hips swaying to the
music of guitar and tambourine and castanets. The carnal
hunger on the fire lit faces of the men surrounding the
young woman, inflamed her own wanton passions, fueled
her limbs till the dancer grew flushed from her exertions.
And still the music would not cease. And still Clovia Madrigal must ride it out like a runaway stallion. But the tight-
ness in her chest and the beating of her heart were from
the rush of power, like lightning in her blood, shooting
through her veins, the power of a primal passion.

These men wanted her. Every man there, from the peon
with his hungry family to the most hardened bandit, not
one of the lot could take his eyes off her. Now she turned
and twisted and her scarlet dress swirled about her legs,
revealing her slender ankles and brown thighs like succu-
lent loaves of warm bread, thighs to wrap about a man's
waist and imprison him in her own exuberant lust, to hold
her lover until he collapsed and shrank and spent himself
and begged for sleep.

In the dance Clovia Madrigal was every man's fantasy.

But when the music stopped she belonged only to Julio
Lopez. And he knew it. And he didn't really care. Lopez
had grown accustomed to her sexual appetites and had a
yen for something different, someone special, a fine lady
with yellow hair and tanned skin. Colleen had been on his
mind for several nights now. Too long. And now it was
time to tame her.

He watched the reckless dancer, let her sweat-streaked
shoulders and heaving breasts and tousled hair start a fire
burning below his belt. But the gratification he needed was

not to be found in the company of Señorita Madrigal. No, not tonight anyway.

Lopez lifted his gaze to the saw-toothed ridges, the dark expanse of the narrow winding pass, then surveyed his own camp, the new arrivals who had begun to build their jacals, begun to dream his dreams. Several days ago, Garza had sent a runner with word that Buell had crossed the border and was leading a wagon loaded with an iron-locked money chest chained to the flatbed. So there it was. His plan had worked. And he had added a new twist. Tomorrow he would bring his men into Huachaca, to await Buell's arrival. At last, the future was within his grasp. Tonight the stars called him by name.

He turned and studied the blockhouse, squat and formidable and black on black upon the sloping land. She was in there, imprisoned in his bedroom, waiting, unwilling of course, but he intended to change all that. She must want him, give him everything, hold nothing back, or she would die.

So Lopez tugged on the hem of his vaquero's coat, patted the dust from the silver-embroidered black sleeves, his ruffled shirt smelling of lilac water; he brushed a hand through his hair and, moistening his fingers, ran them across his thick, black eyebrows. Then he turned and casually strolled away from the fire and the circle of men, his soldiers, numbering seventeen now although several of them were armed only with machetes. *They'll have weapons soon enough*, he thought, as he headed for the blockhouse. Lopez had bragged of his plans, of the ransom demand. He knew Clovia had been as eager as any of the others to see the money. She was a fiery temptress and thoroughly convinced that Julio Lopez was destined for greatness someday and she would be his lady. He allowed Clovia her illusions because it suited him. But no woman had any claim on his heart. Ambition was his only real mistress.

He started up the slope and Clovia watched him as she spun and lifted her arms like sinewy serpents, like rippling water, like spangled flames reaching out to the circle of faces. She watched as Julio left the circular web of her passion and desire to seek another's embrace, another's lust, to go to Buell's woman and spurn the devotion of his sixteen-year-old mistress.

She cried out like a wild thing and spun until the world reeled. How to show him the error of his ways, to teach him a lesson, to punish her lover's unfaithfulness? She searched the hungry faces, chose one brute, a scarred killer with stringy black hair, and another, younger, with a leering smile, now a third; he was older, with a face like a war map. Then she played to them, danced to them, let her swaying hips cast a spell, made a wanton offering of her heat and her forced laughter, of her flesh and fire, given to each of the three.

Yes, she would teach Julio Lopez not to cast her aside.

The three renegades stood and clapped their hands and grabbed for her. Clovia's eyes flashed in reply. *Soon,* she promised as she danced away. But men such as these were unaccustomed to waiting. Her dance had made them bold. *El Jefe*'s absence helped, too. But just to be on the safe side, let them carry her off into one of the dark jacals, ply her with mescal, and have their way. The night belonged to the quick and the dead.

Soon, eh? The men shared that common thought. But never soon enough.

Chapter 31

On a hillside, back beyond the corral and the blockhouse
and the jacals that had begun to spring up almost overnight
since the arrival of the peons from the valley, Chato
perched on a slab of pink granite that jutted out through
the shallow topsoil covering the hard underbelly of the
mountains. The serrated ridge loomed over him, silent,
night-wrapped, marked by narrow deer trails that snaked
along the escarpment. He stared down at the campfire, the
dancing figure that was the center of attention, the unrec-
ognizable faces of the outlaws with whom he had cast his
lot.

Once the valley floor had been dotted with hogans and
the night ablaze with cook fires and the laughter of Apache
children, the throbbing drums and chanted stories, the
boasts of warriors, real fighters and not like the drunken
bandits cheering Clovia to new excess. He lowered his gaze
to the blockhouse, thought of the prisoner it contained, a
link to his past, to the dark deed he had tried to disclaim.
Colleen McDunn's presence plagued him, dragged the sins
of yesterday into the life he had struggled to make for himself. She knew him. And in the knowing lay her death. And
if Buell came for her so much the better. It was her kind
and his that had sealed the demise of his people.

Pain!

He clawed at his chest and threw his head back and his
mouth dropped open and he would have screamed in agony,
but he had no voice. Then on the wings of his suffering

came a dart of pure ice, plunging into his heart, skewering his soul. Let me be. *Let me be. What must I do?*

And then he smelled sage and heard footsteps and in that moment saw beyond seeing and watched as Gray Willow's ghostly figure moved past him, floating on the night, his mother as he remembered her, but in mourning, wreathed with sorrow, and she turned to him and held out her hand and her breast was glistening with blood and her eyes were like pale moonlit shells.

Chato doubled over and pressed his forehead against the granite ledge, unable to bear the image drifting on the night air. *This must not be.* But it was as real as the blood on his hands.

Call yourself a warrior? You could not even make your final stand with Geronimo.

But he was old and tired and sick of battle. I fled to fight on. I fight on.

With such as these? What do they know of the People? Do they hear the earth sing? They cannot see beyond seeing or walk in their souls. Do they know that wisdom sits in places?

"Leave me!" he cried out, and straightened, fists clenched, as if willing to do battle with dreams. He was alone. But the chill remained. And it wasn't of the night. Something, no, someone was coming. Hands sweating, mouth dry, heart racing, all because of one name, one face formed in his mind's eye. "Mickey Free."

* * *

Colleen heard the front door of the blockhouse creak open on its leather hinges and knew her moment of truth had come. Hours earlier, just before sunset, Julio had ordered the woman to make herself ready for him, to remove her torn riding skirt and soiled blouse, and left her a delicately embroidered cotton gown that a bride might choose for her wedding night. Colleen's gaze even now dropped to the gown and she wondered about the delicately embroidered gown's former owner. She was certain Lopez had acquired the finery, like all his other trappings, by thievery or worse.

The bedroom at the rear of the blockhouse had been her prison for several days now. She had only been allowed outside in the company of *El Jefe* or with Clovia Madrigal, the most unpredictable of her captors. Lopez's mistress made no effort to hide her dislike of Senor Buell's lady. The volatile sixteen-year-old never failed to brandish her revolver in Colleen's presence and often went so far as to threaten the Indian agent's daughter with harm if she did anything to "confuse" the bandit chieftain and cause a shift in his affections.

Lantern light flickered across the woman's features as she sat on the edge of the cotton mattress, her forearm resting on the rail at the foot of the bed. The room was, for the most part, as sparsely furnished as the rest of the blockhouse, although Lopez had left her a washstand, a basin, and a clay pitcher of water. But the bed was the main piece and all it represented. "Make yourself ready for me," he had said. Colleen scowled, listening to him approach. "I'll be ready," she whispered.

She rose and crossed to the water pitcher, hefted it. Good solid stoneware, excellent. She poured the water onto the floor in front of the door and, brandishing the pitcher by its curved handle, swung it a couple of times to get used to the weight. The pitcher made a decent weapon. It felt solid enough to do some damage. She fully intended to kill Lopez or render him unconscious; either was acceptable. Afterward she intended to steal one of the horses and make a break for freedom. And if Clovia and the *soldados* shot her down, so be it. Anything was better than sitting here, awaiting whatever horrid fate these brigands had in store for her.

What of James Buell? She knew he would try to rescue her. But he was no match for Lopez and his hardened bunch. And Chato was real trouble. The Apache was cunning, ruthless, and seemed devoid of emotion, as if the legacy of his own murderous act had left him a hollow man . . . a man capable of anything now, for he had purged himself of conscience. No, James Buell would only get himself killed unless she escaped and somehow reached him first. The enormity of the challenge facing her was daunting. But what choice did she have?

The latch on the bedroom door slid open and Lopez appeared in the doorway. He saw Colleen, glanced at the gown still on the bed, frowned, then shrugged. "Have it your way, señorita. I will have what I have come for." He stepped into the room; his boots slid on the water, throwing him momentarily off balance. Colleen lunged for him, the pitcher raised above her head.

Lopez recovered quicker than she had expected and caught her wrist and twisted. The pitcher dropped to the floor and shattered. Though the two were similar in size and weight, Lopez was the more powerful. He forced her back toward the bed. Colleen struggled to escape his grasp. She bit his wrist. He dropped his hold on her arm and backhanded her. The woman staggered, then fell onto the bed. Lopez landed atop her, tore her blouse, and began to fondle her breasts. Colleen dug her fingernails into his cheek. He yelped and hit her again.

Colleen's vision blurred. A dark halo formed around the outlaw's leering visage. She felt him tear her dress; his rough hands pawed her thighs and naked belly. He tossed aside his gunbelt, feverishly unbuttoned the front of his pants. He grabbed her by the hair and arm and leaned down to roughly kiss her. Gone was the civilized veneer, the air of false nobility. He was an animal now, and he hungered like an animal and there was going to be no stopping him until he had slaked his lust.

And still she resisted, her hands raised yet again. She would keep struggling till he killed her if necessary, but she would never surrender. Tears of rage sprang from her eyes. Blood filled her cheeks. She tried to knee him in the groin; he blocked her. His breath, heavy with mescal and tobacco, fanned her features. She almost gagged. Sweat glistened in his black hair. She felt as if she were suffocating. Her naked flesh roused him all the more.

"Fight me. Come on; don't stop. I like it," Lopez taunted, his teeth bared and a feral gleam in his eyes. "The fighting makes it sweet for me."

"Then you ought to love *this*, you son of a bitch." The challenge came from directly behind him. It was a voice he did not recognize.

Lopez shoved clear of the woman and spun around to see who had dared to intrude on his pleasures. The idiot would die, and die hard. "Who the hell . . . ?" A rifle butt stopped him in mid-sentence, flattening his nose. The impact sent Lopez flying head over pants over heels. He landed, groaning, on the opposite side of the bed.

Colleen rose up on her elbows; her vision cleared, allowing her to recognize her savior.

"Mickey Free!" she gasped in astonishment.

Free shot past her as Lopez rose with a revolver in his hand, his once-handsome features now marred by the crushed morsel of flesh and cartilage that used to be his nose.

"Who the hell are you?!" Lopez managed to say through ruined lips.

Mickey reached out and grabbed the revolver and placed his thumb in front of the hammer as the bandit squeezed the trigger. Mickey grimaced as the hammer dug into his flesh. He dropped the rifle to free his right hand and caught the bandit by the throat and drove him back, slamming him into the bedroom wall.

Mickey lifted the bandit off the floor by the neck. Lopez tried to fire a warning shot, but he could not wrest the gun free of Mickey's grasp. And the weight of his own body as Free lifted him cut off his wind.

He kicked. He squirmed. His lungs burned. Eyes bulged. He clawed and pummeled and could not break the iron grip crushing his windpipe. *Soldados. Compañeros, to my aid!* All his plans flashed before his eyes.

As the world went dark and his lungs collapsed in on themselves, the last of his dreams seemed outlined in fire, his future one final vast parade of searing images: Julio Lopez riding at the head of a column of soldiers, as governor, as a man of wealth and influence, as anything but what he was . . .

Muerto.

Chapter 32

The body toppled from its perch, legs and arms flailing in the night air, mouth open in a garbled scream, the things a man will do when his throat is slit. He grazed an outcropping, bounced off a thumblike projection of stone, struck the slope, and landed on loose shale. The body slid another few yards, rolled lazily over, slid more, rolled, legs crossed, doll legs flip-flopping with the momentum, belly-down, then face-up, then belly-down, and this time for good.

Reverend Doctor Jordan staggered back from the precipice, leaned against a wall of pink granite to catch his breath. The knife in his hand was red with the dead man's blood. There would be no sentry to sound the alarm when he and Buell prepared their reception for Lopez and his murderous gang of desperados at the entrance to the narrow pass that led to the Apache *rancheria*.

Hours earlier, before he had departed, Mickey had pointed the sentry out to his two companions where they crouched in the thicket of trees. Free had even identified a path Jordan might use to reach the sentry's watch point under cover of darkness.

"It will be tricky, for an old jehu like yourself," Mickey said before leading off the bay with the muffled hooves.

Well, it had taken Jordan more than an hour to make the ascent without revealing his position. But he had made the climb and caught the bandit napping. The sentry bolted awake at the knife's lethal kiss. By then it was too late.

Jordan closed his eyes and breathed in deep, trying to erase the moment from memory, the resistance of flesh to the blade as it sawed through the man's jugular vein, ravaged muscle and nerve. This was butcher's work. And he took no pleasure in it. Nor did he have the luxury to allow himself any regrets. The bastard had brought it on himself the moment he chose to ride with the likes of Julio Lopez and Chato.

Sometimes a man's gotta do what he's gotta do, he thought. *Reverend Doctor, that's pure poetry. You ought to write it down.* Then he scowled. No, it sounded like an inscription for his tombstone. Leave well enough alone and don't invite bad luck. Anyway, it was time he returned to the thicket. Buell would be getting almighty nervous. Jordan crouched down and wiped the knife blade clean on the pads of a cactus, then straightened and as an afterthought took a moment to glance over the ledge at the patch of shadowy slope that had swallowed up the renegade.

"*Old* jehu?" he sniffed. "Not hardly."

* * *

Mickey Free was alone with the woman he loved and could never possess. But that didn't seem to matter now. He had found her. And for a moment he allowed himself the fantasy that he would steal her away, that she loved him, that they would lose themselves among the ancient mountains and find a life together, drawing their strength from the good earth, from the fuse of creation, from storm and wind and healing sunlight. . . .

But enough of dreams. They were still in the viper's nest. Lopez was dead. Yet Mickey had no doubt there were a number of men out by the raging council fire willing and eager to take his place. And Chato, Free reminded himself. As long his brother lived, his own and Colleen's lives were imperiled.

The blockhouse for the most part had been used for storage. The floor was littered with barrels of various sizes, and stolen goods, the spoils of the bandit's forays on both sides of the border. Mickey stood by one of the front windows, peering through a firing port out toward the great campfire where the *soldados* continued to swill their cheap mescal and boast of the victories to come and the wealth Julio Lopez had promised them.

Mickey turned as Colleen emerged from the bedroom. She had discarded her torn garments and dressed herself in the dead man's clothes. The clothes were a rough fit. Her ample bosom strained the ruffled shirt. For modesty's sake she also wore the bandit's short coat. His embroidered trousers left little to the imagination; they clung to her rounded hips and the contours of her thighs. Despite their predicament, Mickey made time to admire her figure. A good dose of healthy passion did the trick. He felt energized just standing in the room with her. And when she reached out to embrace him it was almost more than he could bear. His knees went weak. One arm went around her shoulders, and he held her, heard her muffled sob as the ordeal of her capture came flooding back, then she drew back, leaned against a barrel of salt pork while she dried her eyes on her coat sleeve.

She stepped toward him and took the revolver jutting from his belt, leaving him the holstered weapon and his rifle. Colleen checked the cylinder and, reassured it was loaded, tucked the Colt in her waistband. "I'll not be taken again." Her voice contained a firm measure of authority. She meant business.

"My God, Mickey, what are you doing here? And what of my father and James?"

"Your father lives. He is at Buell's hacienda. And the major is waiting for you, up the pass a ways. He and Jordan will be arranging a welcome for this bunch."

Colleen breathed a sigh of relief about her father. But the fact that her fiancé and their friend Jordan were also in harm's way offered little comfort. She wanted no one else at risk. She had known how hopeless her situation seemed. And now here before her was the most unexpected help of all. "And you, my dear Mickey . . . how . . . when . . ."

"I escaped from Florida," Mickey bluntly replied. "I returned to Arizona to set things aright."

Colleen wondered what that meant in particular and how it affected the people she loved. She reached out and touched his arm. "Do you still hate me?"

"I never hated you, though it wasn't for lack of trying. It was easier to hate your father and the major, even Jordan for a while."

"And now?"

"And now . . ." His lips pursed as he gave the matter some thought. "And now I think we better wait a couple of hours and let this bunch drink themselves into a stupor. I've got two horses waiting for us by the corral out back. We'll make our break soon enough. And when I tell you to, ride like hell."

Colleen realized he hadn't really answered her question but knew it was the best she could expect. Everything else must come later. For now, better to concentrate on getting out of the Apache *rancheria* alive.

"Mickey?"

"Yes."

"Chato is here." She watched as his face and red hair became illuminated by a silvery shaft of moonlight streaming through a crack in the shutter. His sun-bronzed features looked mottled and bloodless, corpselike in repose. But his hand inadvertently tightened on his rifle. And he nodded.

"I know."

Chapter 33

Grandfather, I ask you.
Give us long life together.

A prayer for the night unfolding, moon drifting on a black velvet sea, hounded by stars, while on earth below the campfire dimmed, untended, the dancer departed with her paramours, and the other *soldados* ambled off to their own blankets, their own mud-and-thatch hovels, some to the arms of the wives they had brought when they fled their hardscrabble farms to swell the ranks of the bandits, others to lonely bedrolls and mescal-fueled dreams.

Bandits? No, Lopez told them they were *soldados,* part of a great revolution that would wrest Sonora from Mexico City's far-off grasp. It had been done before. Why not again? They were tired of poverty; they were ready for Lopez or anyone who promised them golden dreams. Clovia had told them, revealed all she knew, of how the norte americano was coming with a ransom of gold in a chest of iron and wood. Gold for guns, she said. But also a share for each man who chose to ride to the sound of the guns.

And for this bunch, it was going to be first come, first served.

Mickey watched the fire weaken, the dancing flames shrink for lack of fresh timber, the men saunter off, and still he waited and allowed an hour to pass. He stood by the window, his gaze continually checking the path up to the blockhouse, picking up the movement in the camp, remembering a time when hogans littered the valley floor and fresh-killed venison hung above the smoke fires and children warred with blunted arrows and pretended to be warriors like those who raided the cattle ranches and fought to rid the hunting lands from the encroaching villages and farms. Night unfolded and he prayed:

> *May we live until our hair is frosted white*
> *Like the hilltops after the first snow.*
> *May we live till then*
> *This life we hold.*
> *This life we know.*

And finally it was time. He turned back to where Colleen dozed against a barrel, her head drooped forward, chin lowered, asleep despite herself and the desperate situation. But her right hand firmly clasped the Colt revolver. Mickey nodded. He pitied the man who tried to pry it from her grasp. Her spirit was strong.

Tsaaa, I'm thinking like an Apache again, he reflected, unsettled, because he did not know what was happening to him save that the world of the white man and that of the Chiricahua Apache were colliding within him, challenging each other for supremacy. Who was he? Who would he ever be?

He touched her arm. Colleen gasped and bolted awake, recognized him standing over her. She stood and he indicated the door. She understood and followed him across the main room and out onto the porch. Both of them felt intensely vulnerable as they emerged from the stout walls of the blockhouse. They rounded the blockhouse as quickly as they could and headed for the corral where the bay and another mount waited, tethered to the gate.

Colleen climbed into the saddle. Mickey leaped astride the bay. He took the reins in his left hand, held the Winchester in the right. Back in the hills a coyote began to howl. And among the trees, somewhere in the night, a horned owl loosed a cry that sent a chill down Mickey's spine. The creature was a harbinger of death. Something screeched in the night. Blood was flowing. A faint breeze whispered, fanned his sharp features, tugged at the brim of his sombrero. He took the rifle barrel and nudged his hat back from his forehead. His heart pounded; blue eyes like ice chipped from the heart of a glacier swept the surrounding camp one last time, checked the trail leading out of the valley, the narrow twisting passage he had stolen so silently through. The hooves of the bay were no longer muffled by strips of cloth. Now it was time to ride like hell and throw caution to the wind. He glanced toward Colleen and softly instructed her to keep close to him. Then he walked the bay into the corral while Colleen propped the gate open. The horses within began to stir and toss their manes and shift nervously about the confines.

Mickey only intended to scatter the horses, not drive them off. He wanted the *soldados* to be able to follow them, just not too closely. Loosing the horses would delay a pursuit. He and Colleen were going to need time to join Buell and Jordan, who he hoped were in place. If not . . .

"Dabin-ik-eh!" Chato's voice cut through the stillness. "Lift that rifle and I'll cut you in half with this long gun."

Mickey felt his blood run cold and he turned in the direction of the sound and saw his foster brother materialize out of the darkness, several yards from the corral, approaching up the same path Free and the Indian agent's daughter had used. Moonlight glinted off the Apache's rifle. Chato had Free dead in his sights. It would only take a little pressure on the trigger . . .

"I knew it. I knew it was you. I heard the owl call your name," Chato said in a loud voice. His voice cut the stillness like a skinning knife. But the men in the camp con-

·tinued to doze. If any of the *soldados* heard the Chiricahua, they had yet to act. It was going to take a while to shrug off the excesses of the night before. "And you have the agent's daughter with you. I do not see *El Jefe.*" Chato moved slowly toward them. His gaze darted to either side. From what he could see of the corral there was only Free and the woman. "What have you done with Lopez?"

Chato took his time, confident he had the drop on this white Apache. Mickey Free was helpless. His rifle was pointed at the ground. Should he try to bring it up, he'd catch a bullet in the chest for his trouble.

"He's waiting for you," Mickey replied. His voice was iron cold, devoid of fear.

"Waiting where?"

"In hell."

Mickey's rifle spat flame as he squeezed off a round, blasting a hole in the earth. The gunshot startled Chato, who fired on reflex as Mickey twisted in the saddle and flung himself to the side, one foot kicking free of the stirrup. The bullet clipped Mickey's left arm, sliced a furrow through the upper muscle. Colleen opened up with the revolver. Mickey ignored the pain and levered another couple of rounds in the direction of his would-be killer. The gunshots sent the horses in the corral plunging through the gate. Frightened by the sudden explosive exchange, the entire herd, more than two dozen mounts, knocked down part of the fence as they charged from the corral and bore down on Chato. The Apache tried to dive out of harm's way. Mickey saw him disappear beneath their thundering hooves.

Mickey and Colleen turned their mounts toward the passage. Free lingered to see if Chato had perished beneath the stampeding horseflesh. It was impossible to tell with all the commotion. And the camp was coming to life as the panicked animals streamed past the blockhouse and tore through the jacals and scattered the men who had elected to pitch their bedrolls about the smoldering remains of the main campfire.

Colleen leaned forward and clung to the horse beneath her for dear life. More gunfire filled the night. She chanced a brief look over her shoulder and spied Clovia Madrigal racing toward them, naked from the waist up, revolver in hand, firing on the run. She wasn't alone. Gunfire filled the early hours, some of it directed at the escaping couple, other rounds loosed in a number of directions as pockets of desperados mistook their comrades for the enemy and blasted away at one another.

Mickey shoved the Winchester into the saddle boot and hauled out his Colt. His left arm hurt like the devil. Blood was seeping down his shirtsleeve and making his grip slick. But the pain had a way of sharpening his senses. He felt connected to the terrain flashing by, let memory and violence bear him onward, willed himself and the bay to greater effort.

* * *

"Become like the wind; become like the storm."

The boy looked up at Geronimo and nodded. "I hear your words in my heart."

"Then tell me, Dabin-ik-eh."

"Who can stop the rain?"

And Geronimo nodded. The boy understood.

* * *

A bandit rose before him, came scrambling down from his watch point on the ridge to slip and slide and gather his legs beneath him and attempt to block the pass. The bandit was armed with a Spencer carbine, a big .50-caliber weapon with a slower rate of fire. He made the best of it and loosed shot after shot. It would only take one of those heavy slugs to knock a man from the saddle.

Mickey leaned forward and returned fire, snapping off three shots in rapid succession. He hoped to throw the man's aim off until they were past him. But the last of the three found its mark, struck the rifle stock, ricocheted up into the sentry's jaw. The man flung aside the rifle as he spun and toppled over into the spiny embrace of an ocotillo cactus. The pass loomed ahead, open jaws of stone outlined against the lessening dark.

Twenty yards, ten, ride low, but boldly ride. Morning approached. Sweet daylight in another hour or so. A day of reckoning, day of wrath, all of it coming to pass. Mickey Free knew there was no turning back now. Though Lopez was dead, Free and his companions were still outnumbered. And he hadn't seen Chato after the horses had passed. Mickey planned to return to look for the body and set the ghosts to rest. But first, of course, he had to survive the morning.

Chapter 34

Mickey Free and Colleen McDunn reached the far end of the pass in the gray twilight of a new morn. They rode their lathered mounts at a gallop up through the narrow gap in the mountains where the battlements made a natural gateway. Iron-shod hooves beat a harsh cadence upon the broken, barren floor of the passage. Towering over the riders, to either side, loomed the "jaws" of Los Pilares, its stark gray battlements of serrated granite, scored with ledges and pockets of stone eroded by wind and rain and masked by thickets of ocotillo.

They found their escape route blocked by the ransom wagon, its massive strongbox in plain sight. Apparently one of the axles was broken, causing the wagon to rest with a decided tilt to the right. The horses had been freed from the singletree. Mickey studied the steep slopes, noticed the buzzards circling above. He was reaching for his rifle when Jordan and Buell hailed them and came scrambling out from behind the wagon.

Colleen leaped down from horseback and ran to her fiancé. James Buell rushed forward and swept her up in his arms and wrapped her in his embrace. The couple stood locked together in a hungry kiss, their bodies molded to each other by a sense of urgency and desperate love. For the moment they seemed oblivious to their precarious situation and the presence of the other two men. Mickey scowled and started to hail them—it was time someone interjected a note of reality to the moment—but Jordan held him back with a firm but gentle hand.

"Give 'em this, Kid. Lord only knows but it might be all they'll ever have," said the deputy marshal, his big ugly features flushed from the morning's efforts. Somehow, the note of tenderness in the lawman's voice seemed incongruous with his rough, craggy appearance.

Free shrugged and glanced at the buzzards that continued to circle the western escarpment and spied the remains of the bandit lying on the slope where his body had come to rest. "You have any trouble?"

"I was handling trouble when you were a pup in breechclout," Jordan sniffed defensively.

The hint of a smile flashed across Mickey's features. "Even an old bull stumbles now and then."

"I climbed up yonder and found him just where you said he'd be and read him from the book, chapter and verse." Jordan glanced at the blood attempting to coagulate along the flesh wound and the torn sleeve of Free's shirt. "Looks like you got nominated, Kid." Jordan checked the wound; satisfied it wasn't fatal, he tied a bandanna around the younger man's upper arm.

"Yeah, well, the one who did it got *elected*," Mickey dryly explained. He nodded his thanks and, sensing movement behind him, turned as Buell broke away from his intended bride and hurried over to the other two men. The former major looked older, bristly, his youthful features all business now. It was obvious he was firmly resolved to meet whatever came his way, head-on. For the moment, though, iron will gave way to humble gratitude. "Free . . . I, we, don't know what to say. How can we ever repay you?"

"*Tsaaa,* see to your woman," Free replied in a hard-edged tone.

Buell looked puzzled at first; then he changed the subject and gestured toward the wagon. "The wagon's like you wanted; looks as if we broke down and had to run for it."

"That's what I'm counting on," said Mickey, who wasn't any better with words than the former officer. He was not about to share what was in his heart, not with Buell or any other man. He loved Colleen, or then again, maybe he loved the idea of her. The Indian agent's daughter had been kind to him, loved him in her own fashion. And in turn he had glimpsed in the woman the possibility of the life he might have lived. But fate had other plans. "Take Colleen up the slope with you and see she saves the last bullet for herself. Your woman isn't safe. Not yet."

Buell nodded. "Lopez? Is he on the way?"

"Lopez is dead."

Buell's eyes widened in a look of surprise. "Then it's over?" he blurted out, suddenly elated.

"Not till they say so."

"Who?"

Mickey held up his hand, motioning for the man to be quiet. Buell obeyed. And he didn't even chafe at obeying Free's command. He was learning, slow, perhaps, learning all the same. The only rank here was measured in the man who might be able to keep you alive.

"Them."

Buell listened. And now he heard, a sound like rolling thunder, the sound of horses fast approaching from up the canyon. Riders coming at a gallop, renegades like a pack of hungry wolves, without a leader perhaps, but with a lust for the ransom and a determination to recapture the woman who would make each of them a wealthy man.

The ex-officer nodded and hurried off. He took Colleen by the arm and headed for the opposite slope fifty yards away. Jordan checked the action on his rifle and then took a moment to load the shotgun he had taken off Mose Woodard.

"Kid, you sure about staying with the wagon?"

"Someone's got to light the fuse."

"I could do it."

"You're too old and fat to run for cover. I have a chance to make it."

"Keep talking like that and, by God, when this is over I'll clamp you in leg irons and take you back to prison."

"Bold talk for a man without a star."

"I may not have it pinned to my chest," Reverend Doctor Jordan grumbled. "But don't think it ain't there." He fished a cigar from his vest pocket, lit it, and handed the smoke to Mickey, then ambled off to take up his position on the slope across from Buell and the Indian agent's daughter.

Jordan resembled some ungainly crab as he was forced to scramble hand over fist and traverse several yards of loose shale before reaching the first outcropping of boulders about thirty-five feet above the pass. He found a granite slab that had broken away from the face of the ridge and provided him with enough room for him to crouch behind. He pulled his great bulk under cover as the sound of the approaching riders grew louder.

He watched Free climb onto the wagon bed and stand by the chain-secured chest with its load of paper wadding, rolled chains, and dynamite. A fuse poked from the back of the chest a few inches from the bottom seam. Mickey took several drags on the cigar to build up an ash and keep the thing lit. Then satisfied, he set the cigar on top of the ransom chest.

Overhead, the sky brightened, shed its gray mantle. Sunlight tipped the eastern-facing battlements and etched them in gold. A breeze stirred, bringing the clear, sweet smell of the desert. Mickey checked Jordan's position. The big man waved and settled back. Free looked toward the opposite wall where Buell and McDunn's daughter were crouched behind a thicket of cholla cactus and an outcropping of weathered stone.

Was she watching him? Did her heart race just a little faster, fearing for his safety? He wanted to think so. He did not have long to dwell on the issue, for an armed column rounded a corner and rode into view about a hundred yards from the crippled wagon. He knew none of them but recognized the type, lawless renegades for whom life held little meaning other than what they could steal, spend, or screw. These were faceless men, bound by a common lust. Here in the howling wilderness, they were the predators.

And they had found their prey.

Chapter 35

"It will be a tough go for us," Buell said to the woman at his side. He'd held nothing back, minced no words in telling her what the strongbox contained and the illusionary nature of his finances. The hacienda, the land, all of it was a gamble. Nothing would be given to them. "We will have to struggle every season until the herd pays off." Even as he talked and dreamed, his gaze never left the renegades assembling back in the pass. No doubt they were working up the courage to advance on the wagon and the solitary figure attempting to defend it. "And even then it will be a risk."

"I wouldn't have it any other way, James," Colleen replied, placing her hand upon his. "We'll get by." She smiled bravely at Buell, then allowed her attention to return to the lone defender below. She had taken for granted his indomitable strength and iron will. And now Mickey Free seemed almost defenseless, even vulnerable.

"He'll be all right," the man next to her said, reading her thoughts.

"No, he won't," Colleen replied. And her voice grew hushed.

"I swear if any harm comes to him it will not be by my hand," Buell told her. "I don't give a damn how much the army wants him. If nothing else, I've learned when a man needs to set the law aside and do what's right."

"The harm is my doing," Colleen said.

"My dear, you aren't making sense. How could you even think—"

"He loves me."

"Oh." Buell was at a loss now. "Well, I mean, I am sure he cares a great deal about you. After all, you and your father took him in after his mother's death. You befriended him."

"He *loves* me, James. And I fear that will get him killed."

Buell studied the pack of brigands and cutthroats preparing to attack. "None of us came to Sonora at gunpoint," Buell reminded her. "Free knows what he is doing and why he is doing it. Hell, we all do." He touched her arm. "There comes a time to make a stand and earn the right to walk this earth. This is our time. As for Free, you and I are only a part of the story. We are going to live, Colleen; I swear it. We are going to live and tell our children what happened here today."

Perhaps he was right. And if so, then she had better watch. And remember.

Mickey suddenly loosed a wild war cry and held his rifle aloft and in the language of the Chiricahua began to taunt the bandits. His voice rang out like a call to battle; first in the language of the Apache, then in Spanish he summoned his would-be killers to the dance. Still the *soldados* hesitated. They could take this lone defender, but none wanted to die in the process. Then Clovia broke through their ranks and she rode before these men and called them cowards and challenged them to follow her. The gold was theirs for the taking. And the first men to tear into the strongbox would have the lion's share. Let the laggards die poor. At her direction the renegades loosed a volley that sent Free diving for cover behind the box on the wagon bed.

On the hillside, Jordan, Buell, and Colleen all gasped in horror as chips of wood and fragments of the wagon

siding littered the air. If a stray bullet penetrated the strongbox, the whole thing might blow up in Mickey's face. But
Clovia and the others were given renewed courage seeing
the red-haired "Apache" duck out of sight. Her horse led
the charge as the bandits started forward, gathering momentum, guns blazing, horses wild-eyed and spurred onward to greater speed. Now it was a race to see who would
reach the ransom.

A hundred yards became fifty, forty, thirty . . .

"Now!" Colleen shouted. "Mickey, run, for God's sake.
Run!"

Twenty-five yards and blasting away, then twenty. "Run
for it, Kid. Now, damn it!" Jordan shouted from the opposite ridge. Buell echoed the man's sentiment, muttering
it aloud as he brought the rifle to his shoulder.

Mickey crouched by the money chest, then rose up and
leaped from the wagon bed and raced for the western battlements, as if abandoning the wagon and the ransom. But
Colleen could see the narrow ribbon of smoke from the lit
fuse coiling up from the chest. Not so Clovia Madrigal and
the rest of the bandits who peppered the slope with a hail
of lead as Mickey scrambled for cover. He reached a de-
pression in the slope and clawed his way over a jagged slab
of stone as the bandits swarmed over the wagon.

Clovia dismounted onto the wagon bed and with her
revolver began to shoot apart the padlocks securing the
chains. A number of men reined in their mounts around the
wagon, while a couple of hardcases rode straight for the
spot Mickey had reached. The stragglers were the lucky
ones.

Clovia tore away the last of the chains and reached for
the lid and lifted, let it crash back on the wagon bed, her
expression eager, eyes aglow with excitement. She was
about to have everything she had ever dreamed of. For an
instant the young woman stared down, unable to quite

fathom what she beheld, bound strips of paper, iron washers, chains, and bags filled with rocks.

"No," she whimpered. Then the strongbox disappeared in a blinding flash and she with it. Horses were hurled to the ground by the blast; riders went flying; smoke and billowing dust filled the entrance to Los Pilares; the remains of the wagon sailed through the air; shrapnel of stone and iron rings and shattered links of chain sliced through flesh and went ricocheting off the bordering walls.

Then Buell and Jordan opened up, their rifles adding to the din. They poured round after round into the confusion. Men fell to their knees, toppled from horseback; horses pawed the air in their panic. And as the echoes of the explosion were replaced by the noise of battle, the farmers among the *soldados* broke ranks and fled. But the hardened bandits stood their ground; some charged the slopes to root out their attackers.

* * *

Colleen loaded and passed another rifle to her fiancé. She moved slowly, methodically, benumbed by the sight of so much carnage. It sickened her, the wounded clawing at their smoldering clothes and broken limbs, the dead lying where they fell, like discarded toys. Then a bullet struck the ledge inches from her face and spattered her cheek with stone slivers, drawing blood. The pain served to remind her that the remaining renegades wanted her dead. Colleen vigorously began to shove cartridges into the rifle. Remorse was a luxury reserved for the survivors. Buell fired the last of his cartridges and handed the rifle back to her, taking the other one from her hands.

His expression said it all. Here was no great battle where a man might win glory or spoils. This was a personal war brought on him through no fault of his own. The only strategy now was kill or be killed. And victory belonged to the last man standing.

*   *   *

Jordan was blinded by all the dust and the splinters that
filled the air as the wagon erupted with a deafening roar.
A blizzard of wooden shards, fragments of iron and stone,
rained down upon the slope, forcing the ferocious old
plainsman to hunker down behind the nearest boulder until
the worst had passed. He immediately thought of Mickey
and wondered if the younker had survived the explosion.

When the worst had passed, Reverend Doctor levered a
fresh shell into his Winchester and, peering over the outcropping, drew a bead on an outlaw clawing his way up
the slope toward the deputy's position. The bandit had lost
his sombrero, blood streamed from his lacerated scalp, but
the wound hadn't slowed him. His short, powerful legs carried him across the incline without missing a step. He spied
the deputy aiming at him. The bandit's hand dropped to his
cartridge belt and reappeared holding an ancient-looking
Colt dragoon the size of a small cannon. He rose up on one
knee to chance a shot with his cap-and-ball revolver. Jordan's rifle bucked and a plume of dirt erupted from the
bandit's serape. The man yelped, twisted to the right, and
rolled back down the slope, firing as he fell.

Jordan shifted his aim, trying to see through the thick-
ening haze that obscured the pass. He emptied his rifle at
the remaining *soldados,* firing at anything that he could
make out. It was difficult to see. The dust had yet to settle,
and the gunsmoke and smoldering remains of the wagon
didn't help matters. He fired and thought he saw another
of the renegades toss up his hands and slide from
horseback, a lucky shot.

The melee could go either way. Nothing was certain.
But if the remains of the bandit gang reorganized, they
might be able to storm one of the hillsides and drive Buell
or Jordan out from cover. This was the moment. A cross
fire wasn't going to hold them. Jordan knew that he and

Buell weren't enough to turn the tide and break the attack. They needed help.

They got it.

* * *

Mickey Free rose from the dead. At least it seemed that way. He kicked out from the charred remains of a wagon wheel and rose up on his knees. He was practically deaf and the wound on his left arm had opened again and was oozing crimson. His features were soot-streaked and a splinter of wood had sliced open his cheek a couple of inches below his right eye.

The two men who had ridden toward Mickey's position were afoot now and staggering about in the haze, trying to get their bearings. Both were alive but wounded. One of them, a broad-shouldered, powerfully built man, caught a glimpse of Free and fired. The bullet whined past Mickey's ear like an angry bee. The second miscreant had lost his gun but dragged a machete from its sheath and charged through the swirling brown haze.

Mickey lost sight of the man with the blade, knocked the dirt from his rifle, and ducked as a second bullet narrowly missed his skull. He rushed forward, crouched low, and finished clearing the rifle barrel. A patch of haze thinned just enough to reveal the *soldado* with the pistol. Mickey fired.

The man stumbled, tried to bring his pistol to bear. Mickey let him have two more, forcing the man backward. The gunman's legs buckled. He dropped his gun and clawed at his chest and fell over on his backside, slamming into the hard earth.

Mickey sensed rather than saw the flash of the machete blade as it arced through the powder smoke in a vicious swipe intended to behead its victim. Free tried to duck, but what saved him was the bullet that struck the man in the back and knocked him off balance. The cruel-looking steel blade passed overhead close enough to crop a strand of Free's rust-red hair. The man staggered past, carried along by his momentum. A stain spread across his shirt, the legacy of the bullet that had ended his life. Mickey Free squinted, glimpsed the far slope, and for a brief second made out Buell standing in plain sight, his rifle raised in salute.

Mickey held his own rifle up and returned the gesture. Then he bolted out of the pass and ran from the melee, making a mad dash for a cluster of scrub oak where he had tethered the bay for the animal's own protection. As he reached his mount, Free momentarily halted. He was being watched. Mickey searched the shadows, among the trees, and saw a familiar form, the feral eyes, sleek coppery coat, drooping head, and hunched shoulders.

Trickster. Coyote. Have you come to fight?
It is your road, not mine, Dabin-ik-eh.
What do you mean?
And it has brought you to your destiny.

"So be it!" Mickey shouted. He freed the gelding, leaped into the saddle, and stormed off toward the pass. The lust for battle coursed through his limbs; his blood felt like streaming fire, fierce fuel for his veins. He was the land and the wild wind, he was the shadow and the light, the strength of these ancient mountains was his strength now, and there was no stopping him.

He loosed a shrill war cry that pierced the clamor. The haze had begun to clear enough for the remaining *soldados* to see the Apache Kid charging them. Some fled at the sound of his unsettling war cry. Others tried to stand. That was their mistake. For he struck with all the fury of a desert storm. He rode one man down, wounded another, shot a third where he stood.

Even for the most hardened of the lot, the onslaught was almost supernatural. It was as if their own bullets could not strike him and his could not miss. They were faceless to him, he fought without hatred, and they fell before him as before a force of nature. He rode through the ranks of his enemies and they fell like shafts of wheat before the scythe. His Winchester swept from side to side, rattling off shot after shot.

He fired his rifle until it was too hot to hold, and when it was empty he used it as a club, and when the stock shattered he tossed it aside and fought with pistol and knife. He leaped from the saddle and dragged one man from horseback, broke his neck, took the man's carbine, caught the bay as he plunged past, and swung astride the gelding yet again. Another of the *soldados* tried to make a stand and took a bullet in the face for his trouble. Free loosed another war cry and looked for another of the renegades, but the last of the bunch had scattered. They bolted from the pass and vanished into the barrancas, wanting no more of this senseless slaughter.

Mickey resisted the temptation to pursue the last of the bunch. They would meet their fate another day, by another's hand. His walk was here. He glanced down at the carbine, checked the loads. Slowly the rage left him, allowed him to see the dead and the dying, and slowly a sense of sorrow replaced the wrath and he shook his head and muttered, "Enough."

On the slope above him, Colleen barely managed to catch her breath. "It's over," she whispered. "Oh, dear God, it's over." She stood and started to descend the slope, Buell caught her by the arm and stopped her. He indicated Jordan across the way, who was also standing, unharmed, but strangely quiet.

She didn't understand.

They were alive. The nightmare was over. They could go home. And then she saw for herself. A lone figure waited up the valley, a figure of menace, lonely as death.

Chato had come. He had waited out the attack, allowed the bandits to destroy themselves. He owed them no loyalty. Now he waited up the pass, astride a brown stallion painted for war, and he called out to the battered, bleeding rider on the bay. Chato's war cry echoed down the corridor of stone.

Mickey started forward, keeping the bay to a walk. He was in no hurry. It had taken ten long years to arrive at this moment. Another minute or two did not matter. He glanced up at those who had come with him, this far, but could go no further.

Jordan fired his rifle, levering shot after shot into the air, and Buell followed suit until both men emptied their guns in salute. It was all they could do. And in a way, it was enough. Free understood.

"No," Colleen said. But she knew what had to be. One last act remained, the final scene of a drama in which they had no part save to watch and to remember how it was on a day of destiny.

Chapter 36

And so it began, with a challenge made in the silent aftermath of a battle, the stillness after the tempest of violence and death that men had wrought. And lo, nature itself seemed to recoil from the horror. Was there more to come? If not, then why were these two men on horseback walking their mounts toward each other on this sun-drenched morning? Men with guns, always guns, seeking retribution, redemption, peace. Well, death is peace; it's true. And Mickey wondered, *Couldn't life be the same?* The tread of iron-shod hooves beat a distinct cadence on the hard-packed earth, counting off the distance to a dead reckoning.

"You have come a long way to die!" Chato called out. And his voice came back to him, reverberating along the corridor of cliffs, "*. . . die . . . die . . . die.*" He levered a shell into his own rifle. "My brother, do you remember how, as children, we played in the fields of the *rancheria?* My people took you in, yet you betrayed us."

"*betrayed . . . betrayed . . . betrayed . . .*"

Chato shook his fist in the air. "Worse, somehow, you worked magic on my mother and clouded her eyes so she could not see the truth."

"*. . . truth . . . truth . . . truth.*"

Only silence, only the sound of the bay as he whinnied and shook his mane; now came the wind, like a moan, sweeping through the pass. Chato clutched at his chest; it felt like his heart was being torn from his chest. He saw himself, clutching the rifle, the muzzle blast, his mother looking at him with love and pity as she died by his hand.

"I have seen her. I have seen Gray Willow." His voice sounded shrill now, and it broke. "Her ghost walks these mountains. She cannot rest until it is ended between us. You and I. These others mean nothing."

Chato forced the image from his mind and frowned. He was puzzled at Free's lack of response. Had the explosion left him deaf? Had all the killing robbed him of his senses? A nagging fear trailed its icy fingers along Chato's spine. Something was wrong. There was more here in this place of ghosts and dreams than a man with a rifle could resolve. Still he held his course; the two horses plodded toward each other, their gait slow and methodical, bringing the two men ever closer.

Mickey reached down and patted the animal's neck. He breathed in deep. The air here was clear, the farther he rode from the site of battle. He was oddly serene; a calm had settled on him sweet as a dew in spring. He thought of the parents who bore him, the father and mother he had never known, of those who had taken him as their own, who opened him to the power of One. He wasn't alone and knew now he had never been. There was Coyote Trickster slinking along the ridge and, to the right, Geronimo's shade, forged by a war he had not chosen and a purpose that had abandoned him, a phantom from a long-ago time when a young foundling was filled with wonder and a sense of awe. And there was Gray Willow, yes, like a sylph passing along the variegated battlements, a woman of wisdom and beauty whose eyes were filled with sorrow for the sons she loved and in her own way had died for. They were all here, and at long last the Apache Kid understood what had to be done.

Tsaaa. How have you suffered?

I have suffered, no more, no less, than others before me. For that is the way of things.

What have you learned?
I have learned . . . who I am.

A gunshot shattered the stillness. The bullet whined past the man on the bay and ricocheted among the boulders. It had been a risky shot. Chato didn't usually miss. He reined in his mount and snapped his rifle up to his shoulder. He'd make the next one count. He sighted down the rifle barrel, found he had his foster brother dead to rights. Just a little pressure on the trigger to keep from throwing off the aim. But . . . Chato was mystified. Why hadn't Mickey brought up his own carbine? Was he waiting for a better shot? This was a good distance, and still the bay continued.

And then the man in the gun sights did something even more remarkable. He tossed his carbine aside and rode blithely on to his death. Or to his life? Chato blinked, unable to understand. What trick was this? Perhaps Mickey had a hidden gun. But his hands were in plain sight.

"You are a fool. Do you think I won't kill you?" Chato shouted.

But there was only the wind for a reply, a whispering breeze, and the cry of hawks in the fierce blue morning, the warmth rising with the promise of another day and the chance to live it beneath the stark beauty of the sheltering sky. And then he saw her, Gray Willow, watching, so alone, so sad, so full of grief not for herself, but for her sons.

Chato lowered his rifle and allowed Mickey to continue on toward him unharmed. He stopped the bay a mere couple of yards from his brother's mount. Chato bent forward; his shoulders shuddered for a few brief seconds as he struggled to contain his emotions. When he looked up, his eyes that had never known them glistened with tears. The shame was unbearable. A warrior did not weep. But there was a kind of healing there, at least the beginning of healing.

"I never meant to hurt her."

"I know that," said the man on the bay. "And so does she."

Chato lifted his head, amazed at what he heard and that he believed it for the first time since that terrible moment long ago. Then, as gentle as a sunrise, the horror and weight of his deed lifted from his heart . . . and left in its place a great longing.

It was ended. Free sighed with relief and glanced over his shoulder at the people he was leaving behind. Reverend Doctor, and Buell, and Colleen McDunn. *I will never see you again. Go back and have your lives. I have found mine.*

"What shall I do?" Chato asked.

"Ride with me . . . for a while."

"Where?"

"Wherever brothers go."

Chato sat in silence as the bay walked past, carrying his war-torn rider back into the heart of the Apache *rancheria*. And the Chiricahua warrior was amazed that for the first time in his life, he experienced hope. How had this happened? He nudged his heels against the flanks of his mount. The animal dutifully trotted forward until he was abreast of the bay.

"Who are you?" said Chato. It was a simple question asked of a man formed by two worlds, but of one path. His own.

"I am Mickey Free."